P9-CEY-019

THE PENAL COLONY

FRANZ KAFKA

The Penal Colony
STORIES AND SHORT PIECES

TRANSLATED BY WILLA AND EDWIN MUIR

SCHOCKEN BOOKS / NEW YORK

First SCHOCKEN PAPERBACK edition 1961

Twentieth Printing, 1974

Copyright © 1948 by Schocken Books, Inc.
67 Park Avenue, New York 16, N. Y.

Library of Congress Catalog Card No. 48-9743

Printed in the United States of America

CONTENTS

CONVERSATION WITH THE SUPPLICANT

Conversation with the Supplicant

THERE WAS a time when I went every day into a church, since a girl I was in love with knelt there in prayer for half an hour in the evening and I was able to look at her in peace.

Once when she had not come and I was reluctantly eyeing the other supplicants I noticed a young fellow who had thrown his whole lean length along the floor. Every now and then he clutched his head as hard as he could and sighing loudly beat it in his upturned palms on the stone flags.

Only a few old women were in the church, and they kept turning their shawled heads sideways to watch the young man at his devotions. Their awareness of him seemed to please him, for before each of his pious outbursts he cast his eyes around to see whether many of them were looking. This I found unseemly, and I made up my mind to accost him as he left the church and to ask him why he prayed in such a manner. Yes, I felt irritable because my girl had not come.

But an hour elapsed before he stood up, crossed himself punctiliously and strode jerkily towards the basin of holy water. I set myself in a direct line between the basin and the door, knowing that I was not going to let him pass without an explanation. I screwed up my mouth as I always do when I want to speak decisively, I advanced my right leg and rested all my weight upon it, balancing my left leg carelessly on the points of my toes; that too gives me a sense of firmness.

Now it is possible that the young man had already caught sight of me when he was sprinkling himself with the holy water, or he might even have remarked me sooner with some dismay, for he made a sudden unexpected dash out through the doorway. The glass door banged shut. And when I came out immediately behind him I could not see him anywhere, for there were several narrow streets and plenty of traffic.

He stayed away for the next few days, but my girl was there. She was wearing her black dress with the transparent lace top over the shoulders—the crescent of her petticoat showed under it—from the lower edge of which the silk hung down in a beautifully cut ruffle. And since she had come I forgot the young man and did not even concern myself with him when he continued to appear regularly to do his devotions in the usual manner. Yet whenever he passed me he always seemed in a great hurry and turned his face away. Perhaps it was only that I could not think of him except in motion and so even when he was standing still he seemed to me to be slithering past.

One evening I stayed too long in my room. All the same, I went along to the church. My girl was not in it, and I thought of going home again. But there was the young fellow lying on the floor. I was reminded of my first encounter with him and my curiosity revived.

I went on tiptoe to the doorway, gave a coin to the blind beggar who sat there and squeezed in beside him behind the open half of the door; and for a whole hour there I sat, perhaps with a crafty look on my face. I liked being there and made up my mind to come again often. In the second hour I began to think it foolish to sit there because of a man at his prayers. Yet for a third hour in growing irritation I let the spiders creep over my clothes while the last of the people came, drawing deep breaths, out of the darkness of the church.

And then he too came. He was walking cautiously, trying the ground lightly with his feet before setting them down.

I rose up, took a large stride forward and seized him.

"Good evening," I said, and with my hand on his collar pushed him down the steps into the lighted square.

When we were down on the level he said in a fluttering voice: "Good evening, my dear, dear sir, don't be angry with me, your most devoted servant."

"Well," said I, "I want to ask you some questions, sir; you slipped through my fingers the other time but you'll hardly do that tonight."

"Sir, you are a compassionate man and you'll let me go home. I'm a poor creature, that's the truth."

"No," I cried, against the noise of a passing tram, "I won't let you go. This is the kind of encounter I like. You're a lucky catch for me. I congratulate myself."

Then he said: "Oh God, your heart is alive but your head is a block of wood. You call me a lucky catch, what good luck you must be sure of! For my bad luck is like a seesaw teetering on a very fine point, and it will fall on anyone's head who lays a questioning finger on it. Good night, sir."

"Right," said I, and held his right hand fast, "if you don't give me an answer I'll begin to yell here in the street. And all the shopgirls that are coming out now and all their sweethearts waiting for them so happily will come running up, for they'll think a carriage horse has fallen down or some accident has happened. And then I'll point you out to the people."

At that he tearfully kissed my hands, one after the other. "I'll tell you what you want to know, but please let us rather go into the side street over there." I nodded, and we crossed to it.

But it was not enough for him to be in the dusk of the little street where only a few yellow lamps hung at wide intervals, he drew me into the low hallway of an old house underneath a tiny lamp that hung dripping before a wooden stair. There he took out his handkerchief gravely and spread it on a step, saying: "Do sit down, my dear sir, and you will be better able to ask questions, while I stand here, for so I'll be better able to answer them. Only don't torment me."

So I sat down and said, looking up at him with narrowed eyes: "You're an utter lunatic, that's what you are! Look at the way you carry on in the church! How irritating it is and how unpleasant for onlookers! How can anyone compose himself to worship if he has to look at you."

He kept his body pressed against the wall, only his head could move freely to and fro. "Don't be angry—why should you be angry about things that don't concern you. I get angry when I behave badly; but if someone else does the wrong thing I am delighted. So don't be angry if I tell you that it is the aim of my life to get people to look at me."

"What a thing to say," I cried, much too loudly for the low-roofed hallway, but I was afraid to let my voice

die away again, "truly, what a thing to say. Of course
I can guess, of course I guessed the first time I saw
you, what kind of state you are in. I've had some experience, and I don't mean it as a joke when I tell you
it's like being seasick on dry land. It's a condition in
which you can't remember the real names of things and
so in a great hurry you fling temporary names at them.
You do it as fast as you can. But you've hardly turned
your back on them before you've forgotten what you
called them. A poplar in the fields which you called
'the tower of Babel,' since you either didn't or wouldn't
know that it was a poplar, stands wavering anonymously
again, and so you have to call it 'Noah in his cups.'"

I was somewhat disconcerted when he said: "I'm
thankful to say that I don't understand what you've
been talking about."

With annoyance I answered quickly: "Your saying
that you're thankful shows that you do know what I was
talking about."

"Of course it shows that, my dear sir, but what you
said was rather peculiar too."

I laid my hands on a step above me, leaned right back
and in this almost untacklable position, which is the last
resource of a wrestler, asked him: "Haven't you a comic
way of wriggling out of things, projecting your own
state of mind like that on other people?"

That made him pluck up courage. He clasped his
hands together to give his body unity, and put up some
resistance, saying: "No, I don't do that with anyone, not
even with you for instance, because I can't. But I
should be glad if I could, for then I wouldn't need to
make people look at me in church. Do you know why
I need to?"

This question rather dished me. Of course I didn't know, and I believe I didn't want to know. I never wanted to come here, I said to myself, but the creature forced me to give him a hearing. So all I had to do was to shake my head, to convey that I didn't know, yet I found myself unable to move my head at all.

The young man standing opposite me smiled. Then he dropped on his knees and with a dreamy look on his face told me: "There has never been a time in which I have been convinced from within myself that I am alive. You see, I have only such a fugitive awareness of things around me that I always feel they were once real and are now fleeting away. I have a constant longing, my dear sir, to catch a glimpse of things as they may have been before they show themselves to me. I feel that then they were calm and beautiful. It must be so, for I often hear people talking about them as though they were."

Since I made no answer and only through involuntary twitchings in my face betrayed my uneasiness, he asked: "Don't you believe that people talk like that?"

I knew I ought to nod assent but could not do it.

"You don't really believe it? Why, listen; once when I was a child and just waking up from a short afternoon nap, still half asleep, I heard my mother calling down from the balcony in the most natural voice: 'What are you doing, my dear? It's so hot.' And a woman answered from the garden: 'I'm reveling in the grass.' She said it quite simply and without insistence, as if it were to be taken for granted."

I thought an answer was expected from me, so I felt in my hip trouser pocket as if I were looking for something. But I wasn't looking for anything, I only wanted to shift my position to show that I was paying attention. And then I said that the incident was remarkable enough and quite beyond my comprehension. I added also that I didn't believe it was true and that it must have been invented for some special purpose which I could not fathom. Then I shut my eyes for they were hurting me.

"Oh, how glad I am that you agree with me, and it was most unselfish of you to stop me in order to let me know it. Why indeed should I feel ashamed—or why should we feel ashamed—because I don't walk upright and ponderously, striking my walking stick on the pavement and brushing the clothes of the people who pass by so loudly. Shouldn't I rather venture to complain with justified resentment at having to flit along the house walls like a shadow with hunched shoulders, many a time disappearing from sight in the plate glass of the shop windows.

"What dreadful days I have to live through! Why are all our buildings so badly put together that tall houses sometimes collapse without any discernible external cause? I go clambering over the ruins asking everyone I meet: 'Now how could such a thing happen! In our town—a brand new house—that's the fifth one today—just think of it.' And nobody can give me an answer.

"And people often fall down in the street and lie there dead. Then all the tradesmen open their doors that are hung with a litter of goods, come trotting out, carry the dead man into a house, and then appear again, with smiling eyes and lips, saying: 'Good morning—the sky is overcast—I'm selling a lot of kerchiefs—yes, the war.' I go slinking into the house and after timidly raising my hand several times with the fingers ready crooked knock at last on the porter's little glass window. 'My dear fellow,' I say to him in a friendly way, 'a dead man was just brought in here. Do let me see him, please.' And when he shakes his head as if undecided, I say positively: 'My dear chap. I'm from the secret police. Show me that dead man at once.' 'A dead man,' he asks, almost in an injured voice. 'No, there's no dead man here. This is a respectable house.' And I take my leave and go.

"And then if I have to cross a large open space I forget everything. The difficulty of this enterprise confuses me, and I can't help thinking: 'If people must build such large squares out of pure wantonness why don't they add a stone balustrade to help one across. There's a gale from the southwest today. The air in the square is swirling about. The tip of the Town Hall is teetering in small circles. All this agitation should be controlled. Every window pane is rattling and the lamp posts are bending like bamboos. The very robe of the Virgin Mary on her column is fluttering and the stormy wind is snatching at it. Is no one aware of this? The ladies and gentlemen who should be walking on the paving stones are driven along. When the wind slackens they come to a stop, exchange a few words and bow to each other, but when the wind blows again they can't help themselves, all their feet leave the ground at the same moment. They have to hold on to their hats, of course, but their eyes twinkle merrily as if there were only a gentle breeze. No one's afraid but me.' "

Smarting as I was, I said: "The story you told me about your mother and the woman in the garden seems to me not in the least remarkable. Not only have I heard many like it and experienced them, but I've even played a part in some of them. It was quite a natural incident. Do you think that if I had been on the balcony

I couldn't have said the same thing and got the same answer from the garden? Such a simple affair."

When I said that, he seemed very delighted. He remarked that I was well dressed and he particularly liked my tie. And what a fine skin I had. And admissions became most clear and unequivocal when one withdrew them.

MEDITATION

Meditation

Children on a Country Road

I HEARD the wagons rumbling past the garden fence, sometimes I even saw them through gently swaying gaps in the foliage. How the wood of their spokes and shafts creaked in the summer heat! Laborers were coming from the fields and laughing so that it was a scandal.

I was sitting on our little swing, just resting among the trees in my parents' garden.

On the other side of the fence the traffic never stopped. Children's running feet were past in a moment; harvest wagons with men and women perched on and around the sheaves darkened the flower beds; towards evening I saw a gentleman slowly promenading with a walking stick and a couple of girls who met him arm in arm stepped aside into the grass as they greeted him.

Then birds flew up as if in showers, I followed them with my eyes and saw how high they soared in one breath, till I felt not that they were rising but that I was falling, and holding fast to the ropes began to swing a little out of sheer weakness. Soon I was swinging more strongly as the air blew colder and instead of soaring birds trembling stars appeared.

I was given my supper by candle light. Often both my

arms were on the wooden board and I was already weary as I bit into my bread and butter. The coarse-mesh window curtains bellied in the warm wind and many a time some passer-by outside would stay them with his hands as if he wanted to see me better and speak to me. Usually the candle soon went out and in the sooty candle smoke the assembled midges went on circling for a while. If anyone asked me a question from the window I would gaze at him as if at a distant mountain or into vacancy, nor did he particularly care whether he got an answer or not. But if one jumped over the window sill and announced that the others were already waiting, then I did get to my feet with a sigh.

"What are you sighing for? What's wrong? Has something dreadful happened that can never be made good? Shan't we ever recover from it? Is everything lost?"

Nothing was lost. We ran to the front of the house. "Thank God, here you are at last!"—"You're always late!"—"Why just me?"—"Especially you, why don't you stay at home if you don't want to come."—"No quarter!" —"No quarter? What kind of way is that to talk?"

We ran our heads full tilt into the evening. There was no daytime and no nighttime. Now our waistcoat buttons would be clacking together like teeth, again we would be keeping a steady distance from each other as we ran, breathing fire like wild beasts in the tropics. Like cuirassiers in old wars, stamping and springing high, we drove each other down the short alley and with this impetus in our legs a farther stretch along the main road. Stray figures went into the ditch, hardly had they vanished down the dusky escarpment when they were standing like newcomers on the field path above and looking down.

"Come on down!"—"Come on up first!"—"So's you can push us down, no thanks, we're not such fools."—"You're afraid, you mean. Come on up, you cowards!"—"Afraid? Of the likes of you? You're going to push us down, are you? That's a good one."

We made the attempt and were pushed head over heels into the grass of the roadside ditch, tumbling of our own free will. Everything was equably warm to us, we felt neither warmth nor chill in the grass, only one got tired.

Turning on one's right side, with a hand under the ear, one could easily have fallen asleep there. But one wanted to get up again with chin uplifted, only to roll into a deeper ditch. Then with an arm thrust out crosswise and legs threshing to the side one thought to launch into the air again only to fall for certain into a still deeper ditch. And of this one never wanted to make an end.

How one might stretch oneself out, especially in the knees, properly to sleep in the last ditch, was something scarcely thought of, and one simply lay on one's back, like an invalid, inclined to weep a little. One blinked as now and then a youngster with elbows pressed to his sides sprang over one's head with dark-looming soles, in a leap from the escarpment to the roadway.

The moon was already some way up in the sky, in its light a mail coach drove past. A small wind began to blow everywhere, even in the ditch one could feel it, and near by the forest began to rustle. Then one was no longer so anxious to be alone.

"Where are you?"—"Come here!"—"All together!"—
"What are you hiding for, drop your nonsense!"—"Don't
you know the mail's gone past already?"—"Not already?"—"Of course; it went past while you were sleeping."—"I wasn't sleeping. What an idea!"—"Oh shut up,
you're still half asleep."—"But I wasn't."—"Come on!"

We ran bunched more closely together, many of us
linked hands, one's head could not be held high enough,
for now the way was downhill. Someone whooped an
Indian war cry, our legs galloped us as never before,
the wind lifted our hips as we sprang. Nothing could
have checked us; we were in such full stride that even
in overtaking others we could fold our arms and look
quietly around us.

At the bridge over the brook we came to a stop; those
who had overrun it came back. The water below lapped
against stones and roots as if it were not already late
evening. There was no reason why one of us should not
jump on to the parapet of the bridge.

From behind clumps of trees in the distance a railway
train came past, all the carriages were lit up, the window
panes were certainly let down. One of us began to sing
a popular catch, but we all felt like singing. We sang
much faster than the train was going, we waved our
arms because our voices were not enough, our voices
rushed together in an avalanche of sound that did us
good. When one joins in song with others it is like being
drawn on by a fish hook.

So we sang, the forest behind us, for the ears of the
distant travelers. The grownups were still awake in the
village, the mothers were making down the beds for the
night.

Our time was up. I kissed the one next me, reached

hands to the three nearest and began to run home, none called me back. At the first crossroads where they could no longer see me I turned off and ran by the field paths into the forest again. I was making for that city in the south of which it was said in our village:

"There you'll find queer folk! Just think, they never sleep!"

"And why not?"

"Because they never get tired."

"And why not?"

"Because they're fools."

"Don't fools get tired?"

"How could fools get tired!"

Unmasking a Confidence Trickster

AT LAST, about ten o'clock at night, I came to the doorway of the fine house where I was invited to spend the evening, after the man beside me, whom I was barely acquainted with and who had once again thrust himself unasked upon me, had marched me for two long hours around the streets.

"Well!" I said, and clapped my hands to show that I really had to bid him goodbye. I had already made several less explicit attempts to get rid of him. I was tired out.

"Are you going straight in?" he asked. I heard a sound in his mouth that was like the snapping of teeth.

"Yes."

I had been invited out, I told him when I met him. But it was to enter a house where I longed to be that I had been invited, not to stand here at the street door

looking past the ears of the man before me. Nor to
fall silent with him, as if we were doomed to stay for a
long time on this spot. And yet the houses around us
at once took a share in our silence, and the darkness
over them, all the way up to the stars. And the steps of
invisible passers-by, which one could not take the trouble
to elucidate, and the wind persistently buffeting the
other side of the street, and a gramophone singing behind the closed windows of some room—they all announced themselves in this silence, as if it were their own
possession for the time past and to come.

And my companion subscribed to it in his own name
and—with a smile—in mine too, stretched his right arm
up along the wall and leaned his cheek upon it, shutting his eyes.

But I did not wait to see the end of that smile, for
shame suddenly caught hold of me. It had needed that
smile to let me know that the man was a confidence
trickster, nothing else. And yet I had been months in
the town and thought I knew all about confidence
tricksters, how they came slinking out of side streets by
night to meet us with outstretched hands like tavern-
keepers, how they haunted the advertisement pillars we
stood beside, sliding round them as if playing hide-and-
seek and spying on us with at least one eye, how they
suddenly appeared on the curb of the pavement at cross
streets when we were hesitating! I understood them so
well, they were the first acquaintances I had made in
the town's small taverns, and to them I owed my first
inkling of a ruthless hardness which I was now so conscious of, everywhere on earth, that I was even beginning to feel it in myself. How persistently they blocked
our way, even when we had long shaken ourselves free,

even when, that is, they had nothing more to hope for! How they refused to give up, to admit defeat, but kept shooting glances at us that even from a distance were still compelling! And the means they employed were always the same: they planted themselves before us, looking as large as possible, tried to hinder us from going where we purposed, offered us instead a habitation in their own bosoms, and when at last all our balked feelings rose in revolt they welcomed that like an embrace into which they threw themselves face foremost.

And it had taken me such a long time in this man's company to recognize the same old game. I rubbed my finger tips together to wipe away the disgrace.

My companion was still leaning there as before, still believing himself a successful trickster, and his self-complacency glowed pink on his free cheek.

"Caught in the act!" said I, tapping him lightly on the shoulder. Then I ran up the steps, and the disinterested devotion on the servants' faces in the hall delighted me like an unexpected treat. I looked at them all, one after another, while they took my greatcoat off and wiped my shoes clean.

With a deep breath of relief and straightening myself to my full height I then entered the drawing room.

The Sudden Walk

WHEN IT LOOKS as if you had made up your mind finally to stay at home for the evening, when you have put on your house jacket and sat down after supper with a light on the table to the piece of work or the game that usually precedes your going to bed, when the

weather outside is unpleasant so that staying indoors
seems natural, and when you have already been sitting
quietly at the table for so long that your departure must
occasion surprise to everyone, when, besides, the stairs
are in darkness and the front door locked, and in spite of
all that you have started up in a sudden fit of restlessness, changed your jacket, abruptly dressed yourself for
the street, explained that you must go out and with a
few curt words of leave-taking actually gone out, bang-
ing the flat door more or less hastily according to the
degree of displeasure you think you have left behind
you, and when you find yourself once more in the
street with limbs swinging extra freely in answer to the
unexpected liberty you have procured for them, when as
a result of this decisive action you feel concentrated
within yourself all the potentialities of decisive action,
when you recognize with more than usual significance
that your strength is greater than your need to accomplish effortlessly the swiftest of changes and to cope
with it, when in this frame of mind you go striding
down the long streets—then for that evening you have
completely got away from your family, which fades
into insubstantiality, while you yourself, a firm, boldly
drawn black figure, slapping yourself on the thigh,
grow to your true stature.

All this is still heightened if at such a late hour in the
evening you look up a friend to see how he is getting on.

Resolutions

To LIFT yourself out of a miserable mood, even if you
have to do it by strength of will, should be easy. I force

myself out of my chair, stride round the table, exercise my head and neck, make my eyes sparkle, tighten the muscles round them. Defy my own feelings, welcome A. enthusiastically supposing he comes to see me, amiably tolerate B. in my room, swallow all that is said at C.'s, whatever pain and trouble it may cost me, in long draughts.

Yet even if I manage that, one single slip, and a slip cannot be avoided, will stop the whole process, easy and painful alike, and I will have to shrink back into my own circle again.

So perhaps the best resource is to meet everything passively, to make yourself an inert mass, and, if you feel that you are being carried away, not to let yourself be lured into taking a single unnecessary step, to stare at others with the eyes of an animal, to feel no compunction, in short, with your own hand to throttle down whatever ghostly life remains in you, that is, to enlarge the final peace of the graveyard and let nothing survive save that.

A characteristic movement in such a condition is to run your little finger along your eyebrows.

Excursion into the Mountains

"I DON'T KNOW," I cried without being heard, "I do not know. If nobody comes, then nobody comes. I've done nobody any harm, nobody's done me any harm, but nobody will help me. A pack of nobodies. Yet that isn't all true. Only, that nobody helps me—a pack of nobodies would be rather fine, on the other hand. I'd love to go on an excursion—why not?—with a pack of nobodies.

Into the mountains, of course, where else? How these
nobodies jostle each other, all these lifted arms linked
together, these numberless feet treading so close! Of
course they are all in dress suits. We go so gaily, the
wind blows through us and the gaps in our company.
Our throats swell and are free in the mountains! It's a
wonder that we don't burst into song."

Bachelor's Ill Luck

IT SEEMS so dreadful to stay a bachelor, to become an
old man struggling to keep one's dignity while begging
for an invitation whenever one wants to spend an evening in company, to lie ill gazing for weeks into an
empty room from the corner where one's bed is, always
having to say good night at the front door, never to run
up a stairway beside one's wife, to have only side doors
in one's room leading into other people's living rooms,
having to carry one's supper home in one's hand, having
to admire other people's children and not even being
allowed to go on saying: "I have none myself," model-
ing oneself in appearance and behavior on one or two
bachelors remembered from one's youth.

That's how it will be, except that in reality, both today
and later, one will stand there with a palpable body and
a real head, a real forehead, that is, for smiting on with
one's hand.

The Tradesman

IT IS POSSIBLE that some people are sorry for me, but I am not aware of it. My small business fills me with worries that make my forehead and temples ache inside yet without giving any prospect of relief, for my business is a small business.

I have to spend hours beforehand making things ready, jogging the caretaker's memory, warning him about mistakes he is likely to commit, and puzzling out in one season of the year what the next season's fashions are to be, not such as are followed by the people I know but those that will appeal to inaccessible peasants in the depths of the country.

My money is in the hands of strangers; the state of their affairs must be a mystery to me; the ill luck that might overwhelm them I cannot foresee; how could I possibly avert it! Perhaps they are running into extravagance and giving a banquet in some inn garden, some of them may be attending the banquet as a brief respite before their flight to America.

When at the close of a working day I turn the key on my business and suddenly see before me hours in which I shall be able to do nothing to satisfy its never-ending demands, then the excitement which I drove far away from me in the morning comes back like a returning tide, but cannot be contained in me and sweeps me aimlessly away with it.

And yet I can make no use of this impulse, I can only go home, for my face and hands are dirty and sweaty, my clothes are stained and dusty, my working cap is on my head and my shoes are scratched with the nails of crates. I go home as if lifted on a wave, snapping the fingers of both hands, and caress the hair of any children I meet.

But the way is short. Soon I reach my house, open the door of the lift and step in.

I see that now, of a sudden, I am alone. Others who have to climb stairways tire a little as they climb, have to wait with quick panting breath till someone opens the door of the flat, which gives them an excuse for being irritable and impatient, have to traverse the hallway where hats are hung up, and not until they go down a lobby past several glass doors and come into their own room are they alone.

But I am alone in the lift, immediately, and on my knees gaze into the narrow looking glass. As the lift begins to rise, I say:

"Quiet now, back with you, is it the shadow of the trees you want to make for, or behind the window curtains, or into the garden arbor?"

I say that behind my teeth, and the staircase flows down past the opaque glass panes like running water.

"Fly then; let your wings, which I have never seen, carry you into the village hollow or as far as Paris, if that's where you want to go.

"But enjoy yourselves there looking out of the window, see the processions converging out of three streets at once, not giving way to each other but marching through each other and leaving the open space free again as their last ranks draw off. Wave your handkerchiefs, be indignant, be moved, acclaim the beautiful lady who drives past.

"Cross over the stream on the wooden bridge, nod to

the children bathing and gape at the Hurrah! rising from the thousand sailors on the distant battleship.

"Follow the trail of the inconspicuous little man, and when you have pushed him into a doorway, rob him, and then watch him, each with your hands in your pockets, as he sadly goes his way along the left-hand street.

"The police dispersed on galloping horses rein in their mounts and thrust you back. Let them, the empty streets will dishearten them, I know. What did I tell you, they are riding away already in couples, slowly round the corners, at full speed across the squares."

Then I have to leave the lift, send it down again and ring the bell, and the maid opens the door while I say: Good evening.

Absent-minded Window-gazing

WHAT ARE we to do with these spring days that are now fast coming on? Early this morning the sky was gray, but if you go to the window now you are surprised and lean your cheek against the latch of the casement.

The sun is already setting, but down below you see it lighting up the face of the little girl who strolls along looking about her, and at the same time you see her eclipsed by the shadow of the man behind overtaking her.

And then the man has passed by and the little girl's face is quite bright.

The Way Home

SEE WHAT a persuasive force the air has after a thunderstorm! My merits become evident and overpower me, though I don't put up any resistance, I grant you.

I stride along and my tempo is the tempo of all my side of the street, of the whole street, of the whole quarter. Mine is the responsibility, and rightly so, for all the raps on doors or on the flat of a table, for all toasts drunk, for lovers in their beds, in the scaffolding of new buildings, pressed to each other against the house walls in dark alleys, or on the divans of a brothel.

I weigh my past against my future, but find both of them admirable, cannot give either the preference, and find nothing to grumble at save the injustice of Providence that has so clearly favored me.

Only as I come into my room I feel a little meditative, without having met anything on the stairs worth meditating about. It doesn't help me much to open the window wide and hear music still playing in a garden.

Passers-by

WHEN YOU GO walking by night up a street and a man, visible a long way off—for the street mounts uphill and there is a full moon—comes running towards you, well, you don't catch hold of him, not even if he is a feeble and ragged creature, not even if someone chases yelling at his heels, but you let him run on.

For it is night, and you can't help it if the street goes uphill before you in the moonlight, and besides, these two have maybe started that chase to amuse themselves, or perhaps they are both chasing a third, perhaps the first is an innocent man and the second wants to murder him and you would become an accessory, perhaps they don't know anything about each other and are merely running separately home to bed, perhaps they are night birds, perhaps the first man is armed.

And anyhow, haven't you a right to be tired, haven't you been drinking a lot of wine? You're thankful that the second man is now long out of sight.

On the Tram

I STAND on the end platform of the tram and am completely unsure of my footing in this world, in this town, in my family. Not even casually could I indicate any claims that I might rightly advance in any direction. I have not even any defense to offer for standing on this platform, holding on to this strap, letting myself be carried along by this tram, nor for the people who give way to the tram or walk quietly along or stand gazing into shop windows. Nobody asks me to put up a defense, indeed, but that is irrelevant.

The tram approaches a stopping place and a girl takes up her position near the step, ready to alight. She is as distinct to me as if I had run my hands over her. She is dressed in black, the pleats of her skirt hang almost still, her blouse is tight and has a collar of white fine-meshed lace, her left hand is braced flat against the side of the tram, the umbrella in her right hand rests on the second top step. Her face is brown, her nose, slightly pinched at the sides, has a broad round tip. She has a lot of brown hair and stray little tendrils on the right temple. Her small ear is close-set, but since I am near her I can see the whole ridge of the whorl of her right ear and the shadow at the root of it.

At that point I asked myself: How is it that she is not amazed at herself, that she keeps her lips closed and makes no such remark?

Clothes

OFTEN THEN I see clothes with manifold pleats, frills and appendages which fit so smoothly on to lovely bodies I think they won't keep that smoothness long, but will get creases that can't be ironed out, dust lying so thick in the embroidery that it can't be brushed away, and that no one would want to be so unhappy and so foolish as to wear the same valuable gown every day from early morning till night.

And yet I see girls who are lovely enough and display attractive muscles and small bones and smooth skin and masses of delicate hair, and none the less appear day in, day out, in this same natural fancy dress, always propping the same face on the same palms and letting it be reflected from the looking glass.

Only sometimes at night, on coming home late from a party, it seems in the looking glass to be worn out, puffy, dusty, already seen by too many people and hardly wearable any longer.

Rejection

WHEN I MEET a pretty girl and beg her: "Be so good as to come with me," and she walks past without a word, this is what she means to say:

"You are no Duke with a famous name, no broad American with a Red Indian figure, level, brooding eyes and a skin tempered by the air of the prairies and the rivers that flow through them, you have never journeyed to the seven seas and voyaged on them wherever they may be, I don't know where. So why, pray, should a pretty girl like myself go with you?"

"You forget that no automobile swings you through the street in long thrusts; I see no gentlemen escorting you in a close half-circle, pressing on your skirts from behind and murmuring blessings on your head; your breasts are well laced into your bodice, but your thighs and hips make up for that restraint; you are wearing a taffeta dress with a pleated skirt such as delighted all of us last autumn, and yet you smile—inviting mortal danger —from time to time."

"Yes, we're both in the right, and to keep us from being irrevocably aware of it, hadn't we better just go our separate ways home?"

Reflections for Gentlemen-Jockeys

WHEN YOU THINK it over, winning a race is nothing to sigh for.

The fame of being hailed as the best rider in the

country is too intoxicating a pleasure when the applause strikes up not to bring a reaction the morning after.

The envy of your opponents, cunning and fairly influential men, must trouble you in the narrow enclosure you now traverse after the flat racecourse, which soon lay empty before you save for some laggards of the previous round, small figures charging the horizon.

Many of your friends are rushing to gather their winnings and only cry "Hurrah!" to you over their shoulders from distant pay boxes; your best friends laid no bet on your horse, since they feared that they would have to be angry with you if you lost, and now that your horse has come in first and they have won nothing, they turn away as you pass and prefer to look along the stands.

Your rivals behind you, firmly in the saddle, are trying to ignore the bad luck that has befallen them and the injustice they have somehow suffered; they are putting a brave new face on things, as if a different race were due to start, and this time a serious one after such child's play.

For many ladies the victor cuts a ridiculous figure because he is swelling with importance and yet cannot cope with the never-ending hand-shaking, saluting, bowing and waving, while the defeated keep their mouths shut and casually pat the necks of their whinnying horses.

And finally from the now overcast sky rain actually begins to fall.

The Street Window

WHOEVER LEADS a solitary life and yet now and then
wants to attach himself somewhere, whoever, according
to changes in the time of day, the weather, the state of
his business and the like, suddenly wishes to see any arm
at all to which he might cling—he will not be able to
manage for long without a window looking on to the
street. And if he is in the mood of not desiring anything and only goes to his window sill a tired man, with
eyes turning from his public to heaven and back again,
not wanting to look out and having thrown his head up
a little, even then the horses below will draw him down
into their train of wagons and tumult, and so at last
into the human harmony.

The Wish to Be a Red Indian

IF ONE WERE only an Indian, instantly alert, and on a
racing horse, leaning against the wind, kept on quivering
jerkily over the quivering ground, until one shed one's
spurs, for there needed no spurs, threw away the reins,
for there needed no reins, and hardly saw that the land
before one was smoothly shorn heath when horse's neck
and head would be already gone.

The Trees

FOR WE ARE like tree trunks in the snow. In appearance
they lie sleekly and a light push should be enough to set

them rolling. No, it can't be done, for they are firmly wedded to the ground. But see, even that is only appearance.

Unhappiness

WHEN IT WAS becoming unbearable—once towards evening in November—and I ran along the narrow strip of carpet in my room as on a race track, shrank from the sight of the lit-up street, then turning to the interior of the room found a new goal in the depths of the looking glass and screamed aloud, to hear only my own scream which met no answer nor anything that could draw its force away, so that it rose up without check and could not stop even when it ceased being audible, the door in the wall opened towards me, how swiftly, because swiftness was needed and even the cart horses down below on the paving stones were rising in the air like horses driven wild in a battle, their throats bare to the enemy.

Like a small ghost a child blew in from the pitch-dark corridor, where the lamp was not yet lit, and stood a-tiptoe on a floor board that quivered imperceptibly. At once dazzled by the twilight in my room she made to cover her face quickly with her hands, but contented herself unexpectedly with a glance at the window, where the mounting vapor of the street lighting had at last settled under its cover of darkness behind the crossbars. With her right elbow she supported herself against the wall in the open doorway and let the draught from outside play along her ankles, her throat and her temples.

I gave her a brief glance, then said "Good day," and took my jacket from the hood of the stove, since I didn't want to stand there half undressed. For a little while I let my mouth hang open, so that my agitation could find a way out. I had a bad taste in my mouth, my eyelashes were fluttering on my cheeks, in short this visit, though I had expected it, was the one thing needful.

The child was still standing by the wall on the same spot, she had pressed her right hand against the plaster and was quite taken up with finding, her cheeks all pink, that the whitewashed walls had a rough surface and chafed her finger tips. I said: "Are you really looking for me? Isn't there some mistake? Nothing easier than to make a mistake in this big building. I'm called So-and-So and I live on the third floor. Am I the person you want to find?"

"Hush, hush," said the child over her shoulder, "it's all right."

"Then come farther into the room, I'd like to shut the door."

"I've shut it this very minute. Don't bother. Just be easy in your mind."

"It's no bother. But there's a lot of people living on this corridor, and I know them all, of course; most of them are coming back from work now; if they hear someone talking in a room, they simply think they have a right to open the door and see what's happening. They're just like that. They've turned their backs on their daily work and in their provisionally free evenings they're not going to be dictated to by anyone. Besides, you know that as well as I do. Let me shut the door."

"Why, what's the matter with you? I don't mind if the whole house comes in. Anyhow, as I told you, I've already shut the door, do you think you're the only person who can shut doors? I've even turned the key in the lock."

"That's all right then. I couldn't ask for more. You didn't need to turn the key, either. And now that you are here, make yourself comfortable. You are my guest. You can trust me entirely. Just make yourself at home and don't be afraid. I won't compel you either to stay or to go away. Do I have to tell you that? Do you know me so little?"

"No. You really didn't need to tell me that. What's more, you shouldn't have told me. I'm just a child; why stand on so much ceremony with me?"

"It's not so bad as that. A child, of course. But not so very small. You're quite big. If you were a young lady, you wouldn't dare to lock yourself so simply in a room with me."

"We needn't worry about that. I just want to say: my knowing you so well isn't much protection to me, it only relieves you of the effort of keeping up pretenses before me. And yet you're paying me a compliment. Stop it, I beg you, do stop it. Anyhow, I don't know you everywhere and all the time, least of all in this darkness. It would be much better if you were to light up. No, perhaps not. At any rate I'll keep it in mind that you have been threatening me."

"What? Am I supposed to have threatened you? But, look here. I'm so pleased that you've come at last. I say 'at last' because it's already rather late. I can't understand why you've come so late. But it's possible that in the joy of seeing you I have been speaking at random and you took up my words in the wrong sense. I'll admit ten times over that I said something of the kind,

I've made all kinds of threats, anything you like. Only no quarrelling, for Heaven's sake! But how could you think of such a thing? How could you hurt me so? Why do you insist on spoiling this brief moment of your presence here? A stranger would be more oncoming than you are."

"That I can well believe; that's no great discovery. No stranger could come any nearer to you than I am already by nature. You know that, too, so why all this pathos? If you're only wanting to stage a comedy I'll go away immediately."

"What? You have the impudence to tell me that? You make a little too bold. After all, it's my room you're in. It's my wall you're rubbing your fingers on like mad. My room, my wall! And besides, what you are saying is ridiculous as well as impudent. You say your nature forces you to speak to me like that. Is that so? Your nature forces you? That's kind of your nature. Your nature is mine, and if I feel friendly to you by nature, then you mustn't be anything else."

"Is that friendly?"

"I'm speaking of earlier on."

"Do you know how I'll be later on?"

"I don't know anything."

And I went to the bed table and lit the candle on it. At that time I had neither gas nor electric light in my room. Then I sat for a while at the table till I got tired of it, put on my greatcoat, took my hat from the sofa and blew out the candle. As I went out I tripped over the leg of a chair.

On the stairs I met one of the tenants from my floor.

"Going out again already, you rascal?" he asked, pausing with his legs firmly straddled over two steps.

"What can I do?" I said, "I've just had a ghost in my room."

"You say that exactly as if you had just found a hair in your soup."

"You're making a joke of it. But let me tell you, a ghost is a ghost."

"How true. But what if one doesn't believe in ghosts at all?"

"Well, do you think I believe in ghosts? But how can my not believing help me?"

"Quite simply. You don't need to feel afraid if a ghost actually turns up."

"Oh, that's only a secondary fear. The real fear is a fear of what caused the apparition. And that fear doesn't go away. I have it fairly powerfully inside me now." Out of sheer nervousness I began to hunt through all my pockets.

"But since you weren't afraid of the ghost itself, you could easily have asked it how it came to be there."

"Obviously you've never spoken to a ghost. One never gets straight information from them. It's just a hither and thither. These ghosts seem to be more dubious about their existence than we are, and no wonder, considering how frail they are."

"But I've heard that one can feed them up."

"How well informed you are. It's quite true. But is anyone likely to do it?"

"Why not? If it were a feminine ghost, for instance," said he, swinging on to the top step.

"Aha," said I, "but even then it's not worth while."

I thought of something else. My neighbor was already so far up that in order to see me he had to bend over the well of the staircase. "All the same," I called up, "if you steal my ghost from me all is over between us, for ever."

"Oh, I was only joking," he said and drew his head back.

"That's all right," said I, and now I really could have gone quietly for a walk. But because I felt so forlorn I preferred to go upstairs again and so went to bed.

THE JUDGMENT

The Judgment

I⊤ WAS a Sunday morning in the very height of spring. Georg Bendemann, a young merchant, was sitting in his own room on the first floor of one of a long row of small, ramshackle houses stretching beside the river which were scarcely distinguishable from each other except in height and coloring. He had just finished a letter to an old friend of his who was now living abroad, had put it into its envelope in a slow and dreamy fashion, and with his elbows propped on the writing table was gazing out of the window at the river, the bridge and the hills on the farther bank with their tender green.

He was thinking about his friend, who had actually run away to Russia some years before, being dissatisfied with his prospects at home. Now he was carrying on a business in St. Petersburg, which had flourished to begin with but had long been going downhill, as he always complained on his increasingly rare visits. So he was wearing himself out to no purpose in a foreign country, the unfamiliar full beard he wore did not quite conceal the face Georg had known so well since childhood, and his skin was growing so yellow as to indicate some latent disease. By his own account he had no regular connection with the colony of his fellow countrymen out there and almost no social intercourse with Russian families, so that he was resigning himself to becoming a permanent bachelor.

What could one write to such a man, who had obviously run off the rails, a man one could be sorry for but could not help. Should one advise him to come home, to transplant himself and take up his old friendships again—there was nothing to hinder him—and in general to rely on the help of his friends? But that was as good as telling him, and the more kindly the more offensively, that all his efforts hitherto had miscarried, that he should finally give up, come back home, and be gaped at by everyone as a returned prodigal, that only his friends knew what was what and that he himself was just a big child who should do what his successful and home-keeping friends prescribed. And was it certain, besides, that all the pain one would have to inflict on him would achieve its object? Perhaps it would not even be possible to get him to come home at all—he said himself that he was now out of touch with commerce in his native country—and then he would still be left an alien in a foreign land embittered by his friends' advice and more than ever estranged from them. But if he did follow their advice and then didn't fit in at home—not out of malice, of course, but through force of circumstances—couldn't get on with his friends or without them, felt humiliated, couldn't be said to have either friends or a country of his own any longer, wouldn't it have been better for him to stay abroad just as he was? Taking all this into account, how could one be sure that he would make a success of life at home?

For such reasons, supposing one wanted to keep up correspondence with him, one could not send him any

real news such as could frankly be told to the most distant acquaintance. It was more than three years since his
last visit, and for this he offered the lame excuse that the
political situation in Russia was too uncertain, which,
apparently would not permit even the briefest absence
of a small business man while it allowed hundreds of
thousands of Russians to travel peacefully abroad. But
during these three years Georg's own position in life had
changed a lot. Two years ago his mother had died, since
when he and his father had shared the household together, and his friend had of course been informed of
that and had expressed his sympathy in a letter phrased
so dryly that the grief caused by such an event, one had
to conclude, could not be realized in a distant country.
Since that time, however, Georg had applied himself
with greater determination to the business as well as to
everything else.

Perhaps during his mother's lifetime his father's insistence on having everything his own way in the business had hindered him from developing any real activity
of his own, perhaps since her death his father had become
less aggressive, although he was still active in the business, perhaps it was mostly due to an accidental run of
good fortune—which was very probable indeed—but at
any rate during those two years the business had developed in a most unexpected way, the staff had had to
be doubled, the turnover was five times as great, no
doubt about it, farther progress lay just ahead.

But Georg's friend had no inkling of this improvement.
In earlier years, perhaps for the last time in that letter
of condolence, he had tried to persuade Georg to emi-
grate to Russia and had enlarged upon the prospects of
success for precisely Georg's branch of trade. The

figures quoted were microscopic by comparison with
the range of Georg's present operations. Yet he shrank
from letting his friend know about his business success,
and if he were to do it now retrospectively that certainly
would look peculiar.

So Georg confined himself to giving his friend unimportant items of gossip such as rise at random in the
memory when one is idly thinking things over on a
quiet Sunday. All he desired was to leave undisturbed
the idea of the home town which his friend must have
built up to his own content during the long interval.
And so it happened to Georg that three times in three
fairly widely separated letters he had told his friend
about the engagement of an unimportant man to an
equally unimportant girl, until indeed, quite contrary to
his intentions, his friend began to show some interest in
this notable event.

Yet Georg preferred to write about things like these
rather than to confess that he himself had got engaged
a month ago to a Fräulein Frieda Brandenfeld, a girl
from a well-to-do family. He often discussed this friend
of his with his fiancée and the peculiar relationship that
had developed between them in their correspondence.
"So he won't be coming to our wedding," said she, "and
yet I have a right to get to know all your friends." "I
don't want to trouble him," answered Georg, "don't
misunderstand me, he would probably come, at least I
think so, but he would feel that his hand had been forced
and he would be hurt, perhaps he would envy me and
certainly he'd be discontented and without being able to
do anything about his discontent he'd have to go away
again alone. Alone—do you know what that means?"
"Yes, but may he not hear about our wedding in some

other fashion?" "I can't prevent that, of course, but it's unlikely, considering the way he lives." "Since your friends are like that, Georg, you shouldn't ever have got engaged at all." "Well, we're both to blame for that; but I wouldn't have it any other way now." And when, breathing quickly under his kisses, she still brought out: "All the same, I do feel upset," he thought it could not really involve him in trouble were he to send the news to his friend. "That's the kind of man I am and he'll just have to take me as I am," he said to himself, "I can't cut myself to another pattern that might make a more suitable friend for him."

And in fact he did inform his friend, in the long letter he had been writing that Sunday morning, about his engagement, with these words: "I have saved my best news to the end. I have got engaged to a Fräulein Frieda Brandenfeld, a girl from a well-to-do family, who only came to live here a long time after you went away, so that you're hardly likely to know her. There will be time to tell you more about her later, for today let me just say that I am very happy and as between you and me the only difference in our relationship is that instead of a quite ordinary kind of friend you will now have in me a happy friend. Besides that, you will acquire in my fiancée, who sends her warm greetings and will soon write you herself, a genuine friend of the opposite sex, which is not without importance to a bachelor. I know that there are many reasons why you can't come to see us, but would not my wedding be precisely the right occasion for giving all obstacles the go-by? Still, however that may be, do just as seems good to you without regarding any interests but your own."

With this letter in his hand Georg had been sitting a

long time at the writing table, his face turned towards
the window. He had barely acknowledged, with an
absent smile, a greeting waved to him from the street
by a passing acquaintance.

At last he put the letter in his pocket and went out of
his room across a small lobby into his father's room,
which he had not entered for months. There was in fact
no need for him to enter it, since he saw his father
daily at business and they took their midday meal together at an eating house; in the evening, it was true,
each did as he pleased, yet even then, unless Georg—as
mostly happened—went out with friends or, more recently, visited his fiancée, they always sat for a while,
each with his newspaper, in their common sitting room.

It surprised Georg how dark his father's room was
even on this sunny morning. So it was overshadowed as
much as that by the high wall on the other side of the
narrow courtyard. His father was sitting by the window
in a corner hung with various mementoes of Georg's
dead mother, reading a newspaper which he held to one
side before his eyes in an attempt to overcome a defect
of vision. On the table stood the remains of his breakfast, not much of which seemed to have been eaten.

"Ah, Georg," said his father, rising at once to meet
him. His heavy dressing gown swung open as he walked
and the skirts of it fluttered round him.—"My father is
still a giant of a man," said Georg to himself.

"It's unbearably dark here," he said aloud.

"Yes, it's dark enough," answered his father.

"And you've shut the window, too?"

"I prefer it like that."

"Well, it's quite warm outside," said Georg, as if
continuing his previous remark, and sat down.

His father cleared away the breakfast dishes and set them on a chest.

"I really only wanted to tell you," went on Georg, who had been vacantly following the old man's movements, "that I am now sending the news of my engagement to St. Petersburg." He drew the letter a little way from his pocket and let it drop back again.

"To St. Petersburg?" asked his father.

"To my friend there," said Georg, trying to meet his father's eye.—In business hours he's quite different, he was thinking, how solidly he sits here with his arms crossed.

"Oh yes. To your friend," said his father, with peculiar emphasis.

"Well, you know, Father, that I wanted not to tell him about my engagement at first. Out of consideration for him, that was the only reason. You know yourself he's a difficult man. I said to myself that someone else might tell him about my engagement, although he's such a solitary creature that that was hardly likely—I couldn't prevent that—but I wasn't ever going to tell him myself."

"And now you've changed your mind?" asked his father, laying his enormous newspaper on the window sill and on top of it his spectacles, which he covered with one hand.

"Yes, I've been thinking it over. If he's a good friend of mine, I said to myself, my being happily engaged should make him happy too. And so I wouldn't put off telling him any longer. But before I posted the letter I wanted to let you know."

"Georg," said his father, lengthening his toothless mouth, "listen to me! You've come to me about this business, to talk it over with me. No doubt that does you honor. But it's nothing, it's worse than nothing, if you don't tell me the whole truth. I don't want to stir up matters that shouldn't be mentioned here. Since the death of our dear mother certain things have been done that aren't right. Maybe the time will come for mentioning them, and maybe sooner than we think. There's many a thing in the business I'm not aware of, maybe it's not done behind my back—I'm not going to say that it's done behind my back—I'm not equal to things any longer, my memory's failing, I haven't an eye for so many things any longer. That's the course of nature in the first place, and in the second place the death of our dear mother hit me harder than it did you.—But since we're talking about it, about this letter, I beg you, Georg, don't deceive me. It's a trivial affair, it's hardly worth mentioning, so don't deceive me. Do you really have this friend in St. Petersburg?"

Georg rose in embarrassment. "Never mind my friends. A thousand friends wouldn't make up to me for my father. Do you know what I think? You're not taking enough care of yourself. But old age must be taken care of. I can't do without you in the business, you know that very well, but if the business is going to undermine your health, I'm ready to close it down tomorrow forever. And that won't do. We'll have to make a change in your way of living. But a radical change. You sit here in the dark, and in the sitting room you would have plenty of light. You just take a bite of breakfast instead of properly keeping up your strength. You sit by a closed window, and the air would be so good for you. No, Father! I'll get the doctor to come, and we'll follow his orders. We'll change your room, you can move into the front room and I'll move in here. You won't notice the change, all your things will be moved with you. But there's time for all that later, I'll put you to bed now for a little, I'm sure you need to rest. Come, I'll help you to take off your things, you'll see I can do it. Or if you would rather go into the front room at once, you can lie down in my bed for the present. That would be the most sensible thing."

Georg stood close beside his father, who had let his head with its unkempt white hair sink on his chest.

"Georg," said his father in a low voice, without moving.

Georg knelt down at once beside his father, in the old man's weary face he saw the pupils, over-large, fixedly looking at him from the corners of the eyes.

"You have no friend in St. Petersburg. You've always been a leg-puller and you haven't even shrunk from pulling my leg. How could you have a friend out there! I can't believe it."

"Just think back a bit, Father," said Georg, lifting his father from the chair and slipping off his dressing gown as he stood feebly enough, "it'll soon be three years since my friend came to see us last. I remember that you used not to like him very much. At least twice I kept you from seeing him, although he was actually sitting with me in my room. I could quite well understand your dislike of him, my friend has his peculiarities. But then, later, you got on with him very well. I was proud because you listened to him and nodded and asked him questions. If you think back you're bound to remember. He used to tell us the most incredible stories of the Russian Revolution. For instance, when he was on a business trip to Kiev and ran into a riot, and saw a priest on a balcony who cut a broad cross in blood on the palm of his hand and held the hand up and appealed to the mob. You've told that story yourself once or twice since."

Meanwhile Georg had succeeded in lowering his father down again and carefully taking off the woollen drawers he wore over his linen underpants and his socks. The not particularly clean appearance of this underwear made him reproach himself for having been neglectful. It should have certainly been his duty to see that his father had clean changes of underwear. He had not yet explicitly discussed with his bride-to-be what arrangements should be made for his father in the future, for they had both of them silently taken it for granted that the old man would go on living alone in the old house. But now he made a quick, firm decision to take him into his own future establishment. It almost looked, on closer inspection, as if the care he meant to lavish there on his father might come too late.

He carried his father to bed in his arms. It gave him a dreadful feeling to notice that while he took the few steps towards the bed the old man on his breast was playing with his watch chain. He could not lay him down on the bed for a moment, so firmly did he hang on to the watch chain.

But as soon as he was laid in bed, all seemed well. He covered himself up and even drew the blankets farther than usual over his shoulders. He looked up at Georg with a not unfriendly eye.

"You begin to remember my friend, don't you?" asked Georg, giving him an encouraging nod.

"Am I well covered up now?" asked his father, as if he were not able to see whether his feet were properly tucked in or not.

"So you find it snug in bed already," said Georg, and tucked the blankets more closely round him.

"Am I well covered up?" asked the father once more, seeming to be strangely intent upon the answer.

"Don't worry, you're well covered up."

"No!" cried his father, cutting short the answer, threw the blankets off with a strength that sent them all flying in a moment and sprang erect in bed. Only one hand lightly touched the ceiling to steady him.

"You wanted to cover me up, I know, my young sprig, but I'm far from being covered up yet. And even if this is the last strength I have, it's enough for you, too much for you. Of course I know your friend. He would have been a son after my own heart. That's why you've been playing him false all these years. Why else? Do you think I haven't been sorry for him? And that's why you had to lock yourself up in your office—the Chief is busy, mustn't be disturbed—just so that you could write your lying little letters to Russia. But thank goodness a father doesn't need to be taught how to see through his son. And now that you thought you'd got him down, so far down that you could set your bottom on him and sit on him and he wouldn't move, then my fine son makes up his mind to get married!"

Georg stared at the bogey conjured up by his father. His friend in St. Petersburg, whom his father suddenly knew too well, touched his imagination as never before. Lost in the vastness of Russia he saw him. At the door of an empty, plundered warehouse he saw him. Among the wreckage of his showcases, the slashed remnants of his wares, the falling gas brackets, he was just standing up. Why did he have to go so far away!

"But attend to me!" cried his father, and Georg, almost distracted, ran towards the bed to take everything in, yet came to a stop halfway.

"Because she lifted up her skirts," his father began to flute, "because she lifted her skirts like this, the nasty creature," and mimicking her he lifted his shirt so high that one could see the scar on his thigh from his war wound, "because she lifted her skirts like this and this you made up to her, and in order to make free with her undisturbed you have disgraced your mother's memory, betrayed your friend and stuck your father into bed so that he can't move. But he can move, or can't he?"

And he stood up quite unsupported and kicked his legs out. His insight made him radiant.

Georg shrank into a corner, as far away from his father as possible. A long time ago he had firmly made up his mind to watch closely every least movement so that he should not be surprised by any indirect attack, a pounce from behind or above. At this moment he recalled this long-forgotten resolve and forgot it again, like a man drawing a short thread through the eye of a needle.

"But your friend hasn't been betrayed after all!" cried his father, emphasizing the point with stabs of his forefinger. "I've been representing him here on the spot."

"You comedian!" Georg could not resist the retort, realized at once the harm done and, his eyes starting in his head, bit his tongue back, only too late, till the pain made his knees give.

"Yes, of course I've been playing a comedy! A comedy! That's a good expression! What other comfort was left to a poor old widower? Tell me——and while you're answering me be you still my living son—what else was left to me, in my back room, plagued by a disloyal staff, old to the marrow of my bones? And my son strutting through the world, finishing off deals that I had prepared for him, bursting with triumphant glee and stalking away from his father with the closed face of a respectable business man! Do you think I didn't love you, I, from whom you are sprung?"

Now he'll lean forward, thought Georg, what if he topples and smashes himself! These words went hissing through his mind.

His father leaned forward but did not topple. Since Georg did not come any nearer, as he had expected, he straightened himself again.

"Stay where you are, I don't need you! You think you have strength enough to come over here and that you're only hanging back of your own accord. Don't be too sure! I am still much the stronger of us two. All by myself I might have had to give way, but your mother has given me so much of her strength that I've established a fine connection with your friend and I have your customers here in my pocket!"

"He has pockets even in his shirt!" said Georg to himself, and believed that with this remark he could make him an impossible figure for all the world. Only for a moment did he think so, since he kept on forgetting everything.

"Just take your bride on your arm and try getting in my way! I'll sweep her from your very side, you don't know how!"

Georg made a grimace of disbelief. His father only nodded, confirming the truth of his words, towards Georg's corner.

"How you amused me today, coming to ask me if you should tell your friend about your engagement. He

knows it already, you stupid boy, he knows it all! I've
been writing to him, for you forgot to take my writing
things away from me. That's why he hasn't been here
for years, he knows everything a hundred times better
than you do yourself, in his left hand he crumples your
letters unopened while in his right hand he holds up my
letters to read through!"

In his enthusiasm he waved his arm over his head.
"He knows everything a thousand times better!" he
cried.

"Ten thousand times!" said Georg, to make fun of his
father, but in his very mouth the words turned into
deadly earnest.

"For years I've been waiting for you to come with
some such question! Do you think I concern myself
with anything else? Do you think I read my newspapers?
Look!" and he threw Georg a newspaper sheet which he
had somehow taken to bed with him. An old newspaper,
with a name entirely unknown to Georg.

"How long a time you've taken to grow up! Your
mother had to die, she couldn't see the happy day, your
friend is going to pieces in Russia, even three years ago
he was yellow enough to be thrown away, and as for
me, you see what condition I'm in. You have eyes in
your head for that!"

"So you've been lying in wait for me!" cried Georg.

His father said pityingly, in an offhand manner: "I
suppose you wanted to say that sooner. But now it
doesn't matter." And in a louder voice: "So now you
know what else there was in the world besides yourself, till now you've known only about yourself! An
innocent child, yes, that you were, truly, but still more
truly have you been a devilish human being!—And

therefore take note: I sentence you now to death by drowning!"

Georg felt himself urged from the room, the crash with which his father fell on the bed behind him was still in his ears as he fled. On the staircase, which he rushed down as if its steps were an inclined plane, he ran into his charwoman on her way up to do the morning cleaning of the room. "Jesus!" she cried, and covered her face with her apron, but he was already gone. Out of the front door he rushed, across the roadway, driven towards the water. Already he was grasping at the railings as a starving man clutches food. He swung himself over, like the distinguished gymnast he had once been in his youth, to his parents' pride. With weakening grip he was still holding on when he spied between the railings a motor-bus coming which would easily cover the noise of his fall, called in a low voice: "Dear parents, I have always loved you, all the same," and let himself drop.

At this moment an unending stream of traffic was just going over the bridge.

THE METAMORPHOSIS

The Metamorphosis

1

As GREGOR SAMSA awoke one morning from uneasy dreams he found himself transformed in his bed into a gigantic insect. He was lying on his hard, as it were armor-plated, back and when he lifted his head a little he could see his dome-like brown belly divided into stiff arched segments on top of which the bed quilt could hardly keep in position and was about to slide off completely. His numerous legs, which were pitifully thin compared to the rest of his bulk, waved helplessly before his eyes.

What has happened to me? he thought. It was no dream. His room, a regular human bedroom, only rather too small, lay quiet between the four familiar walls. Above the table on which a collection of cloth samples was unpacked and spread out—Samsa was a commercial traveler—hung the picture which he had recently cut out of an illustrated magazine and put into a pretty gilt frame. It showed a lady, with a fur cap on and a fur stole, sitting upright and holding out to the spectator a huge fur muff into which the whole of her forearm had vanished!

Gregor's eyes turned next to the window, and the overcast sky—one could hear rain drops beating on the window gutter—made him quite melancholy. What about sleeping a little longer and forgetting all this nonsense, he thought, but it could not be done, for he was accustomed to sleep on his right side and in his present condition he could not turn himself over. However violently he forced himself towards his right side he always rolled on to his back again. He tried it at least a hundred times, shutting his eyes to keep from seeing his struggling legs, and only desisted when he began to feel in his side a faint dull ache he had never experienced before.

Oh God, he thought, what an exhausting job I've picked on! Traveling about day in, day out. It's much more irritating work than doing the actual business in the office, and on top of that there's the trouble of constant traveling, of worrying about train connections, the bed and irregular meals, casual acquaintances that are always new and never become intimate friends. The devil take it all! He felt a slight itching up on his belly; slowly pushed himself on his back nearer to the top of the bed so that he could lift his head more easily; identified the itching place which was surrounded by many small white spots the nature of which he could not understand and made to touch it with a leg, but drew the leg back immediately, for the contact made a cold shiver run through him.

He slid down again into his former position. This getting up early, he thought, makes one quite stupid. A man needs his sleep. Other commercials live like harem women. For instance, when I come back to the hotel of a morning to write up the orders I've got, these others are only sitting down to breakfast. Let me just try that with my chief; I'd be sacked on the spot. Anyhow, that might be quite a good thing for me, who can tell? If I didn't have to hold my hand because of my parents I'd have given notice long ago, I'd have gone to the chief and told him exactly what I think of him. That would knock him endways from his desk! It's a queer way of doing, too, this sitting on high at a desk and talking down to employees, especially when they have to come quite near because the chief is hard of hearing. Well, there's still hope; once I've saved enough money to pay back my parents' debts to him—that should take another five or six years—I'll do it without fail. I'll cut myself completely loose then. For the moment, though, I'd better get up, since my train goes at five.

He looked at the alarm clock ticking on the chest. Heavenly Father! he thought. It was half-past six o'clock and the hands were quietly moving on, it was even past the half-hour, it was getting on toward a quarter to seven. Had the alarm clock not gone off? From the bed one could see that it had been properly set for four o'clock; of course it must have gone off. Yes, but was it possible to sleep quietly through that ear-splitting noise? Well, he had not slept quietly, yet apparently all the more soundly for that. But what was he to do now? The next train went at seven o'clock; to catch that he would need to hurry like mad and his samples weren't even packed up, and he himself wasn't feeling particularly fresh and active. And even if he did catch the train he wouldn't avoid a row with the chief, since the firm's porter would have been waiting for the five o'clock train and would have long since reported his failure to turn up. The porter was a creature of the chief's, spineless and stupid. Well, supposing he were to say he was sick? But that would be most unpleasant and would look suspicious, since during his five years' employment he

had not been ill once. The chief himself would be sure
to come with the sick-insurance doctor, would reproach
his parents with their son's laziness and would cut all
excuses short by referring to the insurance doctor, who
of course regarded all mankind as perfectly healthy
malingerers. And would he be so far wrong on this
occasion? Gregor really felt quite well, apart from a
drowsiness that was utterly superfluous after such a long
sleep, and he was even unusually hungry.

As all this was running through his mind at top speed
without his being able to decide to leave his bed—the
alarm clock had just struck a quarter to seven—there
came a cautious tap at the door behind the head of his
bed. "Gregor," said a voice—it was his mother's—"it's
a quarter to seven. Hadn't you a train to catch?" That
gentle voice! Gregor had a shock as he heard his own
voice answering hers, unmistakably his own voice, it
was true, but with a persistent horrible twittering squeak
behind it like an undertone, that left the words in their
clear shape only for the first moment and then rose up
reverberating round them to destroy their sense, so that
one could not be sure one had heard them rightly.
Gregor wanted to answer at length and explain everything, but in the circumstances he confined himself to
saying: "Yes, yes, thank you, Mother, I'm getting up
now." The wooden door between them must have kept
the change in his voice from being noticeable outside,
for his mother contented herself with this statement and
shuffled away. Yet this brief exchange of words had
made the other members of the family aware that Gregor
was still in the house, as they had not expected, and at
one of the side doors his father was already knocking,
gently, yet with his fist. "Gregor, Gregor," he called,

"what's the matter with you?" And after a little while he called again in a deeper voice: "Gregor! Gregor!" At the other side door his sister was saying in a low, plaintive tone: "Gregor? Aren't you well? Are you needing anything?" He answered them both at once: "I'm just ready," and did his best to make his voice sound as normal as possible by enunciating the words very clearly and leaving long pauses between them. So his father went back to his breakfast, but his sister whispered: "Gregor, open the door, do." However, he was not thinking of opening the door, and felt thankful for the prudent habit he had acquired in traveling of locking all doors during the night, even at home.

His immediate intention was to get up quietly without being disturbed, to put on his clothes and above all eat his breakfast, and only then to consider what else was to be done, since in bed, he was well aware, his meditations would come to no sensible conclusion. He remembered that often enough in bed he had felt small aches and pains, probably caused by awkward postures, which had proved purely imaginary once he got up, and he looked forward eagerly to seeing this morning's delusions gradually fall away. That the change in his voice was nothing but the precursor of a severe chill, a standing ailment of commercial travelers, he had not the least possible doubt.

To get rid of the quilt was quite easy; he had only to inflate himself a little and it fell off by itself. But the next move was difficult, especially because he was so uncommonly broad. He would have needed arms and hands to hoist himself up; instead he had only the numerous little legs which never stopped waving in all directions and which he could not control in the least. When he tried to bend one of them it was the first to stretch itself straight; and did he succeed at last in making it do what he wanted, all the other legs meanwhile waved the more wildly in a high degree of unpleasant agitation. "But what's the use of lying idle in bed," said Gregor to himself.

He thought that he might get out of bed with the lower part of his body first, but this lower part, which he had not yet seen and of which he could form no clear conception, proved too difficult to move; it shifted so slowly; and when finally, almost wild with annoyance, he gathered his forces together and thrust out recklessly, he had miscalculated the direction and bumped heavily against the lower end of the bed, and the stinging pain he felt informed him that precisely this lower part of his body was at the moment probably the most sensitive.

So he tried to get the top part of himself out first, and cautiously moved his head towards the edge of the bed. That proved easy enough, and despite its breadth and mass the bulk of his body at last slowly followed the movement of his head. Still, when he finally got his head free over the edge of the bed he felt too scared to go on advancing, for after all if he let himself fall in this way it would take a miracle to keep his head from being injured. And at all costs he must not lose consciousness now, precisely now; he would rather stay in bed.

But when after a repetition of the same efforts he lay in his former position again, sighing, and watched his little legs struggling against each other more wildly than ever, if that were possible, and saw no way of bringing any order into this arbitrary confusion, he told himself again that it was impossible to stay in bed and that the most sensible course was to risk everything for the smallest hope of getting away from it. At the same time he did not forget meanwhile to remind himself that cool reflection, the coolest possible, was much better than desperate resolves. In such moments he focused his eyes as sharply as possible on the window, but, unfortunately, the prospect of the morning fog, which muffled even the other side of the narrow street, brought him little encouragement and comfort. "Seven o'clock already," he said to himself when the alarm clock chimed again, "seven o'clock already and still such a thick fog." And for a little while he lay quiet, breathing lightly, as if perhaps expecting such complete repose to restore all things to their real and normal condition.

But then he said to himself: "Before it strikes a quarter past seven I must be quite out of this bed, without fail. Anyhow, by that time someone will have come from the office to ask for me, since it opens before seven." And he set himself to rocking his whole body at once in a regular rhythm, with the idea of swinging it out of the bed. If he tipped himself out in that way he could keep his head from injury by lifting it at an acute angle when he fell. His back seemed to be hard and was not likely to suffer from a fall on the carpet. His biggest worry was the loud crash he would not be able to help making, which would probably cause anxiety, if not terror, behind all the doors. Still, he must take the risk.

When he was already half out of the bed—the new method was more a game than an effort, for he needed only to hitch himself across by rocking to and fro—it struck him how simple it would be if he could get help. Two strong people—he thought of his father and the servant girl—would be amply sufficient; they would only have to thrust their arms under his convex back, lever him out of the bed, bend down with their burden and then be patient enough to let him turn himself right over on to the floor, where it was to be hoped his legs would then find their proper function. Well, ignoring the fact that the doors were all locked, ought he really to call for help? In spite of his misery he could not suppress a smile at the very idea of it.

He had got so far that he could barely keep his equilibrium when he rocked himself strongly, and he would have to nerve himself very soon for the final decision since in five minutes' time it would be a quarter past seven—when the front door bell rang. "That's someone from the office," he said to himself, and grew almost rigid, while his little legs only jigged about all the faster. For a moment everything stayed quiet. "They're not going to open the door," said Gregor to himself, catching at some kind of irrational hope. But then of course the servant girl went as usual to the door with her heavy tread and opened it. Gregor needed only to hear the first good morning of the visitor to know immediately who it was—the chief clerk himself. What a fate, to be condemned to work for a firm where the smallest omission at once gave rise to the gravest suspicion! Were all employees in a body nothing but scoundrels, was there not among them one single loyal devoted man who, had he wasted only an hour or so of the firm's time in a morning, was so tormented by conscience as to be driven out of his mind and actually incapable of leaving his bed? Wouldn't it really have been sufficient to send an apprentice to inquire—if any inquiry were necessary at all—did the chief clerk himself have to come and thus indicate to the entire family, an innocent family, that this suspicious circumstance could be investigated by no one less versed in affairs than himself? And more through the agitation caused by these reflections than through any act of will Gregor swung himself out of bed with all his strength. There was a loud thump, but it was not really a crash. His fall was broken to some extent by the carpet, his back, too, was less stiff than he thought, and so there was merely a dull thud, not so very startling. Only he had not lifted his head carefully enough and had hit it; he turned it and rubbed it on the carpet in pain and irritation.

"That was something falling down in there," said the chief clerk in the next room to the left. Gregor tried to suppose to himself that something like what had happened to him today might some day happen to the chief clerk; one really could not deny that it was possible. But as if in brusque reply to this supposition the chief clerk took a couple of firm steps in the next-door room and his patent leather boots creaked. From the right-hand room his sister was whispering to inform him of the situation: "Gregor, the chief clerk's here." "I know," muttered Gregor to himself; but he didn't dare to make his voice loud enough for his sister to hear it.

"Gregor," said his father now from the left-hand room, "the chief clerk has come and wants to know why you didn't catch the early train. We don't know what to say to him. Besides, he wants to talk to you in person. So open the door, please. He will be good enough to excuse the untidiness of your room." "Good morning, Mr. Samsa," the chief clerk was calling amiably meanwhile. "He's not well," said his mother to the visitor, while his father was still speaking through the door, "he's not well, sir, believe me. What else would make him miss a train! The boy thinks about nothing but his work. It makes me almost cross the way he never goes out in the evenings; he's been here the last eight days and has stayed at home every single evening. He just sits there quietly at the table reading a newspaper or looking through railway timetables. The only amusement he gets is doing fretwork. For instance, he spent two or three evenings cutting out a little picture frame; you would be surprised to see how pretty it is; it's hanging in his room; you'll see it in a minute when Gregor opens the door. I must say I'm glad you've come, sir; we should never have got him to unlock the door by ourselves; he's so obstinate; and I'm sure he's unwell, though he wouldn't have it to be so this morning." "I'm just coming," said Gregor slowly and carefully, not moving an inch for fear of losing one word of the conversation. "I can't think of any other explanation, madam," said the chief clerk, "I hope it's nothing serious. Although on the other hand I must say that we men of business—fortunately or unfortunately—very often simply have to ignore any slight indisposition, since business must be attended to." "Well, can the chief clerk come in now?" asked Gregor's father impatiently, again knocking on the door. "No," said Gregor. In the left-hand room a painful silence followed this refusal, in the right-hand room his sister began to sob.

Why didn't his sister join the others? She was probably newly out of bed and hadn't even begun to put on her clothes yet. Well, why was she crying? Because he wouldn't get up and let the chief clerk in, because he was in danger of losing his job, and because the chief would begin dunning his parents again for the old debts? Surely these were things one didn't need to worry about for the present. Gregor was still at home and not in the least thinking of deserting the family. At the moment, true, he was lying on the carpet and no one who knew the condition he was in could seriously expect him to admit the chief clerk. But for such a small discourtesy, which could plausibly be explained away somehow later on, Gregor could hardly be dismissed on the spot. And it seemed to Gregor that it would be much more sensible to leave him in peace for the present than to trouble him with tears and entreaties. Still, of course, their uncertainty bewildered them all and excused their behavior.

"Mr. Samsa," the chief clerk called now in a louder voice, "what's the matter with you? Here you are, barricading yourself in your room, giving only 'yes' and 'no' for answers, causing your parents a lot of unnecessary trouble and neglecting—I mention this only in passing—neglecting your business duties in an incredible fashion. I am speaking here in the name of your parents and of your chief, and I beg you quite seriously to give me an immediate and precise explanation. You amaze me, you amaze me. I thought you were a quiet, dependable person, and now all at once you seem bent on making a disgraceful exhibition of yourself. The chief did hint to me early this morning a possible explanation for your disappearance—with reference to the cash payments that were entrusted to you recently—but I almost pledged my solemn word of honor that this could not be so. But now that I see how incredibly obstinate you are, I no longer have the slightest desire to take your part at all. And your position in the firm is not so unassailable. I came with the intention of telling you all this in private, but since you are wasting my time so needlessly I don't see why your parents shouldn't hear it too. For some time past your work has been most unsatisfactory; this is not the season of the year for a business boom, of course, we admit that, but a season of the year for doing no business at all, that does not exist, Mr. Samsa, must not exist."

"But, sir," cried Gregor, beside himself and in his agitation forgetting everything else, "I'm just going to open the door this very minute. A slight illness, an attack of giddiness, has kept me from getting up. I'm still lying in bed. But I feel all right again. I'm getting out of bed now. Just give me a moment or two longer! I'm not quite so well as I thought. But I'm all right, really. How a thing like that can suddenly strike one down! Only last night I was quite well, my parents can tell you, or rather I did have a slight presentiment. I must have showed some sign of it. Why didn't I report it at the office! But one always thinks that an indisposition can be got over without staying in the house. Oh sir, do spare my parents! All that you're reproaching me with now has no foundation; no one has ever said a word to me about it. Perhaps you haven't looked at the last orders I sent in. Anyhow, I can still catch the eight o'clock train, I'm much the better for my few hours' rest. Don't let me detain you here, sir; I'll be attending to business very soon, and do be good enough to tell the chief so and to make my excuses to him!"

And while all this was tumbling out pell-mell and Gregor hardly knew what he was saying, he had reached the chest quite easily, perhaps because of the practice he had had in bed, and was now trying to lever himself upright by means of it. He meant actually to open the door, actually to show himself and speak to the chief clerk; he was eager to find out what the others, after all their insistence, would say at the sight of him. If they were horrified then the responsibility was no longer his and he could stay quiet. But if they took it calmly, then he had no reason either to be upset, and could really get to the station for the eight o'clock train if he hurried. At first he slipped down a few times from the polished surface of the chest, but at length with a last heave he stood upright; he paid no more attention to the pains in the lower part of his body, however they smarted. Then he let himself fall against the back of a near-by chair, and clung with his little legs to the edges of it. That brought him into control of himself again and he stopped speaking, for now he could listen to what the chief clerk was saying.

"Did you understand a word of it?" the chief clerk was asking; "surely he can't be trying to make fools of us?" "Oh dear," cried his mother, in tears, "perhaps he's terribly ill and we're tormenting him. Grete! Grete!" she called out then. "Yes Mother?" called his sister from the other side. They were calling to each other across Gregor's room. "You must go this minute for the doctor. Gregor is ill. Go for the doctor, quick. Did you hear how he was speaking?" "That was no human voice," said the chief clerk in a voice noticeably low beside the shrillness of the mother's. "Anna! Anna!" his father was calling through the hall to the kitchen, clapping his hands, "get a locksmith at once!" And the two girls were already running through the hall with a swish of skirts—how could his sister have got dressed so quickly? —and were tearing the front door open. There was no sound of its closing again; they had evidently left it open, as one does in houses where some great misfortune has happened.

But Gregor was now much calmer. The words he uttered were no longer understandable, apparently, although they seemed clear enough to him, even clearer than before, perhaps because his ear had grown accustomed to the sound of them. Yet at any rate people now believed that something was wrong with him, and were ready to help him. The positive certainty with which these first measures had been taken comforted him. He felt himself drawn once more into the human circle and hoped for great and remarkable results from both the doctor and the locksmith, without really distinguishing precisely between them. To make his voice as clear as possible for the decisive conversation that was now imminent he coughed a little, as quietly as he could, of course, since this noise too might not sound like a human cough for all he was able to judge. In the next room meanwhile there was complete silence. Perhaps his parents were sitting at the table with the chief clerk, whispering, perhaps they were all leaning against the door and listening.

Slowly Gregor pushed the chair towards the door, then let go of it, caught hold of the door for support—the soles at the end of his little legs were somewhat sticky—and rested against it for a moment after his efforts. Then he set himself to turning the key in the lock with his mouth. It seemed, unhappily, that he hadn't really any teeth—what could he grip the key with?—but on the other hand his jaws were certainly very strong; with their help he did manage to set the key in motion, heedless of the fact that he was undoubtedly damaging them somewhere, since a brown fluid issued from his mouth, flowed over the key and dripped on the floor. "Just listen to that," said the chief clerk next door; "he's turning the key." That was a great encouragement to Gregor; but they should all have shouted encouragement to him, his father and mother too: "Go on, Gregor," they should have called out, "keep going, hold on to that key!" And in the belief that they were all following his efforts intently, he clenched his jaws recklessly on the key with all the force at his command. As the turning of the key progressed he circled round the lock, holding on now only with his mouth, pushing on the key, as required, or pulling it down again with all the weight of his body. The louder click of the finally yielding lock literally quickened Gregor. With a deep breath of relief he said to himself: "So I didn't need the locksmith," and laid his head on the handle to open the door wide.

Since he had to pull the door towards him, he was still invisible when it was really wide open. He had to edge himself slowly round the near half of the double door, and to do it very carefully if he was not to fall plump upon his back just on the threshold. He was still carrying out this difficult manoeuvre, with no time to observe anything else, when he heard the chief clerk utter a loud "Oh!"—it sounded like a gust of wind—and now he could see the man, standing as he was nearest to the door, clapping one hand before his open mouth and slowly backing away as if driven by some invisible steady pressure. His mother—in spite of the chief clerk's being there her hair was still undone and sticking up in all directions—first clasped her hands and looked at his father, then took two steps towards Gregor and fell on the floor among her outspread skirts, her face quite hidden on her breast. His father knotted his fist with a fierce expression on his face as if he meant to knock Gregor back into his room, then looked uncertainly round the living room, covered his eyes with his hands and wept till his great chest heaved.

Gregor did not go now into the living room, but

leaned against the inside of the firmly shut wing of the door, so that only half his body was visible and his head above it bending sideways to look at the others. The light had meanwhile strengthened; on the other side of the street one could see clearly a section of the endlessly long, dark gray building opposite—it was a hospital—abruptly punctuated by its row of regular windows; the rain was still falling, but only in large singly discernible and literally singly splashing drops. The breakfast dishes were set out on the table lavishly, for breakfast was the most important meal of the day to Gregor's father, who lingered it out for hours over various newspapers. Right opposite Gregor on the wall hung a photograph of himself on military service, as a lieutenant, hand on sword, a carefree smile on his face, inviting one to respect his uniform and military bearing. The door leading to the hall was open, and one could see that the front door stood open too, showing the landing beyond and the beginning of the stairs going down.

"Well," said Gregor, knowing perfectly that he was the only one who had retained any composure, "I'll put my clothes on at once, pack up my samples and start off. Will you only let me go? You see, sir, I'm not obstinate, and I'm willing to work; traveling is a hard life, but I couldn't live without it. Where are you going, sir? To the office? Yes? Will you give a true account of all this? One can be temporarily incapacitated, but that's just the moment for remembering former services and bearing in mind that later on, when the incapacity has been got over, one will certainly work with all the more industry and concentration. I'm loyally bound to serve the chief, you know that very well. Besides, I have to provide for my parents and my sister. I'm in great difficulties, but I'll get out of them again. Don't make things any worse for me than they are. Stand up for me in the firm. Travelers are not popular there, I know. People think they earn sacks of money and just have a good time. A prejudice there's no particular reason for revising. But you, sir, have a more comprehensive view of affairs than the rest of the staff, yes, let me tell you in confidence, a more comprehensive view than the chief himself, who, being the owner, lets his judgment easily be swayed against one of his employees. And you know very well that the traveler, who is never seen in the office almost the whole year round, can so easily fall a victim to gossip and ill luck and unfounded complaints, which he mostly knows nothing about, except when he comes back exhausted from his rounds, and only then suffers in person from their evil consequences, which he can no longer trace back to the original causes. Sir, sir, don't go away without a word to me to show that you think me in the right at least to some extent!"

But at Gregor's very first words the chief clerk had already backed away and only stared at him with parted lips over one twitching shoulder. And while Gregor was speaking he did not stand still one moment but stole away towards the door, without taking his eyes off Gregor, yet only an inch at a time, as if obeying some secret injunction to leave the room. He was already at the hall, and the suddenness with which he took his last step out of the living room would have made one believe he had burned the sole of his foot. Once in the hall he stretched his right arm before him towards the staircase, as if some supernatural power were waiting there to deliver him.

Gregor perceived that the chief clerk must on no account be allowed to go away in this frame of mind if his position in the firm were not to be endangered to the utmost. His parents did not understand this so well; they had convinced themselves in the course of years that Gregor was settled for life in this firm, and besides they were so preoccupied with their immediate troubles that all foresight had forsaken them. Yet Gregor had this foresight. The chief clerk must be detained, soothed, persuaded and finally won over; the whole future of Gregor and his family depended on it! If only his sister had been there! She was intelligent; she had begun to cry while Gregor was still lying quietly on his back. And no doubt the chief clerk, so partial to ladies, would have been guided by her; she would have shut the door of the flat and in the hall talked him out of his horror. But she was not there, and Gregor would have to handle the situation himself. And without remembering that he was still unaware what powers of movement he possessed, without even remembering that his words in all possibility, indeed in all likelihood, would again be unintelligible, he let go the wing of the door, pushed himself through the opening, started to walk towards the chief clerk, who was already ridiculously clinging with both hands to the railing on the landing; but immediately, as he was feeling for a support, he fell down with a little cry upon all his numerous legs. Hardly was he down when he experienced for the first time this morning a sense of physical comfort; his legs had firm ground under them; they were completely obedient, as he noted with joy; they even strove to carry him forward in whatever direction he chose; and he was inclined to believe that a final relief from all his sufferings was at hand. But in the same moment as he found himself on the floor, rocking with suppressed eagerness to move, not far from his mother, indeed just in front of her, she, who had seemed so completely crushed, sprang all at once to her feet, her arms and fingers outspread, cried: "Help, for God's sake, help!" bent her head down as if to see Gregor better, yet on the contrary kept backing senselessly away; had quite forgotten that the laden table stood behind her; sat upon it hastily, as if in absence of mind, when she bumped into it; and seemed altogether unaware that the big coffee pot beside her was upset and pouring coffee in a flood over the carpet.

"Mother, Mother," said Gregor in a low voice, and looked up at her. The chief clerk, for the moment, had quite slipped from his mind; instead, he could not resist snapping his jaws together at the sight of the streaming coffee. That made his mother scream again, she fled from the table and fell into the arms of his father, who hastened to catch her. But Gregor had now no time to spare for his parents; the chief clerk was already on the stairs; with his chin on the banisters he was taking one last backward look. Gregor made a spring, to be as sure as possible of overtaking him; the chief clerk must have divined his intention, for he leaped down several steps and vanished; he was still yelling "Ugh!" and it echoed through the whole staircase.

Unfortunately, the flight of the chief clerk seemed completely to upset Gregor's father, who had remained relatively calm until now, for instead of running after the man himself, or at least not hindering Gregor in his pursuit, he seized in his right hand the walking stick which the chief clerk had left behind on a chair, together with a hat and greatcoat, snatched in his left hand a large newspaper from the table and began stamping his feet and flourishing the stick and the newspaper to drive Gregor back into his room. No entreaty of Gregor's availed, indeed no entreaty was even understood, however humbly he bent his head his father only stamped on the floor the more loudly. Behind his father his mother had torn open a window, despite the cold weather, and was leaning far out of it with her face in her hands. A strong draught set in from the street to the staircase, the window curtains blew in, the newspapers on the table fluttered, stray pages whisked over the floor. Pitilessly Gregor's father drove him back, hissing and crying "Shoo!" like a savage. But Gregor was quite unpracticed in walking backwards, it really was a slow business. If he only had a chance to turn round he could get back to his room at once, but he was afraid of exasperating his father by the slowness of such a rotation and at any moment the stick in his father's hand might hit him a fatal blow on the back or on the head. In the end, however, nothing else was left for him to do since to his horror he observed that in moving backwards he could not even control the direction he took; and so, keeping an anxious eye on his father all the time over his shoulder, he began to turn round as quickly as he could, which was in reality very slowly. Perhaps his father noted his good intentions, for he did not interfere except every now and then to help him in the manoeuvre from a distance with the point of the stick. If only he would have stopped making that unbearable hissing noise! It made Gregor quite lose his head. He had turned almost completely round when the hissing noise so distracted him that he even turned a little the wrong way again. But when at last his head was fortunately right in front of the doorway, it appeared that his body was too broad simply to get through the opening. His father, of course, in his present mood was far from thinking of such a thing as opening the other half of the door, to let Gregor have enough space. He had merely the fixed idea of driving Gregor back into his room as quickly as possible. He would never have suffered Gregor to make the circumstantial preparations for standing up on end and perhaps slipping his way through the door. Maybe he was now making more noise than ever to urge Gregor forward, as if no obstacle impeded him; to Gregor, anyhow, the noise in his rear sounded no longer like the voice of one single father; this was really no joke, and Gregor thrust himself—come what might—into the doorway. One side of his body rose up, he was tilted at an angle in the doorway, his flank was quite bruised, horrid blotches stained the white door, soon he was stuck fast and, left to himself, could not have moved at all, his legs on one side fluttered trembling in the air, those on the other were crushed painfully to the floor—when from behind his father gave him a strong push which was literally a deliverance and he flew far into the room, bleeding freely. The door was slammed behind him with the stick, and then at last there was silence.

II

NOT UNTIL it was twilight did Gregor awake out of a deep sleep, more like a swoon than a sleep. He would certainly have waked up of his own accord not much later, for he felt himself sufficiently rested and well-

slept, but it seemed to him as if a fleeting step and a
cautious shutting of the door leading into the hall had
aroused him. The electric lights in the street cast a pale
sheen here and there on the ceiling and the upper surfaces of the furniture, but down below, where he lay,
it was dark. Slowly, awkwardly trying out his feelers,
which he now first learned to appreciate, he pushed his
way to the door to see what had been happening there.
His left side felt like one single long, unpleasantly tense
scar, and he had actually to limp on his two rows of
legs. One little leg, moreover, had been severely damaged in the course of that morning's events—it was almost a miracle that only one had been damaged—and
trailed uselessly behind him.

He had reached the door before he discovered what
had really drawn him to it: the smell of food. For there
stood a basin filled with fresh milk in which floated
little sops of white bread. He could almost have laughed
with joy, since he was now still hungrier than in the
morning, and he dipped his head almost over the eyes
straight into the milk. But soon in disappointment he
withdrew it again; not only did he find it difficult to
feed because of his tender left side—and he could only
feed with the palpitating collaboration of his whole body
—he did not like the milk either, although milk had
been his favorite drink and that was certainly why his
sister had set it there for him, indeed it was almost with
repulsion that he turned away from the basin and
crawled back to the middle of the room.

He could see through the crack of the door that the
gas was turned on in the living room, but while usually
at this time his father made a habit of reading the afternoon newspaper in a loud voice to his mother and occa-

sionally to his sister as well, not a sound was now to be heard. Well, perhaps his father had recently given up this habit of reading aloud, which his sister had mentioned so often in conversation and in her letters. But there was the same silence all around, although the flat was certainly not empty of occupants. "What a quiet life our family has been leading," said Gregor to himself, and as he sat there motionless staring into the darkness he felt great pride in the fact that he had been able to provide such a life for his parents and sister in such a fine flat. But what if all the quiet, the comfort, the contentment were now to end in horror? To keep himself from being lost in such thoughts Gregor took refuge in movement and crawled up and down the room.

Once during the long evening one of the side doors was opened a little and quickly shut again, later the other side door too; someone had apparently wanted to come in and then thought better of it. Gregor now stationed himself immediately before the living room door, determined to persuade any hesitating visitor to come in or at least to discover who it might be; but the door was not opened again and he waited in vain. In the early morning, when the doors were locked, they had all wanted to come in, now that he had opened one door and the other had apparently been opened during the day, no one came in and even the keys were on the other side of the doors.

It was late at night before the gas went out in the living room, and Gregor could easily tell that his parents and his sister had all stayed awake until then, for he could clearly hear the three of them stealing away on tiptoe. No one was likely to visit him, not until the morning, that was certain; so he had plenty of time to

meditate at his leisure on how he was to arrange his
life afresh. But the lofty, empty room in which he had
to lie flat on the floor filled him with an apprehension
he could not account for, since it had been his very own
room for the past five years—and with a half-uncon-
scious action, not without a slight feeling of shame, he
scuttled under the sofa, where he felt comfortable at
once, although his back was a little cramped and he
could not lift his head up, and his only regret was that
his body was too broad to get the whole of it under the
sofa.

He stayed there all night, spending the time partly in a
light slumber, from which his hunger kept waking him
up with a start, and partly in worrying and sketching
vague hopes, which all led to the same conclusion, that
he must lie low for the present and, by exercising patience and the utmost consideration, help the family to
bear the inconvenience he was bound to cause them in
his present condition.

Very early in the morning, it was still almost night,
Gregor had the chance to test the strength of his new
resolutions, for his sister, nearly fully dressed, opened
the door from the hall and peered in. She did not see
him at once, yet when she caught sight of him under the
sofa—well, he had to be somewhere, he couldn't have
flown away, could he?—she was so startled that without
being able to help it she slammed the door shut again.
But as if regretting her behavior she opened the door
again immediately and came in on tiptoe, as if she were
visiting an invalid or even a stranger. Gregor had pushed
his head forward to the very edge of the sofa and
watched her. Would she notice that he had left the milk
standing, and not for lack of hunger, and would she

bring in some other kind of food more to his taste? If
she did not do it of her own accord, he would rather
starve than draw her attention to the fact, although he
felt a wild impulse to dart out from under the sofa,
throw himself at her feet and beg her for something to
eat. But his sister at once noticed, with surprise, that the
basin was still full, except for a little milk that had been
spilt all around it, she lifted it immediately, not with
her bare hands, true, but with a cloth and carried it
away. Gregor was wildly curious to know what she
would bring instead, and made various speculations about
it. Yet what she actually did next, in the goodness of
her heart, he could never have guessed at. To find out
what he liked she brought him a whole selection of
food, all set out on an old newspaper. There were old,
half-decayed vegetables, bones from last night's supper
covered with a white sauce that had thickened; some
raisins and almonds; a piece of cheese that Gregor would
have called uneatable two days ago; a dry roll of bread,
a buttered roll, and a roll both buttered and salted. Besides all that, she set down again the same basin, into
which she had poured some water, and which was apparently to be reserved for his exclusive use. And with
fine tact, knowing that Gregor would not eat in her
presence, she withdrew quickly and even turned the
key, to let him understand that he could take his ease
as much as he liked. Gregor's legs all whizzed towards
the food. His wounds must have healed completely,
moreover, for he felt no disability, which amazed him
and made him reflect how more than a month ago he had
cut one finger a little with a knife and had still suffered
pain from the wound only the day before yesterday.
Am I less sensitive now? he thought, and sucked greedily

at the cheese, which above all the other edibles attracted him at once and strongly. One after another and with tears of satisfaction in his eyes he quickly devoured the cheese, the vegetables and the sauce; the fresh food, on the other hand, had no charms for him, he could not even stand the smell of it and actually dragged away to some little distance the things he could eat. He had long finished his meal and was only lying lazily on the same spot when his sister turned the key slowly as a sign for him to retreat. That roused him at once, although he was nearly asleep, and he hurried under the sofa again. But it took considerable self-control for him to stay under the sofa, even for the short time his sister was in the room, since the large meal had swollen his body somewhat and he was so cramped he could hardly breathe. Slight attacks of breathlessness afflicted him and his eyes were starting a little out of his head as he watched his unsuspecting sister sweeping together with a broom not only the remains of what he had eaten but even the things he had not touched, as if these were now of no use to anyone, and hastily shoveling it all into a bucket, which she covered with a wooden lid and carried away. Hardly had she turned her back when Gregor came from under the sofa and stretched and puffed himself out.

In this manner Gregor was fed, once in the early morning while his parents and the servant girl were still asleep, and a second time after they had all had their midday dinner, for then his parents took a short nap and the servant girl could be sent out on some errand or other by his sister. Not that they would have wanted him to starve, of course, but perhaps they could not have borne to know more about his feeding than from hearsay, perhaps too his sister wanted to spare them such little anxieties wherever possible, since they had quite enough to bear as it was.

Under what pretext the doctor and the locksmith had been got rid of on that first morning Gregor could not discover, for since what he said was not understood by the others it never struck any of them, not even his sister, that he could understand what they said, and so whenever his sister came into his room he had to content himself with hearing her utter only a sigh now and then and an occasional appeal to the saints. Later on, when she had got a little used to the situation—of course she could never get completely used to it—she sometimes threw out a remark which was kindly meant or could be so interpreted. "Well, he liked his dinner today," she would say when Gregor had made a good clearance of his food; and when he had not eaten, which gradually happened more and more often, she would say almost sadly: "Everything's been left standing again."

But although Gregor could get no news directly, he overheard a lot from the neighboring rooms, and as soon as voices were audible, he would run to the door of the room concerned and press his whole body against it. In the first few days especially there was no conversation that did not refer to him somehow, even if only indirectly. For two whole days there were family consultations at every mealtime about what should be done; but also between meals the same subject was discussed, for there were always at least two members of the family at home, since no one wanted to be alone in the flat and to leave it quite empty was unthinkable. And on the very first of these days the household cook—it was not quite clear what and how much she knew of the situation—

went down on her knees to his mother and begged leave
to go, and when she departed, a quarter of an hour later,
gave thanks for her dismissal with tears in her eyes as
if for the greatest benefit that could have been conferred on her, and without any prompting swore a
solemn oath that she would never say a single word to
anyone about what had happened.

Now Gregor's sister had to cook too, helping her
mother; true, the cooking did not amount to much, for
they ate scarcely anything. Gregor was always hearing
one of the family vainly urging another to eat and getting no answer but: "Thanks, I've had all I want," or
something similar. Perhaps they drank nothing either.
Time and again his sister kept asking his father if he
wouldn't like some beer and offered kindly to go and
fetch it herself, and when he made no answer suggested
that she could ask the concierge to fetch it, so that he
need feel no sense of obligation, but then a round "No"
came from his father and no more was said about it.

In the course of that very first day Gregor's father
explained the family's financial position and prospects to
both his mother and his sister. Now and then he rose
from the table to get some voucher or memorandum out
of the small safe he had rescued from the collapse of
his business five years earlier. One could hear him opening the complicated lock and rustling papers out and
shutting it again. This statement made by his father was
the first cheerful information Gregor had heard since
his imprisonment. He had been of the opinion that
nothing at all was left over from his father's business, at
least his father had never said anything to the contrary,
and of course he had not asked him directly. At that
time Gregor's sole desire was to do his utmost to help

the family to forget as soon as possible the catastrophe which had overwhelmed the business and thrown them all into a state of complete despair. And so he had set to work with unusual ardor and almost overnight had become a commercial traveler instead of a little clerk, with of course much greater chances of earning money, and his success was immediately translated into good round coin which he could lay on the table for his amazed and happy family. These had been fine times, and they had never recurred, at least not with the same sense of glory, although later on Gregor had earned so much money that he was able to meet the expenses of the whole household and did so. They had simply got used to it, both the family and Gregor; the money was gratefully accepted and gladly given, but there was no special uprush of warm feeling. With his sister alone had he remained intimate, and it was a secret plan of his that she, who loved music, unlike himself, and could play movingly on the violin, should be sent next year to study at the Conservatorium, despite the great expense that would entail, which must be made up in some other way. During his brief visits home the Conservatorium was often mentioned in the talks he had with his sister, but always merely as a beautiful dream which could never come true, and his parents discouraged even these innocent references to it; yet Gregor had made up his mind firmly about it and meant to announce the fact with due solemnity on Christmas Day.

Such were the thoughts, completely futile in his present condition, that went through his head as he stood clinging upright to the door and listening. Sometimes out of sheer weariness he had to give up listening and let his head fall negligently against the door, but he always had to pull himself together again at once, for even the slight sound his head made was audible next door and brought all conversation to a stop. "What can he be doing now?" his father would say after a while, obviously turning towards the door, and only then would the interrupted conversation gradually be set going again.

Gregor was now informed as amply as he could wish —for his father tended to repeat himself in his explanations, partly because it was a long time since he had handled such matters and partly because his mother could not always grasp things at once—that a certain amount of investments, a very small amount it was true, had survived the wreck of their fortunes and had even increased a little because the dividends had not been touched meanwhile. And besides that, the money Gregor brought home every month—he had kept only a few dollars for himself—had never been quite used up and now amounted to a small capital sum. Behind the door Gregor nodded his head eagerly, rejoiced at this evidence of unexpected thrift and foresight. True, he could really have paid off some more of his father's debts to the chief with this extra money, and so brought much nearer the day on which he could quit his job, but doubtless it was better the way his father had arranged it.

Yet this capital was by no means sufficient to let the family live on the interest of it; for one year, perhaps, or at the most two, they could live on the principal, that was all. It was simply a sum that ought not to be touched and should be kept for a rainy day; money for living expenses would have to be earned. Now his father was still hale enough but an old man, and he had done no work for the past five years and could not be expected

to do much; during these five years, the first years of
leisure in his laborious though unsuccessful life, he had
grown rather fat and become sluggish. And Gregor's
old mother, how was she to earn a living with her
asthma, which troubled her even when she walked
through the flat and kept her lying on a sofa every other
day panting for breath beside an open window? And
was his sister to earn her bread, she who was still a child
of seventeen and whose life hitherto had been so pleasant, consisting as it did in dressing herself nicely, sleeping long, helping in the housekeeping, going out to a
few modest entertainments and above all playing the
violin? At first whenever the need for earning money
was mentioned Gregor let go his hold on the door and
threw himself down on the cool leather sofa beside it, he
felt so hot with shame and grief.

Often he just lay there the long nights through without sleeping at all, scrabbling for hours on the leather.
Or he nerved himself to the great effort of pushing an
armchair to the window, then crawled up over the
window sill and, braced against the chair, leaned against
the window panes, obviously in some recollection of the
sense of freedom that looking out of a window always
used to give him. For in reality day by day things that
were even a little way off were growing dimmer to his
sight; the hospital across the street, which he used to
execrate for being all too often before his eyes, was now
quite beyond his range of vision, and if he had not
known that he lived in Charlotte Street, a quiet street
but still a city street, he might have believed that his
window gave on a desert waste where gray sky and gray
land blended indistinguishably into each other. His
quick-witted sister only needed to observe twice that

the armchair stood by the window; after that whenever she had tidied the room she always pushed the chair back to the same place at the window and even left the inner casements open.

If he could have spoken to her and thanked her for all she had to do for him, he could have borne her ministrations better; as it was, they oppressed him. She certainly tried to make as light as possible of whatever was disagreeable in her task, and as time went on she succeeded, of course, more and more, but time brought more enlightenment to Gregor too. The very way she came in distressed him. Hardly was she in the room when she rushed to the window, without even taking time to shut the door, careful as she was usually to shield the sight of Gregor's room from the others, and as if she were almost suffocating tore the casements open with hasty fingers, standing then in the open draught for a while even in the bitterest cold and drawing deep breaths. This noisy scurry of hers upset Gregor twice a day; he would crouch trembling under the sofa all the time, knowing quite well that she would certainly have spared him such a disturbance had she found it at all possible to stay in his presence without opening the window.

On one occasion, about a month after Gregor's metamorphosis, when there was surely no reason for her to be still startled at his appearance, she came a little earlier than usual and found him gazing out of the window, quite motionless, and thus well placed to look like a bogey. Gregor would not have been surprised had she not come in at all, for she could not immediately open the window while he was there, but not only did she retreat, she jumped back as if in alarm and banged the door shut; a stranger might well have thought that he had been lying in wait for her there meaning to bite her. Of course he hid himself under the sofa at once, but he had to wait until midday before she came again, and she seemed more ill at ease than usual. This made him realize how repulsive the sight of him still was to her, and that it was bound to go on being repulsive, and what an effort it must cost her not to run away even from the sight of the small portion of his body that stuck out from under the sofa. In order to spare her that, therefore, one day he carried a sheet on his back to the sofa—it cost him four hours' labor—and arranged it there in such a way as to hide him completely, so that even if she were to bend down she could not see him. Had she considered the sheet unnecessary, she would certainly have stripped it off the sofa again, for it was clear enough that this curtaining and confining of himself was not likely to conduce to Gregor's comfort, but she left it where it was, and Gregor even fancied that he caught a thankful glance from her eye when he lifted the sheet carefully a very little with his head to see how she was taking the new arrangement.

For the first fortnight his parents could not bring themselves to the point of entering his room, and he often heard them expressing their appreciation of his sister's activities, whereas formerly they had frequently scolded her for being as they thought a somewhat useless daughter. But now, both of them often waited outside the door, his father and his mother, while his sister tidied his room, and as soon as she came out she had to tell them exactly how things were in the room, what Gregor had eaten, how he had conducted himself this time and whether there was not perhaps some slight improvement in his condition. His mother, moreover, began relatively soon to want to visit him, but his father and sister dissuaded her at first with arguments which Gregor listened to very attentively and altogether approved. Later, however, she had to be held back by main force, and when she cried out: "Do let me in to Gregor, he is my unfortunate son! Can't you understand that I must go to him?" Gregor thought that it might be well to have her come in, not every day, of course, but perhaps once a week; she understood things, after all, much better than his sister, who was only a child despite the efforts she was making and had perhaps taken on so difficult a task merely out of childish thoughtlessness.

Gregor's desire to see his mother was soon fulfilled. During the daytime he did not want to show himself at the window, out of consideration for his parents, but he could not crawl very far around the few square yards of floor space he had, nor could he bear lying quietly at rest all during the night, while he was fast losing any interest he had ever taken in food, so that for mere recreation he had formed the habit of crawling crisscross over the walls and ceiling. He especially enjoyed hanging suspended from the ceiling; it was much better than lying on the floor; one could breathe more freely; one's body swung and rocked lightly; and in the almost blissful absorption induced by this suspension it could happen to his own surprise that he let go and fell plump on the floor. Yet he now had his body much better under control than formerly, and even such a big fall did him no harm. His sister at once remarked the new distraction Gregor had found for himself—he

left traces behind him of the sticky stuff on his soles
wherever he crawled—and she got the idea in her head
of giving him as wide a field as possible to crawl in
and of removing the pieces of furniture that hindered
him, above all the chest of drawers and the writing desk.
But that was more than she could manage all by herself; she did not dare ask her father to help her; and as
for the servant girl, a young creature of sixteen who
had had the courage to stay on after the cook's departure, she could not be asked to help, for she had begged
as an especial favor that she might keep the kitchen
door locked and open it only on a definite summons; so
there was nothing left but to apply to her mother at an
hour when her father was out. And the old lady did
come, with exclamations of joyful eagerness, which,
however, died away at the door of Gregor's room.
Gregor's sister, of course, went in first, to see that
everything was in order before letting his mother enter.
In great haste Gregor pulled the sheet lower and rucked
it more in folds so that it really looked as if it had been
thrown accidentally over the sofa. And this time he did
not peer out from under it; he renounced the pleasure
of seeing his mother on this occasion and was only glad
that she had come at all. "Come in, he's out of sight,"
said his sister, obviously leading her mother in by the
hand. Gregor could now hear the two women struggling to shift the heavy old chest from its place, and
his sister claiming the greater part of the labor for herself, without listening to the admonitions of her mother
who feared she might overstrain herself. It took a long
time. After at least a quarter of an hour's tugging his
mother objected that the chest had better be left where
it was, for in the first place it was too heavy and could

never be got out before his father came home, and standing in the middle of the room like that it would only hamper Gregor's movements, while in the second place it was not at all certain that removing the furniture would be doing a service to Gregor. She was inclined to think to the contrary; the sight of the naked walls made her own heart heavy, and why shouldn't Gregor have the same feeling, considering that he had been used to his furniture for so long and might feel forlorn without it. "And doesn't it look," she concluded in a low voice—in fact she had been almost whispering all the time as if to avoid letting Gregor, whose exact whereabouts she did not know, hear even the tones of her voice, for she was convinced that he could not understand her words—"doesn't it look as if we were showing him, by taking away his furniture, that we have given up hope of his ever getting better and are just leaving him coldly to himself? I think it would be best to keep his room exactly as it has always been, so that when he comes back to us he will find everything unchanged and be able all the more easily to forget what has happened in between."

On hearing these words from his mother Gregor realized that the lack of all direct human speech for the past two months together with the monotony of family life must have confused his mind, otherwise he could not account for the fact that he had quite earnestly looked forward to having his room emptied of furnishing. Did he really want his warm room, so comfortably fitted with old family furniture, to be turned into a naked den in which he would certainly be able to crawl unhampered in all directions but at the price of shedding simultaneously all recollection of his human background? He had indeed been so near the brink of forgetfulness that only the voice of his mother, which he had not heard for so long, had drawn him back from it. Nothing should be taken out of his room; everything must stay as it was; he could not dispense with the good influence of the furniture on his state of mind; and even if the furniture did hamper him in his senseless crawling round and round, that was no drawback but a great advantage.

Unfortunately his sister was of the contrary opinion; she had grown accustomed, and not without reason, to consider herself an expert in Gregor's affairs as against her parents, and so her mother's advice was now enough to make her determined on the removal not only of the chest and the writing desk, which had been her first intention, but of all the furniture except the indispensable sofa. This determination was not, of course, merely the outcome of childish recalcitrance and of the self-confidence she had recently developed so unexpectedly and at such cost; she had in fact perceived that Gregor needed a lot of space to crawl about in, while on the other hand he never used the furniture at all, so far as could be seen. Another factor might have been also the enthusiastic temperament of an adolescent girl, which seeks to indulge itself on every opportunity and which now tempted Grete to exaggerate the horror of her brother's circumstances in order that she might do all the more for him. In a room where Gregor lorded it all alone over empty walls no one save herself was likely ever to set foot.

And so she was not to be moved from her resolve by her mother, who seemed moreover to be ill at ease in Gregor's room and therefore unsure of herself, was soon reduced to silence and helped her daughter as best she could to push the chest outside. Now, Gregor could do without the chest, if need be, but the writing desk he must retain. As soon as the two women had got the chest out of his room, groaning as they pushed it, Gregor stuck his head out from under the sofa to see how he might intervene as kindly and cautiously as possible. But as bad luck would have it, his mother was the first to return, leaving Grete clasping the chest in the room next door where she was trying to shift it all by herself, without of course moving it from the spot. His mother however was not accustomed to the sight of him, it might sicken her and so in alarm Gregor backed quickly to the other end of the sofa, yet could not prevent the sheet from swaying a little in front. That was enough to put her on the alert. She paused, stood still for a moment and then went back to Grete.

Although Gregor kept reassuring himself that nothing out of the way was happening, but only a few bits of furniture were being changed round, he soon had to admit that all this trotting to and fro of the two women, their little ejaculations and the scraping of furniture along the floor affected him like a vast disturbance coming from all sides at once, and however much he tucked in his head and legs and cowered to the very floor he was bound to confess that he would not be able to stand it for long. They were clearing his room out; taking away everything he loved; the chest in which he kept his fret saw and other tools was already dragged off; they were now loosening the writing desk which had almost sunk into the floor, the desk at which he had done all his homework when he was at the commercial academy, at the grammar school before that, and, yes, even at the primary school—he had no more time to waste in weighing the good intentions of the two women, whose existence he had by now almost forgotten, for they were so exhausted that they were laboring in silence and nothing could be heard but the heavy scuffling of their feet.

And so he rushed out—the women were just leaning against the writing desk in the next room to give themselves a breather—and four times changed his direction, since he really did not know what to rescue first, then on the wall opposite, which was already otherwise cleared, he was struck by the picture of the lady muffled in so much fur and quickly crawled up to it and pressed himself to the glass, which was a good surface to hold on to and comforted his hot belly. This picture at least, which was entirely hidden beneath him, was going to be removed by nobody. He turned his head towards the door of the living room so as to observe the women when they came back.

They had not allowed themselves much of a rest and were already coming; Grete had twined her arm round her mother and was almost supporting her. "Well, what shall we take now?" said Grete, looking round. Her eyes met Gregor's from the wall. She kept her composure, presumably because of her mother, bent her head down to her mother, to keep her from looking up, and said, although in a fluttering, unpremeditated voice: "Come, hadn't we better go back to the living room for a moment?" Her intentions were clear enough to Gregor, she wanted to bestow her mother in safety and then chase him down from the wall. Well, just let her try it! He clung to his picture and would not give it up. He would rather fly in Grete's face.

But Grete's words had succeeded in disquieting her mother, who took a step to one side, caught sight of the huge brown mass on the flowered wallpaper, and before she was really conscious that what she saw was Gregor screamed in a loud, hoarse voice: "Oh God, oh God!" fell with outspread arms over the sofa as if giving up and did not move. "Gregor!" cried his sister, shaking her fist and glaring at him. This was the first time she had directly addressed him since his metamorphosis. She ran into the next room for some aromatic essence with which to rouse her mother from her fainting fit. Gregor wanted to help too—there was still time to rescue the picture—but he was stuck fast to the glass and had to tear himself loose; he then ran after his sister into the next room as if he could advise her, as he used to do; but then had to stand helplessly behind her; she meanwhile searched among various small bottles and when she turned round started in alarm at the sight of him; one bottle fell on the floor and broke; a splinter of glass cut Gregor's face and some kind of corrosive medicine splashed him; without pausing a moment longer Grete gathered up all the bottles she could carry and ran to her mother with them; she banged the door shut with her foot. Gregor was now cut off from his mother, who was perhaps nearly dying because of him; he dared not open the door for fear of frightening away his sister, who had to stay with her mother; there was nothing he could do but wait; and harassed by self-reproach and worry he began now to crawl to and fro, over everything, walls, furniture and ceiling, and finally in his despair, when the whole room seemed to be reeling round him, fell down on to the middle of the big table.

A little while elapsed, Gregor was still lying there feebly and all around was quiet, perhaps that was a good omen. Then the doorbell rang. The servant girl was of course locked in her kitchen, and Grete would have to open the door. It was his father. "What's been happening?" were his first words; Grete's face must have told him everything. Grete answered in a muffled voice, apparently hiding her head on his breast: "Mother has been fainting, but she's better now. Gregor's broken loose." "Just what I expected," said his father, "just what I've been telling you, but you women would never listen." It was clear to Gregor that his father had taken the worst interpretation of Grete's all too brief statement and was assuming that Gregor had been guilty of some violent act. Therefore Gregor must now try to propitiate his father, since he had neither time nor means tor an explanation. And so he fled to the door of his own room and crouched against it, to let his father see as soon as he came in from the hall that his son had the good intention of getting back into his room immediately and that it was not necessary to drive him there, but that if only the door were opened he would disappear at once.

Yet his father was not in the mood to perceive such fine distinctions. "Ah!" he cried as soon as he appeared, in a tone which sounded at once angry and exultant. Gregor drew his head back from the door and lifted it to look at his father. Truly, this was not the father he had imagined to himself; admittedly he had been too absorbed of late in his new recreation of crawling over the ceiling to take the same interest as before in what was happening elsewhere in the flat, and he ought really to be prepared for some changes. And yet, and

yet, could that be his father? The man who used to lie
wearily sunk in bed whenever Gregor set out on a
business journey; who welcomed him back of an evening
lying in a long chair in a dressing gown; who could not
really rise to his feet but only lifted his arms in greeting,
and on the rare occasions when he did go out with
his family, on one or two Sundays a year and on high
holidays, walked between Gregor and his mother, who
were slow walkers anyhow, even more slowly than they
did, muffled in his old greatcoat, shuffling laboriously
forward with the help of his crook-handled stick which
he set down most cautiously at every step and, whenever he wanted to say anything, nearly always came to
a full stop and gathered his escort around him? Now
he was standing there in fine shape; dressed in a smart
blue uniform with gold buttons, such as bank messengers wear; his strong double chin bulged over the stiff
high collar of his jacket; from under his bushy eyebrows his black eyes darted fresh and penetrating
glances; his onetime tangled white hair had been combed
flat on either side of a shining and carefully exact part-
ing. He pitched his cap, which bore a gold monogram,
probably the badge of some bank, in a wide sweep
across the whole room on to a sofa and with the tail-
ends of his jacket thrown back, his hands in his trouser
pockets, advanced with a grim visage towards Gregor.
Likely enough he did not himself know what he meant
to do; at any rate he lifted his feet uncommonly high,
and Gregor was dumbfounded at the enormous size of
his shoe soles. But Gregor could not risk standing up to
him, aware as he had been from the very first day of
his new life that his father believed only the severest
measures suitable for dealing with him. And so he ran

before his father, stopping when he stopped and scuttling forward again when his father made any kind of
move. In this way they circled the room several times
without anything decisive happening, indeed the whole
operation did not even look like a pursuit because it
was carried out so slowly. And so Gregor did not leave
the floor, for he feared that his father might take as a
piece of peculiar wickedness any excursion of his over
the walls or the ceiling. All the same, he could not stay
this course much longer, for while his father took one
step he had to carry out a whole series of movements.
He was already beginning to feel breathless, just as in
his former life his lungs had not been very dependable.
As he was staggering along, trying to concentrate his
energy on running, hardly keeping his eyes open; in his
dazed state never even thinking of any other escape
than simply going forward; and having almost forgotten that the walls were free to him, which in this room
were well provided with finely carved pieces of furniture full of knobs and crevices—suddenly something
lightly flung landed close behind him and rolled before
him. It was an apple; a second apple followed immediately; Gregor came to a stop in alarm; there was no
point in running on, for his father was determined to
bombard him. He had filled his pockets with fruit from
the dish on the sideboard and was now shying apple
after apple, without taking particularly good aim for
the moment. The small red apples rolled about the floor
as if magnetized and cannoned into each other. An
apple thrown without much force grazed Gregor's
back and glanced off harmlessly. But another following
immediately landed right on his back and sank in;
Gregor wanted to drag himself forward, as if this

startling, incredible pain could be left behind him; but
he felt as if nailed to the spot and flattened himself out
in a complete derangement of all his senses. With his
last conscious look he saw the door of his room being
torn open and his mother rushing out ahead of his
screaming sister, in her underbodice, for her daughter
had loosened her clothing to let her breathe more freely
and recover from her swoon, he saw his mother rushing
towards his father, leaving one after another behind
her on the floor her loosened petticoats, stumbling over
her petticoats straight to his father and embracing him,
in complete union with him—but here Gregor's sight
began to fail—with her hands clasped round his father's
neck as she begged for her son's life.

III

THE SERIOUS INJURY done to Gregor, which disabled
him for more than a month—the apple went on sticking
in his body as a visible reminder, since no one ventured to remove it—seemed to have made even his
father recollect that Gregor was a member of the
family, despite his present unfortunate and repulsive
shape, and ought not to be treated as an enemy, that, on
the contrary, family duty required the suppression of
disgust and the exercise of patience, nothing but
patience.

And although his injury had impaired, probably for
ever, his powers of movement, and for the time being
it took him long, long minutes to creep across his room
like an old invalid—there was no question now of
crawling up the wall—yet in his own opinion he was

sufficiently compensated for this worsening of his condition by the fact that towards evening the living-room
door, which he used to watch intently for an hour or
two beforehand, was always thrown open, so that lying
in the darkness of his room, invisible to the family, he
could see them all at the lamp-lit table and listen to their
talk, by general consent as it were, very different from
his earlier eavesdropping.

True, their intercourse lacked the lively character of
former times, which he had always called to mind with
a certain wistfulness in the small hotel bedrooms where
he had been wont to throw himself down, tired out,
on damp bedding. They were now mostly very silent.
Soon after supper his father would fall asleep in his
armchair; his mother and sister would admonish each
other to be silent; his mother, bending low over the
lamp, stitched at fine sewing for an underwear firm; his
sister, who had taken a job as a salesgirl, was learning
shorthand and French in the evenings on the chance of
bettering herself. Sometimes his father woke up, and
as if quite unaware that he had been sleeping said to his
mother: "What a lot of sewing you're doing today!"
and at once fell asleep again, while the two women
exchanged a tired smile.

With a kind of mulishness his father persisted in
keeping his uniform on even in the house; his dressing
gown hung uselessly on its peg and he slept fully
dressed where he sat, as if he were ready for service at
any moment and even here only at the beck and call
of his superior. As a result, his uniform, which was
not brand-new to start with, began to look dirty, despite
all the loving care of the mother and sister to keep it
clean, and Gregor often spent whole evenings gazing

at the many greasy spots on the garment, gleaming with gold buttons always in a high state of polish, in which the old man sat sleeping in extreme discomfort and yet quite peacefully.

As soon as the clock struck ten his mother tried to rouse his father with gentle words and to persuade him after that to get into bed, for sitting there he could not have a proper sleep and that was what he needed most, since he had to go on duty at six. But with the mulishness that had obsessed him since he became a bank messenger he always insisted on staying longer at the table, although he regularly fell asleep again and in the end only with the greatest trouble could be got out of his armchair and into his bed. However insistently Gregor's mother and sister kept urging him with gentle reminders, he would go on slowly shaking his head for a quarter of an hour, keeping his eyes shut, and refuse to get to his feet. The mother plucked at his sleeve, whispering endearments in his ear, the sister left her lessons to come to her mother's help, but Gregor's father was not to be caught. He would only sink down deeper in his chair. Not until the two women hoisted him up by the armpits did he open his eyes and look at them both, one after the other, usually with the remark: "This is a life. This is the peace and quiet of my old age." And leaning on the two of them he would heave himself up, with difficulty, as if he were a great burden to himself, suffer them to lead him as far as the door and then wave them off and go on alone, while the mother abandoned her needlework and the sister her pen in order to run after him and help him farther.

Who could find time, in this overworked and tired-out family, to bother about Gregor more than was absolutely needful? The household was reduced more and more; the servant girl was turned off; a gigantic bony charwoman with white hair flying round her head came in morning and evening to do the rough work; everything else was done by Gregor's mother, as well as great piles of sewing. Even various family ornaments, which his mother and sister used to wear with pride at parties and celebrations, had to be sold, as Gregor discovered of an evening from hearing them all discuss the prices obtained. But what they lamented most was the fact that they could not leave the flat which was much too big for their present circumstances, because they could not think of any way to shift Gregor. Yet Gregor saw well enough that consideration for him was not the main difficulty preventing the removal, for they could have easily shifted him in some suitable box with a few air holes in it; what really kept them from moving into another flat was rather their own complete hopelessness and the belief that they had been singled out for a misfortune such as had never happened to any of their relations or acquaintances. They fulfilled to the uttermost all that the world demands of poor people, the father fetched breakfast for the small clerks in the bank, the mother devoted her energy to making underwear for strangers, the sister trotted to and fro behind the counter at the behest of customers, but more than this they had not the strength to do. And the wound in Gregor's back began to nag at him afresh when his mother and sister, after getting his father into bed, came back again, left their work lying, drew close to each other and sat cheek by cheek; when his mother, pointing towards his room, said: "Shut

that door now, Grete," and he was left again in darkness, while next door the women mingled their tears or
perhaps sat dry-eyed staring at the table.

Gregor hardly slept at all by night or by day. He
was often haunted by the idea that next time the door
opened he would take the family's affairs in hand again
just as he used to do; once more, after this long interval, there appeared in his thoughts the figures of the
chief and the chief clerk, the commercial travelers and
the apprentices, the porter who was so dull-witted, two
or three friends in other firms, a chambermaid in one
of the rural hotels, a sweet and fleeting memory, a
cashier in a milliner's shop, whom he had wooed earnestly but too slowly—they all appeared, together with
strangers or people he had quite forgotten, but instead
of helping him and his family they were one and all
unapproachable and he was glad when they vanished.
At other times he would not be in the mood to bother
about his family, he was only filled with rage at the way
they were neglecting him, and although he had no clear
idea of what he might care to eat he would make
plans for getting into the larder to take the food that
was after all his due, even if he were not hungry. His
sister no longer took thought to bring him what might
especially please him, but in the morning and at noon
before she went to business hurriedly pushed into his
room with her foot any food that was available, and
in the evening cleared it out again with one sweep of
the broom, heedless of whether it had been merely
tasted, or—as most frequently happened—left untouched.
The cleaning of his room, which she now did always
in the evenings, could not have been more hastily done.
Streaks of dirt stretched along the walls, here and

there lay balls of dust and filth. At first Gregor used to station himself in some particularly filthy corner when his sister arrived, in order to reproach her with it, so to speak. But he could have sat there for weeks without getting her to make any improvement; she could see the dirt as well as he did, but she had simply made up her mind to leave it alone. And yet, with a touchiness that was new to her, which seemed anyhow to have infected the whole family, she jealously guarded her claim to be the sole caretaker of Gregor's room. His mother once subjected his room to a thorough cleaning, which was achieved only by means of several buckets of water—all this dampness of course upset Gregor too and he lay widespread, sulky and motionless on the sofa—but she was well punished for it. Hardly had his sister noticed the changed aspect of his room that evening than she rushed in high dudgeon into the living room and, despite the imploringly raised hands of her mother, burst into a storm of weeping, while her parents—her father had of course been startled out of his chair—looked on at first in helpless amazement; then they too began to go into action; the father reproached the mother on his right for not having left the cleaning of Gregor's room to his sister; shrieked at the sister on his left that never again was she to be allowed to clean Gregor's room; while the mother tried to pull the father into his bedroom, since he was beyond himself with agitation; the sister, shaken with sobs, then beat upon the table with her small fists; and Gregor hissed loudly with rage because not one of them thought of shutting the door to spare him such a spectacle and so much noise.

Still, even if the sister, exhausted by her daily work,

had grown tired of looking after Gregor as she did
formerly, there was no need for his mother's intervention or for Gregor's being neglected at all. The charwoman was there. This old widow, whose strong bony
frame had enabled her to survive the worst a long life
could offer, by no means recoiled from Gregor. Without being in the least curious she had once by chance
opened the door of his room and at the sight of Gregor,
who, taken by surprise, began to rush to and fro although no one was chasing him, merely stood there with
her arms folded. From that time she never failed to open
his door a little for a moment, morning and evening, to
have a look at him. At first she even used to call him to
her, with words which apparently she took to be
friendly, such as: "Come along, then, you old dung
beetle!" or "Look at the old dung beetle, then!" To such
allocutions Gregor made no answer, but stayed motionless where he was, as if the door had never been opened.
Instead of being allowed to disturb him so senselessly
whenever the whim took her, she should rather have
been ordered to clean out his room daily, that charwoman! Once, early in the morning—heavy rain was
lashing on the windowpanes, perhaps a sign that spring
was on the way—Gregor was so exasperated when she
began addressing him again that he ran at her, as if to
attack her, although slowly and feebly enough. But the
charwoman instead of showing fright merely lifted high
a chair that happened to be beside the door, and as she
stood there with her mouth wide open it was clear that
she meant to shut it only when she brought the chair
down on Gregor's back. "So you're not coming any
nearer?" she asked, as Gregor turned away again, and
quietly put the chair back into the corner.

Gregor was now eating hardly anything. Only when he happened to pass the food laid out for him did he take a bit of something in his mouth as a pastime, kept it there for an hour at a time and usually spat it out again. At first he thought it was chagrin over the state of his room that prevented him from eating, yet he soon got used to the various changes in his room. It had become a habit in the family to push into his room things there was no room for elsewhere, and there were plenty of these now, since one of the rooms had been let to three lodgers. These serious gentlemen—all three of them with full beards, as Gregor once observed through a crack in the door—had a passion for order, not only in their own room but, since they were now members of the household, in all its arrangements, especially in the kitchen. Superfluous, not to say dirty, objects they could not bear. Besides, they had brought with them most of the furnishings they needed. For this reason many things could be dispensed with that it was no use trying to sell but that should not be thrown away either. All of them found their way into Gregor's room. The ash can likewise and the kitchen garbage can. Anything that was not needed for the moment was simply flung into Gregor's room by the charwoman, who did everything in a hurry; fortunately Gregor usually saw only the object, whatever it was, and the hand that held it. Perhaps she intended to take the things away again as time and opportunity offered, or to collect them until she could throw them all out in a heap, but in fact they just lay wherever she happened to throw them, except when Gregor pushed his way through the junk heap and shifted it somewhat, at first out of necessity, because he had not room enough to crawl, but later with increasing enjoy-

ment, although after such excursions, being sad and
weary to death, he would lie motionless for hours. And
since the lodgers often ate their supper at home in the
common living room, the living-room door stayed shut
many an evening, yet Gregor reconciled himself quite
easily to the shutting of the door, for often enough on
evenings when it was opened he had disregarded it entirely and lain in the darkest corner of his room, quite
unnoticed by the family. But on one occasion the charwoman left the door open a little and it stayed ajar even
when the lodgers came in for supper and the lamp was
lit. They set themselves at the top end of the table where
formerly Gregor and his father and mother had eaten
their meals, unfolded their napkins and took knife and
fork in hand. At once his mother appeared in the other
doorway with a dish of meat and close behind her his sister with a dish of potatoes piled high. The food steamed
with a thick vapor. The lodgers bent over the food set
before them as if to scrutinize it before eating, in fact
the man in the middle, who seemed to pass for an au-
thority with the other two, cut a piece of meat as it lay
on the dish, obviously to discover if it were tender or
should be sent back to the kitchen. He showed satisfaction, and Gregor's mother and sister, who had been
watching anxiously, breathed freely and began to smile.

The family itself took its meals in the kitchen. None
the less, Gregor's father came into the living room before going into the kitchen and with one prolonged bow,
cap in hand, made a round of the table. The lodgers all
stood up and murmured something in their beards.
When they were alone again they ate their food in almost
complete silence. It seemed remarkable to Gregor that
among the various noises coming from the table he could

always distinguish the sound of their masticating teeth, as if this were a sign to Gregor that one needed teeth in order to eat, and that with toothless jaws even of the finest make one could do nothing. "I'm hungry enough," said Gregor sadly to himself, "but not for that kind of food. How these lodgers are stuffing themselves, and here am I dying of starvation!"

On that very evening—during the whole of his time there Gregor could not remember ever having heard the violin—the sound of violin-playing came from the kitchen. The lodgers had already finished their supper, the one in the middle had brought out a newspaper and given the other two a page apiece, and now they were leaning back at ease reading and smoking. When the violin began to play they pricked up their ears, got to their feet, and went on tiptoe to the hall door where they stood huddled together. Their movements must have been heard in the kitchen, for Gregor's father called out: "Is the violin-playing disturbing you, gentlemen? It can be stopped at once." "On the contrary," said the middle lodger, "could not Fräulein Samsa come and play in this room, beside us, where it is much more convenient and comfortable?" "Oh certainly," cried Gregor's father, as if he were the violin-player. The lodgers came back into the living room and waited. Presently Gregor's father arrived with the music stand, his mother carrying the music and his sister with the violin. His sister quietly made everything ready to start playing; his parents, who had never let rooms before and so had an exaggerated idea of the courtesy due to lodgers, did not venture to sit down on their own chairs; his father leaned against the door, the right hand thrust between two buttons of his livery coat, which was

formally buttoned up; but his mother was offered a
chair by one of the lodgers and, since she left the chair
just where he had happened to put it, sat down in a
corner to one side.

Gregor's sister began to play; the father and mother,
from either side, intently watched the movements of
her hands. Gregor, attracted by the playing, ventured to
move forward a little until his head was actually inside
the living room. He felt hardly any surprise at his growing lack of consideration for the others; there had been
a time when he prided himself on being considerate. And
yet just on this occasion he had more reason than ever
to hide himself, since owing to the amount of dust which
lay thick in his room and rose into the air at the slightest movement, he too was covered with dust; fluff and
hair and remnants of food trailed with him, caught on
his back and along his sides; his indifference to everything was much too great for him to turn on his back
and scrape himself clean on the carpet, as once he had
done several times a day. And in spite of his condition,
no shame deterred him from advancing a little over the
spotless floor of the living room.

To be sure, no one was aware of him. The family was
entirely absorbed in the violin-playing; the lodgers, however, who first of all had stationed themselves, hands in
pockets, much too close behind the music stand so that
they could all have read the music, which must have
bothered his sister, had soon retreated to the window,
half-whispering with downbent heads, and stayed there
while his father turned an anxious eye on them. Indeed,
they were making it more than obvious that they had
been disappointed in their expectation of hearing good
or enjoyable violin-playing, that they had had more

than enough of the performance and only out of courtesy suffered a continued disturbance of their peace. From the way they all kept blowing the smoke of their cigars high in the air through nose and mouth one could divine their irritation. And yet Gregor's sister was playing so beautifully. Her face leaned sideways, intently and sadly her eyes followed the notes of music. Gregor crawled a little farther forward and lowered his head to the ground so that it might be possible for his eyes to meet hers. Was he an animal, that music had such an effect upon him? He felt as if the way were opening before him to the unknown nourishment he craved. He was determined to push forward till he reached his sister, to pull at her skirt and so let her know that she was to come into his room with her violin, for no one here appreciated her playing as he would appreciate it. He would never let her out of his room, at least, not so long as he lived; his frightful appearance would become, for the first time, useful to him; he would watch all the doors of his room at once and spit at intruders; but his sister should need no constraint, she should stay with him of her own free will; she should sit beside him on the sofa, bend down her ear to him and hear him confide that he had had the firm intention of sending her to the Conservatorium, and that, but for his mishap, last Christmas—surely Christmas was long past?—he would have announced it to everybody without allowing a single objection. After this confession his sister would be so touched that she would burst into tears, and Gregor would then raise himself to her shoulder and kiss her on the neck, which, now that she went to business, she kept free of any ribbon or collar.

"Mr. Samsa!" cried the middle lodger, to Gregor's father, and pointed, without wasting any more words, at Gregor, now working himself slowly forwards. The violin fell silent, the middle lodger first smiled to his friends with a shake of the head and then looked at Gregor again. Instead of driving Gregor out, his father seemed to think it more needful to begin by soothing down the lodgers, although they were not at all agitated and apparently found Gregor more entertaining than the violin-playing. He hurried towards them and, spreading out his arms, tried to urge them back into their own room and at the same time to block their view of Gregor. They now began to be really a little angry, one could not tell whether because of the old man's behavior or because it had just dawned on them that all unwittingly they had such a neighbor as Gregor next door. They demanded explanations of his father, they waved their arms like him, tugged uneasily at their beards, and only with reluctance backed towards their room. Meanwhile Gregor's sister, who stood there as if lost when her playing was so abruptly broken off, came to life again, pulled herself together all at once after standing for a while holding violin and bow in nervelessly hanging hands and staring at her music, pushed her violin into the lap of her mother, who was still sitting in her chair fighting asthmatically for breath, and ran into the lodgers' room to which they were now being shepherded by her father rather more quickly than before. One could see the pillows and blankets on the beds flying under her accustomed fingers and being laid in order. Before the lodgers had actually reached their room she had finished making the beds and slipped out.

The old man seemed once more to be so possessed by his mulish self-assertiveness that he was forgetting all the respect he should show to his lodgers. He kept driving them on and driving them on until in the very door of the bedroom the middle lodger stamped his foot loudly on the floor and so brought him to a halt. "I beg to announce," said the lodger, lifting one hand and looking also at Gregor's mother and sister, "that because of the disgusting conditions prevailing in this household and family"—here he spat on the floor with emphatic brevity—"I give you notice on the spot. Naturally I won't pay you a penny for the days I have lived here, on the contrary I shall consider bringing an action for damages against you, based on claims—believe me—that will be easily susceptible of proof." He ceased and stared straight in front of him, as if he expected something. In fact his two friends at once rushed into the breach with these words: "And we too give notice on the spot." On that he seized the door-handle and shut the door with a slam.

Gregor's father, groping with his hands, staggered forward and fell into his chair; it looked as if he were stretching himself there for his ordinary evening nap, but the marked jerkings of his head, which was as if uncontrollable, showed that he was far from asleep. Gregor had simply stayed quietly all the time on the spot where the lodgers had espied him. Disappointment at the failure of his plan, perhaps also the weakness arising from extreme hunger, made it impossible for him to move. He feared, with a fair degree of certainty, that at any moment the general tension would discharge itself in a combined attack upon him, and he lay waiting. He did not react even to the noise made by the violin as it fell off his mother's lap from under her trembling fingers and gave out a resonant note.

"My dear parents," said his sister, slapping her hand on the table by way of introduction, "things can't go on like this. Perhaps you don't realize that, but I do. I won't utter my brother's name in the presence of this creature, and so all I say is: we must try to get rid of it. We've tried to look after it and to put up with it as far as is humanly possible, and I don't think anyone could reproach us in the slightest."

"She is more than right," said Gregor's father to himself. His mother, who was still choking for lack of breath, began to cough hollowly into her hand with a wild look in her eyes.

His sister rushed over to her and held her forehead. His father's thoughts seemed to have lost their vagueness at Grete's words, he sat more upright, fingering his service cap that lay among the plates still lying on the table from the lodgers' supper, and from time to time looked at the still form of Gregor.

"We must try to get rid of it," his sister now said explicitly to her father, since her mother was coughing too much to hear a word, "it will be the death of both of you, I can see that coming. When one has to work as hard as we do, all of us, one can't stand this continual torment at home on top of it. At least I can't stand it any longer." And she burst into such a passion of sobbing that her tears dropped on her mother's face, where she wiped them off mechanically.

"My dear," said the old man sympathetically, and with evident understanding, "but what can we do?"

Gregor's sister merely shrugged her shoulders to indicate the feeling of helplessness that had now overmastered her during her weeping fit, in contrast to her former confidence.

"If he could understand us," said her father, half questioningly; Grete, still sobbing, vehemently waved a hand to show how unthinkable that was.

"If he could understand us," repeated the old man, shutting his eyes to consider his daughter's conviction that understanding was impossible, "then perhaps we might come to some agreement with him. But as it is—"

"He must go," cried Gregor's sister, "that's the only solution, Father. You must just try to get rid of the idea that this is Gregor. The fact that we've believed it for so long is the root of all our trouble. But how can it be Gregor? If this were Gregor, he would have realized long ago that human beings can't live with such a creature, and he'd have gone away on his own accord. Then we wouldn't have any brother, but we'd be able to go on living and keep his memory in honor. As it is, this creature persecutes us, drives away our lodgers, obviously wants the whole apartment to himself and would have us all sleep in the gutter. Just look, Father," she shrieked all at once, "he's at it again!" And in an access of panic that was quite incomprehensible to Gregor she even quitted her mother, literally thrusting the chair from her as if she would rather sacrifice her mother than stay so near to Gregor, and rushed behind her father, who also rose up, being simply upset by her agitation, and half-spread his arms out as if to protect her.

Yet Gregor had not the slightest intention of frightening anyone, far less his sister. He had only begun to turn round in order to crawl back to his room, but it was certainly a startling operation to watch, since because of his disabled condition he could not execute the difficult turning movements except by lifting his head and then bracing it against the floor over and over again. He paused and looked round. His good intentions seemed to have been recognized; the alarm had only been momentary. Now they were all watching him in melancholy silence. His mother lay in her chair, her legs stiffly outstretched and pressed together, her eyes almost closing for sheer weariness; his father and his sister were sitting beside each other, his sister's arm around the old man's neck.

Perhaps I can go on turning round now, thought Gregor, and began his labors again. He could not stop himself from panting with the effort, and had to pause now and then to take breath. Nor did anyone harass him, he was left entirely to himself. When he had completed the turn-round he began at once to crawl straight back. He was amazed at the distance separating him from his room and could not understand how in his weak state he had managed to accomplish the same journey so recently, almost without remarking it. Intent on crawling as fast as possible, he barely noticed that not a single word, not an ejaculation from his family, interfered with his progress. Only when he was already in the doorway did he turn his head round, not completely, for his neck muscles were getting stiff, but enough to see that nothing had changed behind him except that his sister had risen to her feet. His last glance fell on his mother, who was not quite overcome by sleep.

Hardly was he well inside his room when the door was hastily pushed shut, bolted and locked. The sudden noise in his rear startled him so much that his little legs gave beneath him. It was his sister who had shown such haste. She had been standing ready waiting

and had made a light spring forward, Gregor had not
even heard her coming, and she cried "At last!" to her
parents as she turned the key in the lock.

"And what now?" said Gregor to himself, looking
round in the darkness. Soon he made the discovery that
he was now unable to stir a limb. This did not surprise
him, rather it seemed unnatural that he should ever
actually have been able to move on these feeble little
legs. Otherwise he felt relatively comfortable. True, his
whole body was aching, but it seemed that the pain
was gradually growing less and would finally pass away.
The rotting apple in his back and the inflamed area
around it, all covered with soft dust, already hardly
troubled him. He thought of his family with tenderness
and love. The decision that he must disappear was one
that he held to even more strongly than his sister, if that
were possible. In this state of vacant and peaceful meditation he remained until the tower clock struck three in
the morning. The first broadening of light in the world
outside the window entered his consciousness once more.
Then his head sank to the floor of its own accord
and from his nostrils came the last faint flicker of his
breath.

When the charwoman arrived early in the morning—
what between her strength and her impatience she
slammed all the doors so loudly, never mind how often
she had been begged not to do so, that no one in the
whole apartment could enjoy any quiet sleep after her
arrival—she noticed nothing unusual as she took her
customary peep into Gregor's room. She thought he
was lying motionless on purpose, pretending to be in
the sulks; she credited him with every kind of intelligence. Since she happened to have the long-handled

broom in her hand she tried to tickle him up with it from the doorway. When that too produced no reaction she felt provoked and poked at him a little harder, and only when she had pushed him along the floor without meeting any resistance was her attention aroused. It did not take her long to establish the truth of the matter, and her eyes widened, she let out a whistle, yet did not waste much time over it but tore open the door of the Samsas' bedroom and yelled into the darkness at the top of her voice: "Just look at this, it's dead; it's lying here dead and done for!"

Mr. and Mrs. Samsa started up in their double bed and before they realized the nature of the charwoman's announcement had some difficulty in overcoming the shock of it. But then they got out of bed quickly, one on either side, Mr. Samsa throwing a blanket over his shoulders, Mrs. Samsa in nothing but her nightgown; in this array they entered Gregor's room. Meanwhile the door of the living room opened, too, where Grete had been sleeping since the advent of the lodgers; she was completely dressed as if she had not been to bed, which seemed to be confirmed also by the paleness of her face. "Dead?" said Mrs. Samsa, looking questioningly at the charwoman, although she could have investigated for herself, and the fact was obvious enough without investigation. "I should say so," said the charwoman, proving her words by pushing Gregor's corpse a long way to one side with her broomstick. Mrs. Samsa made a movement as if to stop her, but checked it. "Well," said Mr. Samsa, "now thanks be to God." He crossed himself, and the three women followed his example. Grete, whose eyes never left the corpse, said: "Just see how thin he was. It's such a long time since he's eaten anything. The food came out again just as it went in." Indeed, Gregor's body was completely flat and dry, as could only now be seen when it was no longer supported by the legs and nothing prevented one from looking closely at it.

"Come in beside us, Grete, for a little while," said Mrs. Samsa with a tremulous smile, and Grete, not without looking back at the corpse, followed her parents into their bedroom. The charwoman shut the door and opened the window wide. Although it was so early in the morning a certain softness was perceptible in the fresh air. After all, it was already the end of March.

The three lodgers emerged from their room and were surprised to see no breakfast; they had been forgotten. "Where's our breakfast?" said the middle lodger peevishly to the charwoman. But she put her finger to her lips and hastily, without a word, indicated by gestures that they should go into Gregor's room. They did so and stood, their hands in the pockets of their somewhat shabby coats, around Gregor's corpse in the room where it was now fully light.

At that the door of the Samsas' bedroom opened and Mr. Samsa appeared in his uniform, his wife on one arm, his daughter on the other. They all looked a little as if they had been crying; from time to time Grete hid her face on her father's arm.

"Leave my house at once!" said Mr. Samsa, and pointed to the door without disengaging himself from the women. "What do you mean by that?" said the middle lodger, taken somewhat aback, with a feeble smile. The two others put their hands behind them and kept rubbing them together, as if in gleeful expectation of a fine set-to in which they were bound to come off the winners. "I mean just what I say," answered Mr. Samsa, and advanced in a straight line with his two companions towards the lodger. He stood his ground at first quietly, looking at the floor as if his thoughts were taking a new pattern in his head. "Then let us go, by all means," he said, and looked up at Mr. Samsa as if in a sudden access of humility he were expecting some renewed sanction for this decision. Mr. Samsa merely nodded briefly once or twice with meaning eyes. Upon that the lodger really did go with long strides into the hall, his two friends had been listening and had quite stopped rubbing their hands for some moments and now went scuttling after him as if afraid that Mr. Samsa might get into the hall before them and cut them off from their leader. In the hall they all three took their hats from the rack, their sticks from the umbrella stand, bowed in silence and quitted the apartment. With a suspiciousness which proved quite unfounded Mr. Samsa and the two women followed them out to the landing; leaning over the banister they watched the three figures slowly but surely going down the long stairs, vanishing from sight at a certain turn of the staircase on every floor and coming into view again after a moment or so; the more they dwindled, the more the Samsa family's interest in them dwindled, and when a butcher's boy met them and passed them on the stairs coming up proudly with a tray on his head, Mr. Samsa and the two women soon left the landing and as if a burden had been lifted from them went back into their apartment.

They decided to spend this day in resting and going for a stroll; they had not only deserved such a respite from work, but absolutely needed it. And so they sat down at the table and wrote three notes of excuse, Mr. Samsa to his board of management, Mrs. Samsa to her employer and Grete to the head of her firm. While they were writing, the charwoman came in to say that she was going now, since her morning's work was finished. At first they only nodded without looking up, but as she kept hovering there they eyed her irritably. "Well?" said Mr. Samsa. The charwoman stood grinning in the doorway as if she had good news to impart to the family but meant not to say a word unless properly questioned. The small ostrich feather standing upright on her hat, which had annoyed Mr. Samsa ever since she was engaged, was waving gaily in all directions. "Well, what is it then?" asked Mrs. Samsa, who obtained more respect from the charwoman than the others. "Oh," said the charwoman, giggling so amiably that she could not at once continue, "just this, you don't need to bother about how to get rid of the thing next door. It's been seen to already." Mrs. Samsa and Grete bent over their letters again, as if preoccupied; Mr. Samsa, who perceived that she was eager to begin describing it all in detail, stopped her with a decisive hand. But since she was not allowed to tell her story, she remembered the great hurry she was in, being obviously deeply huffed: "Bye, everybody," she said, whirling off violently, and departed with a frightful slamming of doors.

"She'll be given notice tonight," said Mr. Samsa, but neither from his wife nor his daughter did he get any answer, for the charwoman seemed to have shattered again the composure they had barely achieved. They rose, went to the window and stayed there, clasping each other tight. Mr. Samsa turned in his chair to look at them and quietly observed them for a little. Then he called out: "Come along, now, do. Let bygones be bygones. And you might have some consideration for me." The two of them complied at once, hastened to him, caressed him and quickly finished their letters.

Then they all three left the apartment together, which was more than they had done for months, and went by tram into the open country outside the town. The tram, in which they were the only passengers, was filled with warm sunshine. Leaning comfortably back in their seats they canvassed their prospects for the future, and it appeared on closer inspection that these were not at all bad, for the jobs they had got, which so far they had never really discussed with each other, were all three admirable and likely to lead to better things later on. The greatest immediate improvement in their condition would of course arise from moving to another house; they wanted to take a smaller and cheaper but also better situated and more easily run apartment than the one they had, which Gregor had selected. While they were thus conversing, it struck both Mr. and Mrs. Samsa, almost at the same moment, as they became aware of their daughter's increasing vivacity, that in spite of all the sorrow of recent times, which had made her cheeks pale, she had bloomed into a pretty girl with a good figure. They grew quieter and half unconsciously exchanged glances of complete agreement, having come to the conclusion that it would soon be time to find a good husband for her. And it was like a confirmation of their new dreams and excellent intentions that at the end of their journey their daughter sprang to her feet first and stretched her young body.

A COUNTRY DOCTOR

A Country Doctor

The New Advocate

WE HAVE a new advocate, Dr. Bucephalus. There is little in his appearance to remind you that he was once Alexander of Macedon's battle charger. Of course, if you know his story, you are aware of something. But even a simple usher whom I saw the other day on the front steps of the Law Courts, a man with the professional appraisal of the regular small punter in a racecourse, was running an admiring eye over the advocate as he mounted the marble steps with a high action that made them ring beneath his feet.

In general the Bar approves the admission of Bucephalus. With astonishing insight people tell themselves that, modern society being what it is, Bucephalus is in a difficult position, and therefore, considering also his importance in the history of the world, he deserves at least a friendly reception. Nowadays—it cannot be denied—there is no Alexander the Great. There are plenty of men who know how to murder people; the skill needed to reach over a banqueting table and pink a friend with a lance is not lacking; and for many Macedonia is too confining, so that they curse Philip, the father—but no one, no one at all, can blaze a trail to India. Even in his day the gates of India were beyond reach, yet the King's sword pointed the way to them. Today the gates have receded to remoter and loftier places; no one points the way; many carry swords, but only to brandish them, and the eye that tries to follow them is confused.

So perhaps it is really best to do as Bucephalus has done and absorb oneself in law books. In the quiet lamplight, his flanks unhampered by the thighs of a rider, free and far from the clamor of battle, he reads and turns the pages of our ancient tomes.

A Country Doctor

I WAS in great perplexity; I had to start on an urgent journey; a seriously ill patient was waiting for me in a village ten miles off; a thick blizzard of snow filled all the wide spaces between him and me; I had a gig, a light gig with big wheels, exactly right for our country roads; muffled in furs, my bag of instruments in my hand, I was in the courtyard all ready for the journey; but there was no horse to be had, no horse. My own horse had died in the night, worn out by the fatigues of this icy winter; my servant girl was now running round the village trying to borrow a horse; but it was hopeless, I knew it, and I stood there forlornly, with the snow gathering more and more thickly upon me, more and more unable to move. In the gateway the girl appeared, alone, and waved the lantern; of course, who would lend a horse at this time for such a journey? I strode through the courtyard once more; I could see no way out; in my confused distress I kicked at the dilapidated door of the yearlong uninhabited pigsty.

It flew open and flapped to and fro on its hinges. A steam and smell as of horses came out from it. A dim stable lantern was swinging inside from a rope. A man, crouching on his hams in that low space, showed an open blue-eyed face. "Shall I yoke up?" he asked, crawling out on all fours. I did not know what to say and merely stooped down to see what else was in the sty. The servant girl was standing beside me. "You never know what you're going to find in your own house," she said, and we both laughed. "Hey there, Brother, hey there, Sister!" called the groom, and two horses, enormous creatures with powerful flanks, one after the other, their legs tucked close to their bodies, each well-shaped head lowered like a camel's, by sheer strength of buttocking squeezed out through the door hole which they filled entirely. But at once they were standing up, their legs long and their bodies steaming thickly. "Give him a hand," I said, and the willing girl hurried to help the groom with the harnessing. Yet hardly was she beside him when the groom clipped hold of her and pushed his face against hers. She screamed and fled back to me; on her cheek stood out in red the marks of two rows of teeth. "You brute," I yelled in fury, "do you want a whipping?" but in the same moment reflected that the man was a stranger; that I did not know where he came from, and that of his own free will he was helping me out when everyone else had failed me. As if he knew my thoughts he took no offense at my threat but, still busied with the horses, only turned round once towards me. "Get in," he said then, and indeed: everything was ready. A magnificent pair of horses, I observed, such as I had never sat behind, and I climbed in happily. "But I'll drive, you don't know the way," I

said. "Of course," said he, "I'm not coming with you
anyway, I'm staying with Rose." "No," shrieked Rose,
fleeing into the house with a justified presentiment that
her fate was inescapable; I heard the door chain rattle
as she put it up; I heard the key turn in the lock; I
could see, moreover, how she put out the lights in the
entrance hall and in further flight all through the rooms
to keep herself from being discovered. "You're coming
with me," I said to the groom, "or I won't go, urgent
as my journey is. I'm not thinking of paying for it by
handing the girl over to you." "Gee up!" he said;
clapped his hands; the gig whirled off like a log in a
freshet; I could just hear the door of my house splitting
and bursting as the groom charged at it and then I
was deafened and blinded by a storming rush that
steadily buffeted all my senses. But this only for a
moment, since, as if my patient's farmyard had opened
out just before my courtyard gate, I was already there;
the horses had come quietly to a standstill; the blizzard
had stopped; moonlight all around; my patient's parents
hurried out of the house, his sister behind them; I was
almost lifted out of the gig; from their confused ejaculations I gathered not a word; in the sickroom the air
was almost unbreathable; the neglected stove was smoking; I wanted to push open a window; but first I had to
look at my patient. Gaunt, without any fever, not cold,
not warm, with vacant eyes, without a shirt, the youngster heaved himself up from under the feather bedding,
threw his arms round my neck, and whispered in my
ear: "Doctor, let me die." I glanced round the room;
no one had heard it; the parents were leaning forward
in silence waiting for my verdict; the sister had set a
chair for my handbag; I opened the bag and hunted

among my instruments; the boy kept clutching at me from his bed to remind me of his entreaty; I picked up a pair of tweezers, examined them in the candlelight and laid them down again. "Yes," I thought blasphemously, "in cases like this the gods are helpful, send the missing horse, add to it a second because of the urgency, and to crown everything bestow even a groom—" And only now did I remember Rose again; what was I to do, how could I rescue her, how could I pull her away from under that groom at ten miles' distance, with a team of horses I couldn't control. These horses, now, they had somehow slipped the reins loose, pushed the windows open from outside, I did not know how; each of them had stuck a head in at a window and, quite unmoved by the startled cries of the family, stood eyeing the patient. "Better go back at once," I thought, as if the horses were summoning me to the return journey, yet I permitted the patient's sister, who fancied that I was dazed by the heat, to take my fur coat from me. A glass of rum was poured out for me, the old man clapped me on the shoulder, a familiarity justified by this offer of his treasure. I shook my head; in the narrow confines of the old man's thoughts I felt ill; that was my only reason for refusing the drink. The mother stood by the bedside and cajoled me towards it; I yielded, and, while one of the horses whinnied loudly to the ceiling, laid my head to the boy's breast, which shivered under my wet beard. I confirmed what I already knew; the boy was quite sound, something a little wrong with his circulation, saturated with coffee by his solicitous mother, but sound and best turned out of bed with one shove. I am no world reformer and so I let him lie. I was the district doctor and did my duty

to the uttermost, to the point where it became almost
too much. I was badly paid and yet generous and helpful to the poor. I had still to see that Rose was all right,
and then the boy might have his way and I wanted to
die too. What was I doing there in that endless winter! My horse was dead, and not a single person in the
village would lend me another. I had to get my team
out of the pigsty; if they hadn't chanced to be horses
I should have had to travel with swine. That was how
it was. And I nodded to the family. They knew nothing
about it, and, had they known, would not have believed
it. To write prescriptions is easy, but to come to an understanding with people is hard. Well, this should be
the end of my visit, I had once more been called out
needlessly, I was used to that, the whole district made
my life a torment with my night bell, but that I should
have to sacrifice Rose this time as well, the pretty girl
who had lived in my house for years almost without my
noticing her—that sacrifice was too much to ask, and I
had somehow to get it reasoned out in my head with the
help of what craft I could muster, in order not to let fly
at this family, which with the best will in the world
could not restore Rose to me. But as I shut my bag and
put an arm out for my fur coat, the family meanwhile
standing together, the father sniffing at the glass of rum
in his hand, the mother, apparently disappointed in me
—why, what do people expect?—biting her lips with
tears in her eyes, the sister fluttering a blood-soaked
towel, I was somehow ready to admit conditionally that
the boy might be ill after all. I went towards him, he
welcomed me smiling as if I were bringing him the
most nourishing invalid broth—ah, now both horses
were whinnying together; the noise, I suppose, was or-

dained by heaven to assist my examination of the patient
—and this time I discovered that the boy was indeed ill.
In his right side, near the hip, was an open wound as
big as the palm of my hand. Rose-red, in many variations of shade, dark in the hollows, lighter at the edges,
softly granulated, with irregular clots of blood, open as
a surface mine to the daylight. That was how it looked
from a distance. But on a closer inspection there was
another complication. I could not help a low whistle of
surprise. Worms, as thick and as long as my little finger,
themselves rose-red and blood-spotted as well, were
wriggling from their fastness in the interior of the
wound towards the light, with small white heads and
many little legs. Poor boy, you were past helping. I
had discovered your great wound; this blossom in your
side was destroying you. The family was pleased; they
saw me busying myself; the sister told the mother, the
mother the father, the father told several guests who
were coming in, through the moonlight at the open
door, walking on tiptoe, keeping their balance with
outstretched arms. "Will you save me?" whispered the
boy with a sob, quite blinded by the life within his
wound. That is what people are like in my district.
Always expecting the impossible from the doctor. They
have lost their ancient beliefs; the parson sits at home
and unravels his vestments, one after another; but the
doctor is supposed to be omnipotent with his merciful
surgeon's hand. Well, as it pleases them; I have not
thrust my services on them; if they misuse me for sacred
ends, I let that happen to me too; what better do I
want, old country doctor that I am, bereft of my
servant girl! And so they came, the family and the village elders, and stripped my clothes off me; a school

choir with the teacher at the head of it stood before the
house and sang these words to an utterly simple tune:

Strip his clothes off, then he'll heal us,
If he doesn't, kill him dead!
Only a doctor, only a doctor.

Then my clothes were off and I looked at the people
quietly, my fingers in my beard and my head cocked
to one side. I was altogether composed and equal to the
situation and remained so, although it was no help to me,
since they now took me by the head and feet and
carried me to the bed. They laid me down in it next
to the wall, on the side of the wound. Then they all
left the room; the door was shut; the singing stopped;
clouds covered the moon; the bedding was warm around
me; the horses' heads in the open windows wavered
like shadows. "Do you know," said a voice in my ear,
"I have very little confidence in you. Why, you were
only blown in here, you didn't come on your own
feet. Instead of helping me, you're cramping me on my
deathbed. What I'd like best is to scratch your eyes
out." "Right," I said, "it is a shame. And yet I am a
doctor. What am I to do? Believe me, it is not too
easy for me either." "Am I supposed to be content with
this apology? Oh, I must be, I can't help it. I always
have to put up with things. A fine wound is all I
brought into the world; that was my sole endowment."
"My young friend," said I, "your mistake is: you have
not a wide enough view. I have been in all the sick-
rooms, far and wide, and I tell you: your wound is not
so bad. Done in a tight corner with two strokes of the
ax. Many a one proffers his side and can hardly hear
the ax in the forest, far less that it is coming nearer to
him." "Is that really so, or are you deluding me in my

fever?" "It is really so, take the word of honor of an official doctor." And he took it and lay still. But now it was time for me to think of escaping. The horses were still standing faithfully in their places. My clothes, my fur coat, my bag were quickly collected; I didn't want to waste time dressing; if the horses raced home as they had come, I should only be springing, as it were, out of this bed into my own. Obediently a horse backed away from the window; I threw my bundle into the gig; the fur coat missed its mark and was caught on a hook only by the sleeve. Good enough. I swung myself on to the horse. With the reins loosely trailing, one horse barely fastened to the other, the gig swaying behind, my fur coat last of all in the snow. "Gee up!" I said, but there was no galloping; slowly, like old men, we crawled through the snowy wastes; a long time echoed behind us the new but faulty song of the children:

> O be joyful, all you patients,
> The doctor's laid in bed beside you!

Never shall I reach home at this rate; my flourishing practice is done for; my successor is robbing me, but in vain, for he cannot take my place; in my house the disgusting groom is raging; Rose is his victim; I do not want to think about it any more. Naked, exposed to the frost of this most unhappy of ages, with an earthly vehicle, unearthly horses, old man that I am, I wander astray. My fur coat is hanging from the back of the gig, but I cannot reach it, and none of my limber pack of patients lifts a finger. Betrayed! Betrayed! A false alarm on the night bell once answered—it cannot be made good, not ever.

Up in the Gallery

IF SOME FRAIL, consumptive equestrienne in the circus were to be urged round and round on an undulating horse for months on end without respite by a ruthless, whip-flourishing ringmaster, before an insatiable public, whizzing along on her horse, throwing kisses, swaying from the waist, and if this performance were likely to continue in the infinite perspective of a drab future to the unceasing roar of the orchestra and hum of the ventilators, accompanied by ebbing and renewed swelling bursts of applause which are really steam hammers —then, perhaps, a young visitor to the gallery might race down the long stairs through all the circles, rush into the ring, and yell: Stop! against the fanfares of the orchestra still playing the appropriate music.

But since that is not so; a lovely lady, pink and white, floats in between the curtains, which proud lackeys open before her; the ringmaster, deferentially catching her eye, comes towards her breathing animal devotion; tenderly lifts her up on the dapple-gray, as if she were his own most precious granddaughter about to start on a dangerous journey; cannot make up his mind to give the signal with his whip, finally masters himself enough to crack the whip loudly; runs along beside the horse, open-mouthed; follows with a sharp eye the leaps taken by its rider; finds her artistic skill almost beyond belief; calls to her with English shouts of warning; angrily exhorts the grooms who hold the hoops to be most closely attentive; before the great somersault lifts up his arms and implores the orchestra to be silent; finally lifts the little one down from her trembling horse, kisses her on both cheeks and finds that all the ovation she gets from the audience is barely sufficient; while she herself, supported by him, right up on the tips of her toes, in a cloud of dust, with outstretched arms and small head thrown back, invites the whole circus to share her triumph—since that is so, the visitor to the gallery lays his face on the rail before him and, sinking into the closing march as into a heavy dream, weeps without knowing it.

An Old Manuscript

IT LOOKS as if much had been neglected in our country's system of defense. We have not concerned ourselves with it until now and have gone about our daily work; but things that have been happening recently begin to trouble us.

I have a cobbler's workshop in the square that lies before the Emperor's palace. Scarcely have I taken my shutters down, at the first glimmer of dawn, when I see armed soldiers already posted in the mouth of every street opening on the square. But these soldiers are not ours, they are obviously nomads from the North. In some way that is incomprehensible to me they have pushed right into the capital, although it is a long way from the frontier. At any rate, here they are; it seems that every morning there are more of them.

As is their nature, they camp under the open sky, for they abominate dwelling houses. They busy themselves sharpening swords, whittling arrows and practicing horsemanship. This peaceful square, which was always kept so scrupulously clean, they have made literally into

a stable. We do try every now and then to run out of
our shops and clear away at least the worst of the
filth, but this happens less and less often, for the labor
is in vain and brings us besides into danger of falling
under the hoofs of the wild horses or of being crippled
with lashes from the whips.

Speech with the nomads is impossible. They do not
know our language, indeed they hardly have a language
of their own. They communicate with each other much
as jackdaws do. A screeching as of jackdaws is always
in our ears. Our way of living and our institutions they
neither understand nor care to understand. And so they
are unwilling to make sense even out of our sign language. You can gesture at them till you dislocate your
jaws and your wrists and still they will not have understood you and will never understand. They often
make grimaces; then the whites of their eyes turn up
and foam gathers on their lips, but they do not mean
anything by that, not even a threat; they do it because it
is their nature to do it. Whatever they need, they take.
You cannot call it taking by force. They grab at something and you simply stand aside and leave them to it.

From my stock, too, they have taken many good
articles. But I cannot complain when I see how the
butcher, for instance, suffers across the street. As soon
as he brings in any meat the nomads snatch it all from
him and gobble it up. Even their horses devour flesh;
often enough a horseman and his horse are lying side by
side, both of them gnawing at the same joint, one at
either end. The butcher is nervous and does not dare
to stop his deliveries of meat. We understand that, however, and subscribe money to keep him going. If the
nomads got no meat, who knows what they might think

of doing; who knows anyhow what they may think of, even though they get meat every day.

Not long ago the butcher thought he might at least spare himself the trouble of slaughtering, and so one morning he brought along a live ox. But he will never dare to do that again. I lay for a whole hour flat on the floor at the back of my workshop with my head muffled in all the clothes and rugs and pillows I had, simply to keep from hearing the bellowing of that ox, which the nomads were leaping on from all sides, tearing morsels out of its living flesh with their teeth. It had been quiet for a long time before I risked coming out; they were lying overcome round the remains of the carcass like drunkards round a wine cask.

This was the occasion when I fancied I actually saw the Emperor himself at a window of the palace; usually he never enters these outer rooms but spends all his time in the innermost garden; yet on this occasion he was standing, or so at least it seemed to me, at one of the windows, watching with bent head the ongoings before his residence.

"What is going to happen?" we all ask ourselves. "How long can we endure this burden and torment? The Emperor's palace has drawn the nomads here but does not know how to drive them away again. The gate stays shut; the guards, who used to be always marching out and in with ceremony, keep close behind barred windows. It is left to us artisans and tradesmen to save our country; but we are not equal to such a task; nor have we ever claimed to be capable of it. This is a misunderstanding of some kind; and it will be the ruin of us."

Before the Law

BEFORE THE LAW stands a doorkeeper. To this doorkeeper there comes a man from the country and prays
for admittance to the Law. But the doorkeeper says that
he cannot grant admittance at the moment. The man
thinks it over and then asks if he will be allowed in
later. "It is possible," says the doorkeeper, "but not at
the moment." Since the gate stands open, as usual, and
the doorkeeper steps to one side, the man stoops to peer
through the gateway into the interior. Observing that,
the doorkeeper laughs and says: "If you are so drawn
to it, just try to go in despite my veto. But take note:
I am powerful. And I am only the least of the doorkeepers. From hall to hall there is one doorkeeper after
another, each more powerful than the last. The third
doorkeeper is already so terrible that even I cannot bear
to look at him." These are difficulties the man from the
country has not expected; the Law, he thinks, should
surely be accessible at all times and to everyone, but as
he now takes a closer look at the doorkeeper in his fur
coat, with his big sharp nose and long, thin, black Tar-
tar beard, he decides that it is better to wait until he
gets permission to enter. The doorkeeper gives him a
stool and lets him sit down at one side of the door.
There he sits for days and years. He makes many attempts to be admitted, and wearies the doorkeeper by
his importunity. The doorkeeper frequently has little
interviews with him, asking him questions about his
home and many other things, but the questions are put
indifferently, as great lords put them, and always finish
with the statement that he cannot be let in yet. The

man, who has furnished himself with many things for
his journey, sacrifices all he has, however valuable, to
bribe the doorkeeper. The doorkeeper accepts everything, but always with the remark: "I am only taking
it to keep you from thinking you have omitted anything." During these many years the man fixes his attention almost continuously on the doorkeeper. He forgets the other doorkeepers, and this first one seems to
him the sole obstacle preventing access to the Law. He
curses his bad luck, in his early years boldly and loudly,
later, as he grows old, he only grumbles to himself. He
becomes childish, and since in his yearlong contempla-
tion of the doorkeeper he has come to know even the
fleas in his fur collar, he begs the fleas as well to help
him and to change the doorkeeper's mind. At length
his eyesight begins to fail, and he does not know whether
the world is really darker or whether his eyes are only
deceiving him. Yet in his darkness he is now aware
of a radiance that streams inextinguishably from the
gateway of the Law. Now he has not very long to
live. Before he dies, all his experiences in these long
years gather themselves in his head to one point, a question he has not yet asked the doorkeeper. He waves
him nearer, since he can no longer raise his stiffening
body. The doorkeeper has to bend low towards him,
for the difference in height between them has altered
much to the man's disadvantage. "What do you want
to know now?" asks the doorkeeper; "you are insatiable." "Everyone strives to reach the Law," says the
man, "so how does it happen that for all these many
years no one but myself has ever begged for admittance?" The doorkeeper recognizes that the man has
reached his end, and to let his failing senses catch the

words roars in his ear: "No one else could ever be admitted here, since this gate was made only for you. I am now going to shut it."

Jackals and Arabs

WE WERE CAMPING in the oasis. My companions were asleep. The tall, white figure of an Arab passed by; he had been seeing to the camels and was on his way to his own sleeping place.

I threw myself on my back in the grass; I tried to fall asleep; I could not; a jackal howled in the distance; I sat up again. And what had been so far away was all at once quite near. Jackals were swarming round me, eyes gleaming dull gold and vanishing again, lithe bodies moving nimbly and rhythmically, as if at the crack of a whip.

One jackal came from behind me, nudging right under my arm, pressing against me, as if he needed my warmth, and then stood before me and spoke to me almost eye to eye.

"I am the oldest jackal far and wide. I am delighted to have met you here at last. I had almost given up hope, since we have been waiting endless years for you; my mother waited for you, and her mother, and all our fore-mothers right back to the first mother of all the jackals. It is true, believe me!"

"That is surprising," said I, forgetting to kindle the pile of firewood which lay ready to smoke away jackals, "that is very surprising for me to hear. It is by pure chance that I have come here from the far North, and I am making only a short tour of your country. What do you jackals want, then?"

As if emboldened by this perhaps too friendly inquiry the ring of jackals closed in on me; all were panting and openmouthed.

"We know," began the eldest, "that you have come from the North; that is just what we base our hopes on. You Northerners have the kind of intelligence that is not to be found among Arabs. Not a spark of intelligence, let me tell you, can be struck from their cold arrogance. They kill animals for food, and carrion they despise."

"Not so loud," said I, "there are Arabs sleeping near by."

"You are indeed a stranger here," said the jackal, "or you would know that never in the history of the world has any jackal been afraid of an Arab. Why should we fear them? Is it not misfortune enough for us to be exiled among such creatures?"

"Maybe, maybe," said I, "matters so far outside my province I am not competent to judge; it seems to me a very old quarrel; I suppose it's in the blood, and perhaps will only end with it."

"You are very clever," said the old jackal; and they all began to pant more quickly; the air pumped out of their lungs although they were standing still; a rank smell which at times I had to set my teeth to endure streamed from their open jaws, "you are very clever; what you have just said agrees with our old tradition. So we shall draw blood from them and the quarrel will be over."

"Oh!" said I, more vehemently than I intended, "they'll defend themselves; they'll shoot you down in dozens with their muskets."

"You misunderstand us," said he, "a human failing which persists apparently even in the far North. We're not proposing to kill them. All the water in the Nile couldn't cleanse us of that. Why, the mere sight of their living flesh makes us turn tail and flee into cleaner air, into the desert, which for that very reason is our home."

And all the jackals around, including many new-comers from farther away, dropped their muzzles between their forelegs and wiped them with their paws; it was as if they were trying to conceal a disgust so overpowering that I felt like leaping over their heads to get away.

"Then what are you proposing to do?" I asked, trying to rise to my feet; but I could not get up; two young beasts behind me had locked their teeth through my coat and shirt; I had to go on sitting. "These are your trainbearers," explained the old jackal, quite seriously, "a mark of honor." "They must let go!" I cried, turning now to the old jackal, now to the youngsters. "They will, of course," said the old one, "if that is your wish. But it will take a little time, for they have got their teeth well in, as is our custom, and must first loosen their jaws bit by bit. Meanwhile, give ear to our peti-tion." "Your conduct hasn't exactly inclined me to grant it," said I. "Don't hold it against us that we are clumsy," said he, and now for the first time had re-course to the natural plaintiveness of his voice, "we are poor creatures, we have nothing but our teeth; whatever we want to do, good or bad, we can tackle it only with our teeth." "Well, what do you want?" I asked, not much mollified.

"Sir," he cried, and all the jackals howled together; very remotely it seemed to resemble a melody. "Sir, we want you to end this quarrel that divides the world. You are exactly the man whom our ancestors foretold as born to do it. We want to be troubled no more by Arabs; room to breathe; a skyline cleansed of them; no more bleating of sheep knifed by an Arab; every beast to die a natural death; no interference till we have drained the carcass empty and picked its bones clean. Cleanliness, nothing but cleanliness is what we want"— and now they were all lamenting and sobbing—"how can you bear to live in such a world, O noble heart and kindly bowels? Filth is their white; filth is their black; their beards are a horror; the very sight of their eye sockets makes one want to spit; and when they lift an arm, the murk of hell yawns in the armpit. And so, sir, and so, dear sir, by means of your all-powerful hands slit their throats through with these scissors!" And in answer to a jerk of his head a jackal came trotting up with a small pair of sewing scissors, covered with ancient rust, dangling from an eyetooth.

"Well, here's the scissors at last, and high time to stop!" cried the Arab leader of our caravan who had crept upwind towards us and now cracked his great whip.

The jackals fled in haste, but at some little distance rallied in a close huddle, all the brutes so tightly packed and rigid that they looked as if penned in a small fold girt by flickering will-o'-the-wisps.

"So you've been treated to this entertainment too, sir," said the Arab, laughing as gaily as the reserve of his race permitted. "You know, then, what the brutes are after?" I asked. "Of course," said he, "it's common knowledge; so long as Arabs exist, that pair of scissors goes wandering through the desert and will wander with us to the end of our days. Every European is offered it for the great work; every European is just the man that

Fate has chosen for them. They have the most lunatic hopes, these beasts; they're just fools, utter fools. That's why we like them; they are our dogs; finer dogs than any of yours. Watch this, now, a camel died last night and I have had it brought here."

Four men came up with the heavy carcass and threw it down before us. It had hardly touched the ground before the jackals lifted up their voices. As if irresistibly drawn by cords each of them began to waver forward, crawling on his belly. They had forgotten the Arabs, forgotten their hatred, the all-obliterating immediate presence of the stinking carrion bewitched them. One was already at the camel's throat, sinking his teeth straight into an artery. Like a vehement small pump endeavoring with as much determination as hopefulness to extinguish some raging fire, every muscle in his body twitched and labored at the task. In a trice they were all on top of the carcass, laboring in common, piled mountain-high.

And now the caravan leader lashed his cutting whip crisscross over their backs. They lifted their heads; half swooning in ecstasy; saw the Arabs standing before them; felt the sting of the whip on their muzzles; leaped and ran backwards a stretch. But the camel's blood was already lying in pools, reeking to heaven, the carcass was torn wide open in many places. They could not resist it; they were back again; once more the leader lifted his whip; I stayed his arm.

"You are right, sir," said he, "we'll leave them to their business; besides, it's time to break camp. Well, you've seen them. Marvelous creatures, aren't they? And how they hate us!"

A Visit to a Mine

TODAY THE CHIEF engineers have been down to our part
of the mine. The management has issued some instructions or other about boring new galleries, and so the
engineers arrived to make the initial survey. How young
these men are and yet how different from each other!
They have all grown up in freedom and show clearly
defined characters without self-consciousness even in
their youth.

One, a lively man with black hair, has eyes that take
in everything.

A second with a notebook makes jottings as he goes,
looks round him, compares, notes down.

A third, his hands in his coat pockets, so that everything about him is taut, walks very upright; maintains
his dignity; only the fact that he keeps biting his lips
betrays his impatient, irrepressible youth.

A fourth showers explanations on the third, who does
not ask for them; smaller than the other, trotting beside
him like a tempter, his index finger always in the air,
he seems to be making a running commentary on everything he sees.

A fifth, perhaps the senior in rank, suffers no one to
accompany him; now he is in front, now behind; the
group accommodates its pace to him; he is pallid and
frail; responsibility has made his eyes hollow; he often
presses his hand to his forehead in thought.

The sixth and seventh walk leaning forward a little,
their heads close together, arm in arm, in confidential
talk; if this were not unmistakably our coal mine and
our working station in the deepest gallery, one could

easily believe that these bony, clean-shaven, knobbly-nosed gentlemen were young clerics. One of them laughs mostly to himself with a catlike purring; the other, smiling too, leads the conversation and beats some kind of time to it with his free hand. How sure these two must be of their position; yes, what services must they have already rendered to our mine in spite of their youth, to be able here, on such an important survey, under the eyes of their chief, to devote themselves so unwaveringly to their own affairs, or at least to affairs that have nothing to do with the immediate task? Or might it be possible that, in spite of their laughter and apparent inattention, they are very well aware of whatever is needful? One scarcely ventures to pass a decisive judgment on gentlemen like these.

On the other hand, there is no doubt at all that the eighth man, for instance, is incomparably more intent on his work than these two, indeed more than all the other gentlemen. He has to touch everything and tap it with a little hammer which he keeps taking out of his pocket and putting back again. He often goes down on his knees in the dirt, despite his elegant attire, and taps the ground, then again taps the walls as he walks along or the roof over his head. Once he stretched himself out at full length and lay still; we were beginning to think something had gone wrong with him; then with a sudden recoil of his lithe body he sprang to his feet. He had only been making another investigation. We fancy that we know our mine and its rock formations, but what this engineer can be sounding all the time in such a manner lies beyond our comprehension.

A ninth man pushes a kind of perambulator in front of him with the surveying instruments. Extremely expensive apparatus, deeply embedded in the softest cotton wool. The office porter ought really to be pushing this vehicle, but he is not trusted with it; an engineer has to do it, and one can see that he does it with good will. He is probably the youngest, perhaps he doesn't even understand all the apparatus yet, but he keeps his eye on the instruments all the time, which brings him often into danger of running his vehicle into the wall.

But there is another engineer walking alongside who prevents that from happening. Obviously he understands the apparatus thoroughly and seems to be really the man in charge of it. From time to time, without stopping the vehicle, he takes up a part of some instrument, peers through it, screws it open or shut, shakes it and taps it, holds it to his ear and listens; and finally, while the man pushing the instruments usually stands still, he lays the small thing, which one can scarcely discern at a distance, back into its packing with great care. This engineer is a little domineering, but only in the service of his instruments. Ten paces ahead of the perambulator we have to give way to it at a wordless sign of his finger, even where there is no room for us to make way.

Behind these two gentlemen stalks the office porter, with nothing to do. The gentlemen, as is to be expected from men of their great knowledge, have long dropped any arrogance they ever had, but the porter seems to have picked it all up and kept it. With one hand tucked behind him, the other in front fingering the gilt buttons or fine facecloth of his uniform, he keeps bowing to right and left as if we had saluted him and he were answering, or rather as if he assumed that we had saluted him, he being too high and mighty to see any salutes.

Of course we do not salute him, yet one could almost believe, to look at him, that it is a great distinction to be a porter at the head office of the mine. Behind his back, to be sure, we burst out laughing, but as not even a thunderbolt could make him look round, he remains an unsolved riddle for us to respect.

Today we shall not do much work; the interruption has been too interesting; such a visit draws away with it all thoughts of work. It is too tempting to stand gazing after the gentlemen as they vanish into the darkness of the trial gallery. Besides, our shift will soon come to an end; we shall not be here to see them coming back.

The Next Village

MY GRANDFATHER used to say: "Life is astoundingly short. To me, looking back over it, life seems so foreshortened that I scarcely understand, for instance, how a young man can decide to ride over to the next village without being afraid that—not to mention accidents—even the span of a normal happy life may fall far short of the time needed for such a journey."

An Imperial Message

THE EMPEROR—so the story goes—has sent a message to you, the lone individual, the meanest of his subjects, the shadow that has fled before the Imperial sun until it is microscopic in the remotest distance, just to you has the Emperor sent a message from his deathbed. He made the messenger kneel by his bed and whispered the message into his ear; he felt it to be so important that he made the man repeat it into his own ear. With a nod of the head he confirmed that the repetition was accurate. And then, before the whole retinue gathered to witness his death—all the walls blocking the view had been broken down and on the wide high curve of the open stairway stood the notables of the Empire in a circle—before them all he dispatched the messenger. The messenger set off at once; a strong, an indefatigable man; thrusting out now one arm, now the other, he forces his way through the crowd; where he finds obstacles he points to the sign of the sun on his breast; he gets through easily, too, as no one else could. Yet the throng is so numerous; there is no end to their dwelling places. If he only had a free field before him, how he would run, and soon enough you would hear the glorious tattoo of his fists on your door. But instead of that, how vain are his efforts; he is still forcing his way through the chambers of the innermost palace; he will never get to the end of them; and even if he did, he would be no better off; he would have to fight his way down the stairs; and even if he did that, he would be no better off; he would still have to get through the courtyards; and after the courtyards, the second outer palace inclosing the first; and more stairways and more courtyards; and still another palace; and so on for thousands of years; and did he finally dash through the outermost gate—but never, never can that happen—he would still have the capital city before him, the center of the world, overflowing with the dregs of humanity. No one can force a way through that, least of all with a message from a dead man.—But you sit by your window and dream it all true, when evening falls.

The Cares of a Family Man

SOME SAY the word Odradek is of Slavonic origin, and try to account for it on that basis. Others again believe it to be of German origin, only influenced by Slavonic. The uncertainty of both interpretations allows one to assume with justice that neither is accurate, especially as neither of them provides an intelligent meaning of the word.

No one, of course, would occupy himself with such studies if there were not a creature called Odradek. At first glance it looks like a flat star-shaped spool for thread, and indeed it does seem to have thread wound upon it; to be sure, they are only old, broken-off bits of thread, knotted and tangled together, of the most varied sorts and colors. But it is not only a spool, for a small wooden crossbar sticks out of the middle of the star, and another small rod is joined to that at a right angle. By means of this latter rod on one side and one of the points of the star on the other, the whole thing can stand upright as if on two legs.

One is tempted to believe that the creature once had some sort of intelligible shape and is now only a broken-down remnant. Yet this does not seem to be the case; at least there is no sign of it; nowhere is there an unfinished or unbroken surface to suggest anything of the kind; the whole thing looks senseless enough, but in its own way perfectly finished. In any case, closer scrutiny is impossible, since Odradek is extraordinarily nimble and can never be laid hold of.

He lurks by turns in the garret, the stairway, the lobbies, the entrance hall. Often for months on end he is not to be seen; then he has presumably moved into other houses; but he always comes faithfully back to our house again. Many a time when you go out of the door and he happens just to be leaning directly beneath you against the banisters you feel inclined to speak to him. Of course, you put no difficult questions to him, you treat him—he is so diminutive that you cannot help it—rather like a child. "Well, what's your name?" you ask him. "Odradek," he says. "And where do you live?" "No fixed abode," he says and laughs; but it is only the kind of laughter that has no lungs behind it. It sounds rather like the rustling of fallen leaves. And that is usually the end of the conversation. Even these answers are not always forthcoming; often he stays mute for a long time, as wooden as his appearance.

I ask myself, to no purpose, what is likely to happen to him? Can he possibly die? Anything that dies has had some kind of aim in life, some kind of activity, which has worn out; but that does not apply to Odradek. Am I to suppose, then, that he will always be rolling down the stairs, with ends of thread trailing after him, right before the feet of my children, and my children's children? He does no harm to anyone that one can see; but the idea that he is likely to survive me I find almost painful.

Eleven Sons

I HAVE eleven sons.

The first is outwardly very plain, but serious and clever; yet, although I love him as I love all my children, I do not rate him very highly. His mental processes seem to me to be too simple. He looks neither to

right nor to left, nor into the far distance; he runs
round all the time, or rather revolves, within his own
little circle of thoughts.

The second is handsome, slim, well made; one draws
one's breath with delight to watch him with a fencing
foil. He is clever too, but has experience of the world as
well; he has seen much, and therefore even our native
country seems to yield more secrets to him than to
the stay-at-home. Yet I am sure that this advantage is
not only and not even essentially due to his travels, it
is rather an attribute of his own inimitable nature, which
is acknowledged for instance by everyone who has ever
tried to copy him in, let us say, the fancy high dive
he does into the water, somersaulting several times over,
yet with almost violent self-control. To the very end
of the springboard the emulator keeps up his courage
and his desire to follow; but at that point, instead of
leaping into the air, he sits down suddenly and lifts his
arms in excuse.—And despite all this (I ought really to
feel blessed with such a son) my attachment to him
is not untroubled. His left eye is a little smaller than
his right and blinks a good deal; only a small fault, certainly, and one which even lends more audacity to his
face than it would otherwise have, nor, considering his
unapproachable self-sufficiency, would anyone think of
noticing and finding fault with this smaller eye and
the way it blinks. Yet I, his father, do so. Of course, it
is not the physical blemish that worries me, but a small
irregularity of the spirit that somehow corresponds to
it, a kind of stray poison in the blood, a kind of inability to develop to the full the potentialities of his
nature which I alone can see. On the other hand, this is
just what makes him again my own true son, for this

fault of his is a fault of our whole family and in him it is only too apparent.

My third son is handsome too, but not in a way that I appreciate. He has the good looks of a singer: the curving lips; the dreaming eye; the kind of head that asks for drapery behind it to make it effective; the too deeply arched chest; hands that are quick to fly up and much too quick to fall limp; legs that move delicately because they cannot support a weight. And besides: the tone of his voice is not round and full; it takes you in for a moment; the connoisseur pricks up his ears; but almost at once its breath gives out.—Although, in general, everything tempts me to bring this son of mine into the limelight, I prefer to keep him in the background; he himself is not insistent, yet not because he is aware of his shortcomings but out of innocence. Moreover, he does not feel at home in our age; as if he admitted belonging to our family, yet knew that he belonged also to another which he has lost forever, he is often melancholy and nothing can cheer him.

My fourth son is perhaps the most companionable of all. A true child of his age, he is understood by everyone, he stands on what is common ground to all men and everyone feels inclined to give him a nod. Perhaps this universal appreciation is what makes his nature rather facile, his movements rather free, his judgments rather unconcerned. Many of his remarks are worth quoting over and over again, but by no means all of them, for by and large his extreme facility becomes irritating. He is like a man who makes a wonderful take-off from the ground, cleaves the air like a swallow and after all comes down helplessly in a desert waste, a nothing. Such reflections gall me when I look at him.

My fifth son is kind and good; promised less than he performed; used to be so insignificant that one literally felt alone in his presence; but has achieved a certain reputation. If I were asked how this came about, I could hardly tell you. Perhaps innocence makes its way easiest through the elemental chaos of this world, and innocent he certainly is. Perhaps too innocent. Friendly to everyone. Perhaps too friendly. I confess: I don't feel comfortable when I hear him praised. It seems to make praise rather too cheap to bestow it on anyone so obviously praiseworthy as this son of mine.

My sixth son seems, at first glance anyhow, the most thoughtful of all. He is given to hanging his head, and yet he is a great talker. So he is not easy to get at. If he is on the down grade, he falls into impenetrable melancholy; if he is in the ascendant, he maintains his advantage by sheer talk. Yet I grant him a certain self-forgetful passionate absorption; in the full light of day he often fights his way through a tangle of thoughts as if in a dream. Without being ill—his health on the contrary is very good—he sometimes staggers, especially in the twilight, but he needs no help, he never falls. Perhaps his physical growth is the cause of this phenomenon, he is much too tall for his age. That makes him look ugly in general, although he has remarkable beauty in detail, in hands and feet, for instance. His forehead, too, is ugly; both its skin and its bone formation are somehow arrested in their development.

The seventh son belongs to me perhaps more than all the others. The world would not know how to appreciate him; it does not understand his peculiar brand of wit. I do not overvalue him; I know he is of little enough importance; if the world had no other fault than that of not appreciating him, it would still be blameless. But within the family circle I should not care to be without this son of mine. He contributes a certain restlessness as well as a reverence for tradition, and combines them both, at least that is how I feel it, into an incontestable whole. True, he knows less than anyone what to do with this achievement; the wheel of the future will never be started rolling by him; but his disposition is so stimulating, so rich in hope; I wish that he had children and children's children. Unfortunately he does not seem inclined to fulfil my wish. With a self-satisfaction that I understand as much as I deplore, and which stands in magnificent contrast to the verdict of the world, he goes everywhere alone, pays no attention to girls and yet will never lose his good humor.

My eighth son is my child of sorrow, and I do not really know why. He keeps me at a distance and yet I feel a close paternal tie binding me to him. Time has done much to lessen the pain; but once I used often to tremble at the mere thought of him. He goes his own way; he has broken off all communication with me; and certainly with his hard head, his small athletic body— only his legs were rather frail when he was a boy, but perhaps that has meanwhile righted itself—he will make a success of anything he chooses. Many a time I used to want to call him back, to ask him how things really were with him, why he cut himself off so completely from his father and what his fundamental purpose was in life, but now he is so far away and so much time has passed that things had better stay as they are. I hear that he is the only one of my sons to grow a full beard; that cannot look well, of course, on a man so small as he is.

My ninth son is very elegant and has what women consider a definitely melting eye. So melting that there are occasions when he can cajole even me, although I know that a wet sponge is literally enough to wipe away all that unearthly brilliance. But the curious thing about the boy is that he makes no attempt to be seductive; he would be content to spend his life lying on the sofa and wasting his glances on the ceiling, or still better, keeping them to himself under his eyelids. When he is lying in this favorite position, he enjoys talking and talks quite well; concisely and pithily; but still only within narrow limits; once he oversteps these, which he cannot avoid doing since they are so narrow, what he says is quite empty. One would sign him to stop, if one had any hope that such slumbrous eyes were even aware of the gesture.

My tenth son is supposed to be an insincere character. I shall not entirely deny or confirm this supposition. Certainly anyone who sees him approaching with the pomposity of a man twice his age, in a frock coat always tightly buttoned, an old but meticulously brushed black hat, with an expressionless face, slightly jutting chin, protruding eyelids that mask the light behind them, two fingers very often at his lips—anyone seeing him thus is bound to think: what an utter hypocrite. But then, just listen to him talking! With understanding; thoughtfully; brusquely; cutting across questions with satirical vivacity; in complete accord with the universe, an accord that is surprising, natural and gay; an accord that of necessity straightens the neck and makes the body proud. Many who think themselves very clever and for this reason, as they fancied, felt a dislike for his outward appearance, have become strongly attached to him because of his conversation. There are other people, again, who are unaffected by his appearance but who find his conversation hypocritical. I, being his father, will not pronounce a verdict, but I must admit that the latter critics are at least to be taken more seriously than the former.

My eleventh son is delicate, probably the frailest of my sons; but deceptive in his weakness; for at times he can be strong and resolute, though even then there is somehow always an underlying weakness. Yet it is not a weakness to be ashamed of, merely something that appears as weakness only on this solid earth of ours. For instance, is not a readiness for flight a kind of weakness too, since it consists in a wavering, an unsteadiness, a fluttering? Something of that nature characterizes my son. These are not, of course, the characteristics to rejoice a father; they tend obviously to destroy a family. Sometimes he looks at me as if he would say: "I shall take you with me, Father." Then I think: "You are the last person I would trust myself to." And again his look seems to say: "Then let me be at least the last."

These are my eleven sons.

A Fratricide

THE EVIDENCE shows that this is how the murder was committed:

Schmar, the murderer, took up his post about nine o'clock one night in clear moonlight by the corner where Wese, his victim, had to turn from the street where his office was into the street he lived in.

The night air was shivering cold. Yet Schmar was wearing only a thin blue suit; the jacket was unbuttoned, too. He felt no cold; besides, he was moving about all the time. His weapon, half a bayonet and half a kitchen knife, he kept firmly in his grasp, quite naked. He looked at the knife against the light of the moon; the blade glittered; not enough for Schmar; he struck it against the bricks of the pavement till the sparks flew; regretted that, perhaps; and to repair the damage drew it like a violin bow across his boot sole while he bent forward, standing on one leg, and listened both to the whetting of the knife on his boot and for any sound out of the fateful side street.

Why did Pallas, the private citizen who was watching it all from his window near by in the second story, permit it to happen? Unriddle the mysteries of human nature! With his collar turned up, his dressing gown girt round his portly body, he stood looking down, shaking his head.

And five houses further along, on the opposite side of the street, Mrs. Wese, with a fox-fur coat over her nightgown, peered out to look for her husband who was lingering unusually late tonight.

At last there rang out the sound of the doorbell before Wese's office, too loud for a doorbell, right over the town and up to heaven, and Wese, the industrious nightworker, issued from the building, still invisible in that street, only heralded by the sound of the bell; at once the pavement registered his quiet footsteps.

Pallas bent far forward; he dared not miss anything. Mrs. Wese, reassured by the bell, shut her window with a clatter. But Schmar knelt down; since he had no other parts of his body bare, he pressed only his face and his hands against the pavement; where everything else was freezing, Schmar was glowing hot.

At the very corner dividing the two streets Wese paused, only his walking stick came round into the other street to support him. A sudden whim. The night sky invited him, with its dark blue and its gold. Unknowing, he gazed up at it, unknowing he lifted his hat and stroked his hair; nothing up there drew together in a pattern to interpret the immediate future for him; everything stayed in its senseless, inscrutable place. In itself it was a highly reasonable action that Wese should walk on, but he walked on to Schmar's knife.

"Wese!" shrieked Schmar, standing on tiptoe, his arm outstretched, the knife sharply lowered, "Wese! You will never see Julia again!" And right into the throat and left into the throat and a third time deep into the belly stabbed Schmar's knife. Water rats, slit open, give out such a sound as came from Wese.

"Done," said Schmar, and pitched the knife, now superfluous blood-stained ballast, against the nearest house front. "The bliss of murder! The relief, the soaring ecstasy from the shedding of another's blood! Wese, old nightbird, friend, alehouse crony, you are oozing away into the dark earth below the street. Why aren't you simply a bladder of blood so that I could stamp on you and make you vanish into nothingness. Not all we want comes true, not all the dreams that blossomed have borne fruit, your solid remains lie here, already indifferent to every kick. What's the good of the dumb question you are asking?"

Pallas, choking on the poison in his body, stood at the double-leafed door of his house as it flew open. "Schmar! Schmar! I saw it all, I missed nothing." Pallas and

Schmar scrutinized each other. The result of the scrutiny satisfied Pallas, Schmar came to no conclusion.

Mrs. Wese, with a crowd of people on either side, came rushing up, her face grown quite old with the shock. Her fur coat swung open, she collapsed on top of Wese, the nightgowned body belonged to Wese, the fur coat spreading over the couple like the smooth turf of a grave belonged to the crowd.

Schmar, fighting down with difficulty the last of his nausea, pressed his mouth against the shoulder of the policeman who, stepping lightly, led him away.

A Dream

JOSEF K. was dreaming.

It was a beautiful day and K. felt like going for a walk. But hardly had he taken a couple of steps when he was already at the cemetery. The paths there were very winding, ingeniously made and unpractical, but he glided along one of them as if on a rushing stream with unshaken poise and balance. From a long way off his eye was caught by a freshly heaped grave mound which he wanted to pause beside. This grave mound exerted almost a fascination over him and he felt he could not reach it fast enough. But he often nearly lost sight of it, for his view was obscured by banners which veered and flapped against each other with great force; one could not see the standard-bearers, but there seemed to be a very joyous celebration going on.

While he was still peering into the distance, he suddenly saw the grave mound quite near his path, indeed he was almost leaving it behind him. He made a hasty spring on to the grass. But since the path went rushing on under his shifting foot, he tottered and fell on his knees just in front of the grave mound. Two men were standing behind the grave and were holding a gravestone between them in the air; scarcely had K. arrived when they thrust the stone into the earth and it stood as if cemented there. Out of some bushes there came at once a third man, whom K. recognized immediately as an artist. He was clad only in trousers and a badly buttoned shirt; on his head was a velvet cap; in his hand he held an ordinary pencil with which he was already drawing figures in the air as he approached.

With this pencil he now addressed himself to the top end of the gravestone; the stone was very tall, he did not have to bend down, though he had to bend forward, since the grave mound, on which he shrank from setting foot, came between him and the stone. So he stood on tiptoe and steadied himself with his left hand on the stone's flat surface. With an astonishing turn of skill he managed to produce golden letters from his ordinary pencil; he wrote: HERE LIES— Every letter was clear and beautifully made, deeply incised and of the purest gold. When he had inscribed these two words he looked at K. over his shoulder; K., who was very eager to know how the inscription would go, paid hardly any attention to the man but was intent only on the stone. And in fact the man turned again to continue writing, but he could not go on, something was hindering him, he let the pencil sink and once more turned towards K. This time K. looked back at him and noted that he was deeply embarrassed and yet unable to explain himself. All his earlier vivacity had vanished. That made K. feel embarrassed too; they exchanged helpless glances; there was some dreadful misunderstanding between them which neither could resolve. An untimely little bell now began to ring from the cemetery chapel, but the artist made a sign with uplifted hand and the bell stopped. In a little while it began again; this time quite softly and without any insistence, breaking off again at once; as if it were only testing its own tone. K. felt miserable because of the artist's predicament, he began to cry and sobbed for a long time into his cupped hands. The artist waited until K. had calmed down and then decided, since there was no help for it, just to go on with the inscription. The first small stroke that he made was a relief to K., but the artist obviously achieved it only with the greatest reluctance; the work, too, was no longer beautifully finished, above all there seemed to be a lack of gold leaf, pale and uncertain the stroke straggled down, only it turned into a very big letter. It was a J, it was almost finished, and at that moment the artist stamped angrily on the grave mound with one foot so that the soil all around flew up in the air. At long last K. understood him; it was too late to start apologizing now; with all his fingers he dug into the earth which offered almost no resistance; everything seemed prepared beforehand; a thin crust of earth had been constructed only for the look of the thing; immediately beneath it a great hole opened out, with steep sides, into which K. sank, wafted onto his back by a gentle current. And while he was already being received into impenetrable depths, his head still straining upwards on his neck, his own name raced across the stone above him in great flourishes.

Enchanted by the sight, he woke up.

A Report to an Academy

HONORED MEMBERS of the Academy!

You have done me the honor of inviting me to give your Academy an account of the life I formerly led as an ape.

I regret that I cannot comply with your request to the extent you desire. It is now nearly five years since I was an ape, a short space of time, perhaps, according to the calendar, but an infinitely long time to gallop through at full speed, as I have done, more or less accompanied by excellent mentors, good advice, applause and orchestral music, and yet essentially alone, since all my escorters, to keep the image, kept well off the course. I could never have achieved what I have done had I been stubbornly set on clinging to my origins, to the remembrances of my youth. In fact, to give up being stubborn was the supreme commandment I laid upon myself; free ape as I was, I submitted myself to that yoke. In revenge, however, my memory of the past has closed the door against me more and more. I could have returned at first, had human beings allowed it, through an archway as wide as the span of heaven over the earth, but as I spurred myself on in my forced career, the opening narrowed and shrank behind me; I felt more comfortable in the world of men and fitted it better; the strong wind that blew after me out of my past began to slacken; today it is only a gentle puff of air that plays around my heels; and the opening in the distance, through which it comes and through which I once came myself, has grown so small that, even if my strength and my will power sufficed to get me back to it, I should have to scrape the very skin from my body to crawl through. To put it plainly, much as I like expressing myself in images, to put it plainly: your life as apes, gentlemen, insofar as something of that kind lies behind you, cannot be farther removed from you than mine is from me. Yet everyone on earth feels a tickling at the heels; the small chimpanzee and the great Achilles alike.

But to a lesser extent I can perhaps meet your demand, and indeed I do so with the greatest pleasure. The first thing I learned was to give a handshake; a handshake betokens frankness; well, today, now that I stand at the very peak of my career, I hope to add frankness in words to the frankness of that first handshake. What I have to tell the Academy will contribute nothing essentially new, and will fall far behind what you have asked of me and what with the best will in the world I cannot communicate—none the less, it should indicate the line an erstwhile ape has had to follow in entering and establishing himself in the world of men. Yet I could not risk putting into words even such insignificant information as I am going to give you if I were not quite sure of myself and if my position on all the great variety stages of the civilized world had not become quite unassailable.

I belong to the Gold Coast. For the story of my capture I must depend on the evidence of others. A hunting expedition sent out by the firm of Hagenbeck—by the way, I have drunk many a bottle of good red wine since then with the leader of that expedition—had taken up its position in the bushes by the shore when I came down for a drink at evening among a troop of apes. They shot at us; I was the only one that was hit; I was hit in two places.

Once in the cheek; a slight wound; but it left a large, naked, red scar which earned me the name of Red Peter, a horrible name, utterly inappropriate, which only some ape could have thought of, as if the only difference between me and the performing ape Peter, who died not so long ago and had some small local reputation, were the red mark on my cheek. This by the way.

The second shot hit me below the hip. It was a severe wound, it is the cause of my limping a little to this day. I read an article recently by one of the ten thousand windbags who vent themselves concerning me in the newspapers, saying: my ape nature is not yet quite under control; the proof being that when visitors come to see me, I have a predilection for taking down my trousers to show them where the shot went in. The hand which wrote that should have its fingers shot away one by one. As for me, I can take my trousers down before anyone if I like; you would find nothing but a well-groomed fur and the scar made—let me be particular in the choice of a word for this particular purpose, to avoid misunderstanding—the scar made by a wanton shot. Everything is open and aboveboard; there is nothing to conceal; when the plain truth is in question, great minds discard the niceties of refinement. But if the writer of the article were to take down his trousers before a visitor, that would be quite another story, and I will let it stand to his credit that he does not do it. In return, let him leave me alone with his delicacy!

After these two shots I came to myself—and this is where my own memories gradually begin—between decks in the Hagenbeck steamer, inside a cage. It was not a four-sided barred cage; it was only a three-sided cage nailed to a locker; the locker made the fourth side of it. The whole construction was too low for me to stand up in and too narrow to sit down in. So I had to squat with my knees bent and trembling all the time, and also, since probably for a time I wished to see no one, and to stay in the dark, my face was turned towards the locker while the bars of the cage cut into my flesh behind. Such a method of confining wild beasts is supposed to have its advantages during the first days of captivity, and out of my own experiences I cannot deny that from the human point of view this is really the case.

But that did not occur to me then. For the first time in my life I could see no way out; at least no direct way out; directly in front of me was the locker, board fitted close to board. True, there was a gap running right through the boards which I greeted with the blissful howl of ignorance when I first discovered it, but the hole was not even wide enough to stick one's tail through and not all the strength of an ape could enlarge it.

I am supposed to have made uncommonly little noise, as I was later informed, from which the conclusion was drawn that I would either soon die or if I managed to survive the first critical period would be very amenable to training. I did survive this period. Hopelessly sobbing, painfully hunting for fleas, apathetically licking a cocoanut, beating my skull against the locker, sticking out my tongue at anyone who came near me—that was how I filled in time at first in my new life. But over and above it all only the one feeling: no way out. Of course what I felt then as an ape I can represent now only in human terms, and therefore I misrepresent it, but although I cannot reach back to the truth of the old ape life, there is no doubt that it lies somewhere in the direction I have indicated.

Until then I had had so many ways out of everything,

and now I had none. I was pinned down. Had I been nailed down, my right to free movement would not have been lessened. Why so? Scratch your flesh raw between your toes, but you won't find the answer. Press yourself against the bar behind you till it nearly cuts you in two, you won't find the answer. I had no way out but I had to devise one, for without it I could not live. All the time facing that locker—I should certainly have perished. Yet as far as Hagenbeck was concerned, the place for apes was in front of a locker—well then, I had to stop being an ape. A fine, clear train of thought, which I must have constructed somehow with my belly, since apes think with their bellies.

I fear that perhaps you do not quite understand what I mean by "way out." I use the expression in its fullest and most popular sense. I deliberately do not use the word "freedom." I do not mean the spacious feeling of freedom on all sides. As an ape, perhaps, I knew that, and I have met men who yearn for it. But for my part I desired such freedom neither then nor now. In passing: may I say that all too often men are betrayed by the word freedom. And as freedom is counted among the most sublime feelings, so the corresponding disillusionment can be also sublime. In variety theaters I have often watched, before my turn came on, a couple of acrobats performing on trapezes high in the roof. They swung themselves, they rocked to and fro, they sprang into the air, they floated into each other's arms, one hung by the hair from the teeth of the other. "And that too is human freedom," I thought, "self-controlled movement." What a mockery of holy Mother Nature! Were the apes to see such a spectacle, no theater walls could stand the shock of their laughter.

No, freedom was not what I wanted. Only a way out;

right or left, or in any direction; I made no other demand; even should the way out prove to be an illusion;
the demand was a small one, the disappointment could be
no bigger. To get out somewhere, to get out! Only not
to stay motionless with raised arms, crushed against a
wooden wall.

Today I can see it clearly; without the most profound
inward calm I could never have found my way out. And
indeed perhaps I owe all that I have become to the calm
that settled within me after my first few days in the ship.
And again for that calmness it was the ship's crew I had
to thank.

They were good creatures, in spite of everything. I
find it still pleasant to remember the sound of their heavy
footfalls which used to echo through my half-dreaming
head. They had a habit of doing everything as slowly as
possible. If one of them wanted to rub his eyes, he lifted
a hand as if it were a drooping weight. Their jests were
coarse, but hearty. Their laughter had always a gruff
bark in it that sounded dangerous but meant nothing.
They always had something in their mouths to spit out
and did not care where they spat it. They always grum-
bled that they got fleas from me; yet they were not seriously angry about it; they knew that my fur fostered
fleas, and that fleas jump; it was a simple matter of fact
to them. When they were off duty some of them often
used to sit down in a semicircle round me; they hardly
spoke but only grunted to each other; smoked their
pipes, stretched out on lockers; smacked their knees as
soon as I made the slightest movement; and now and
then one of them would take a stick and tickle me where
I liked being tickled. If I were to be invited today to
take a cruise on that ship I should certainly refuse the

invitation, but just as certainly the memories I could recall between its decks would not all be hateful.

The calmness I acquired among these people kept me above all from trying to escape. As I look back now, it seems to me I must have had at least an inkling that I had to find a way out or die, but that my way out could not be reached through flight. I cannot tell now whether escape was possible, but I believe it must have been; for an ape it must always be possible. With my teeth as they are today I have to be careful even in simply cracking nuts, but at that time I could certainly have managed by degrees to bite though the lock of my cage. I did not do it. What good would it have done me? As soon as I had poked out my head I should have been caught again and put in a worse cage; or I might have slipped among the other animals without being noticed, among the pythons, say, who were opposite me, and so breathed out my life in their embrace; or supposing I had actually succeeded in sneaking out as far as the deck and leaping overboard, I should have rocked for a little on the deep sea and then been drowned. Desperate remedies. I did not think it out in this human way, but under the influence of my surroundings I acted as if I had thought it out.

I did not think things out; but I observed everything quietly. I watched these men go to and fro, always the same faces, the same movements, often it seemed to me there was only the same man. So this man or these men walked about unimpeded. A lofty goal faintly dawned before me. No one promised me that if I became like them the bars of my cage would be taken away. Such promises for apparently impossible contingencies are not given. But if one achieves the impossible, the promises appear later retrospectively precisely where one had looked in vain for them before. Now, these men in themselves had no great attraction for me. Had I been devoted to the aforementioned idea of freedom, I should certainly have preferred the deep sea to the way out that suggested itself in the heavy faces of these men. At any rate, I watched them for a long time before I even thought of such things, indeed, it was only the mass weight of my observations that impelled me in the right direction.

It was so easy to imitate these people. I learned to spit in the very first days. We used to spit in each other's faces; the only difference was that I licked my face clean afterwards and they did not. I could soon smoke a pipe like an old hand; and if I also pressed my thumb into the bowl of the pipe, a roar of appreciation went up between-decks; only it took me a very long time to understand the difference between a full pipe and an empty one.

My worst trouble came from the schnapps bottle. The smell of it revolted me; I forced myself to it as best I could; but it took weeks for me to master my repulsion. This inward conflict, strangely enough, was taken more seriously by the crew than anything else about me. I cannot distinguish the men from each other in my recollection, but there was one of them who came again and again, alone or with friends, by day, by night, at all kinds of hours; he would post himself before me with the bottle and give me instructions. He could not understand me, he wanted to solve the enigma of my being. He would slowly uncork the bottle and then look at me to see if I had followed him; I admit that I always watched him with wildly eager, too eager attention; such a student of humankind no human teacher ever found on earth. After the bottle was uncorked he lifted it to his mouth; I followed it with my eyes right up to his jaws; he would nod, pleased with me, and set the bottle to his lips; I, enchanted with my gradual enlightenment, squealed and scratched myself comprehensively wherever scratching was called for; he rejoiced, tilted the bottle and took a drink; I, impatient and desperate to emulate him, be-fouled myself in my cage, which again gave him great satisfaction; and then, holding the bottle at arm's length and bringing it up with a swing, he would empty it at one draught, leaning back at an exaggerated angle for my better instruction. I, exhausted by too much effort, could follow him no farther and hung limply to the bars, while he ended his theoretical exposition by rubbing his belly and grinning.

After theory came practice. Was I not already quite exhausted by my theoretical instruction? Indeed I was; utterly exhausted. That was part of my destiny. And yet I would take hold of the proffered bottle as well as I was able; uncork it, trembling; this successful action would gradually inspire me with new energy; I would lift the bottle, already following my original model almost ex-actly; put it to my lips and—and then throw it down in disgust, utter disgust, although it was empty and filled only with the smell of the spirit, throw it down on the floor in disgust. To the sorrow of my teacher, to the greater sorrow of myself; neither of us being really com-forted by the fact that I did not forget, even though I had thrown away the bottle, to rub my belly most admirably and to grin.

Far too often my lesson ended in that way. And to the credit of my teacher, he was not angry; sometimes indeed he would hold his burning pipe against my fur, until it began to smolder in some place I could not easily reach, but then he would himself extinguish it with his own kind, enormous hand; he was not angry with me, he perceived that we were both fighting on the same side against the nature of apes and that I had the more difficult task.

What a triumph it was then both for him and for me, when one evening before a large circle of spectators—perhaps there was a celebration of some kind, a gramophone was playing, an officer was circulating among the crew—when on this evening, just as no one was looking, I took hold of a schnapps bottle that had been carelessly left standing before my cage, uncorked it in the best style, while the company began to watch me with mounting attention, set it to my lips without hesitation, with no grimace, like a professional drinker, with rolling eyes and full throat, actually and truly drank it empty; then threw the bottle away, not this time in despair but as an artistic performer; forgot, indeed, to rub my belly; but instead of that, because I could not help it, because my senses were reeling, called a brief and unmistakable "Hallo!" breaking into human speech, and with this outburst broke into the human community, and felt its echo: "Listen, he's talking!" like a caress over the whole of my sweat-drenched body.

I repeat: there was no attraction for me in imitating human beings; I imitated them because I needed a way out, and for no other reason. And even that triumph of mine did not achieve much. I lost my human voice again at once; it did not come back for months; my aversion for the schnapps bottle returned again with even greater force. But the line I was to follow had in any case been decided, once for all.

When I was handed over to my first trainer in Hamburg I soon realized that there were two alternatives before me: the Zoological Gardens or the variety stage. I did not hesitate. I said to myself: do your utmost to get on to the variety stage; the Zoological Gardens means only a new cage; once there, you are done for.

And so I learned things, gentlemen. Ah, one learns when one has to; one learns when one needs a way out; one learns at all costs. One stands over oneself with a whip; one flays oneself at the slightest opposition. My ape nature fled out of me, head over heels and away, so that my first teacher was almost himself turned into an ape by it, had soon to give up teaching and was taken away to a mental hospital. Fortunately he was soon let out again.

But I used up many teachers, indeed, several teachers at once. As I became more confident of my abilities, as the public took an interest in my progress and my future began to look bright, I engaged teachers for myself, established them in five communicating rooms and took lessons from them all at once by dint of leaping from one room to the other.

That progress of mine! How the rays of knowledge penetrated from all sides into my awakening brain! I do not deny it: I found it exhilarating. But I must also confess: I did not overestimate it, not even then, much less now. With an effort which up till now has never been repeated I managed to reach the cultural level of an average European. In itself that might be nothing to speak of, but it is something insofar as it has helped me out of my cage and opened a special way out for me, the way of humanity. There is an excellent idiom: to fight one's way through the thick of things; that is what I have done, I have fought through the thick of things.

There was nothing else for me to do, provided always that freedom was not to be my choice.

As I look back over my development and survey what I have achieved so far, I do not complain, but I am not complacent either. With my hands in my trouser pockets, my bottle of wine on the table, I half lie and half sit in my rocking chair and gaze out of the window: if a visitor arrives, I receive him with propriety. My manager sits in the anteroom; when I ring, he comes and listens to what I have to say. Nearly every evening I give a performance, and I have a success which could hardly be increased. When I come home late at night from banquets, from scientific receptions, from social gatherings, there sits waiting for me a half-trained little chimpanzee and I take comfort from her as apes do. By day I cannot bear to see her; for she has the insane look of the bewildered half-broken animal in her eye; no one else sees it, but I do, and I cannot bear it. On the whole, at any rate, I have achieved what I set out to achieve. But do not tell me that it was not worth the trouble. In any case, I am not appealing for any man's verdict, I am only imparting knowledge, I am only making a report. To you also, honored Members of the Academy, I have only made a report.

The Bucket Rider

COAL ALL SPENT; the bucket empty; the shovel useless; the stove breathing out cold; the room freezing; the leaves outside the window rigid, covered with rime; the sky a silver shield against any one who looks for help from it. I must have coal; I cannot freeze to death;

behind me is the pitiless stove, before me the pitiless sky, so I must ride out between them and on my journey seek aid from the coaldealer. But he has already grown deaf to ordinary appeals; I must prove irrefutably to him that I have not a single grain of coal left, and that he means to me the very sun in the firmament. I must approach like a beggar, who, with the death rattle already in his throat, insists on dying on the doorstep, and to whom the grand people's cook accordingly decides to give the dregs of the coffeepot; just so must the coaldealer, filled with rage, but acknowledging the command, "Thou shalt not kill," fling a shovelful of coal into my bucket.

My mode of arrival must decide the matter; so I ride off on the bucket. Seated on the bucket, my hands on the handle, the simplest kind of bridle, I propel myself with difficulty down the stairs; but once down below my bucket ascends, superbly, superbly; camels humbly squatting on the ground do not rise with more dignity, shaking themselves under the sticks of their drivers. Through the hard frozen streets we go at a regular canter; often I am upraised as high as the first story of a house; never do I sink as low as the house doors. And at last I float at an extraordinary height above the vaulted cellar of the dealer, whom I see far below crouching over his table, where he is writing; he has opened the door to let out the excessive heat.

"Coaldealer!" I cry in a voice burned hollow by the frost and muffled in the cloud made by my breath, "please, coaldealer, give me a little coal. My bucket is so light that I can ride on it. Be kind. When I can I'll pay you."

The dealer puts his hand to his ear. "Do I hear

rightly?" he throws the question over his shoulder to his wife. "Do I hear rightly? A customer."

"I hear nothing," says his wife, breathing in and out peacefully while she knits on, her back pleasantly warmed by the heat.

"Oh, yes, you must hear," I cry. "It's me; an old customer; faithful and true; only without means at the moment."

"Wife," says the dealer, "it's someone, it must be; my ears can't have deceived me so much as that; it must be an old, a very old customer, that can move me so deeply."

"What ails you, man?" says his wife, ceasing from her work for a moment and pressing her knitting to her bosom. "It's nobody, the street is empty, all our customers are provided for; we could close down the shop for several days and take a rest."

"But I'm sitting up here on the bucket," I cry, and unfeeling frozen tears dim my eyes, "please look up here, just once; you'll see me directly; I beg you, just a shovelful; and if you give me more it'll make me so happy that I won't know what to do. All the other customers are provided for. Oh, if I could only hear the coal clattering into the bucket!"

"I'm coming," says the coaldealer, and on his short legs he makes to climb the steps of the cellar, but his wife is already beside him, holds him back by the arm and says: "You stay here; seeing you persist in your fancies I'll go myself. Think of the bad fit of coughing you had during the night. But for a piece of business, even if it's one you've only fancied in your head, you're prepared to forget your wife and child and sacrifice your lungs. I'll go."

"Then be sure to tell him all the kinds of coal we have in stock; I'll shout out the prices after you."

"Right," says his wife, climbing up to the street. Naturally she sees me at once. "Frau Coaldealer," I cry, "my humblest greetings; just one shovelful of coal; here in my bucket; I'll carry it home myself. One shovelful of the worst you have. I'll pay you in full for it, of course, but not just now, not just now." What a knell-like sound the words "not just now" have, and how bewilderingly they mingle with the evening chimes that fall from the church steeple near by!

"Well, what does he want?" shouts the dealer. "Nothing," his wife shouts back, "there's nothing here; I see nothing, I hear nothing; only six striking, and now we must shut up the shop. The cold is terrible; tomorrow we'll likely have lots to do again."

She sees nothing and hears nothing; but all the same she loosens her apron strings and waves her apron to waft me away. She succeeds, unluckily. My bucket has all the virtues of a good steed except powers of resistance, which it has not; it is too light; a woman's apron can make it fly through the air.

"You bad woman!" I shout back, while she, turning into the shop, half contemptuous, half reassured, flourishes her fist in the air. "You bad woman! I begged you for a shovelful of the worst coal and you would not give it me." And with that I ascend into the regions of the ice mountains and am lost for ever.

IN THE PENAL COLONY

In the Penal Colony

"IT'S A REMARKABLE piece of apparatus," said the officer to the explorer and surveyed with a certain air of admiration the apparatus which was after all quite familiar to him. The explorer seemed to have accepted merely out of politeness the Commandant's invitation to witness the execution of a soldier condemned to death for disobedience and insulting behavior to a superior. Nor did the colony itself betray much interest in this execution. At least, in the small sandy valley, a deep hollow surrounded on all sides by naked crags, there was no one present save the officer, the explorer, the condemned man, who was a stupid-looking wide-mouthed creature with bewildered hair and face, and the soldier who held the heavy chain controlling the small chains locked on the prisoner's ankles, wrists and neck, chains which were themselves attached to each other by communicating links. In any case, the condemned man looked so like a submissive dog that one might have thought he could be left to run free on the surrounding hills and would only need to be whistled for when the execution was due to begin.

The explorer did not much care about the apparatus and walked up and down behind the prisoner with almost visible indifference while the officer made the last adjustments, now creeping beneath the structure, which was bedded deep in the earth, now climbing a ladder to inspect its upper parts. These were tasks that might well have been left to a mechanic, but the officer performed them with great zeal, whether because he was a devoted admirer of the apparatus or because of other reasons the work could be entrusted to no one else. "Ready now!" he called at last and climbed down from the ladder. He looked uncommonly limp, breathed with his mouth wide open and had tucked two fine ladies' handkerchiefs under the collar of his uniform. "These uniforms are too heavy for the tropics, surely," said the explorer, instead of making some inquiry about the apparatus, as the officer had expected. "Of course," said the officer, washing his oily and greasy hands in a bucket of water that stood ready, "but they mean home to us; we don't want to forget about home. Now just have a look at this machine," he added at once, simultaneously drying his hands on a towel and indicating the apparatus. "Up till now a few things still had to be set by hand, but from this moment it works all by itself." The explorer nodded and followed him. The officer, anxious to secure himself against all contingencies, said: "Things sometimes go wrong, of course; I hope that nothing goes wrong today, but we have to allow for the possibility. The machinery should go on working continuously for twelve hours. But if anything does go wrong it will only be some small matter that can be set right at once."

"Won't you take a seat?" he asked finally, drawing a cane chair out from among a heap of them and offering it to the explorer, who could not refuse it. He was now sitting at the edge of a pit, into which he glanced for a

fleeting moment. It was not very deep. On one side of
the pit the excavated soil had been piled up in a rampart, on the other side of it stood the apparatus. "I don't
know," said the officer, "if the Commandant has already
explained this apparatus to you." The explorer waved
one hand vaguely; the officer asked for nothing better,
since now he could explain the apparatus himself. "This
apparatus," he said, taking hold of a crank handle and
leaning against it, "was invented by our former Commandant. I assisted at the very earliest experiments and
had a share in all the work until its completion. But the
credit of inventing it belongs to him alone. Have you ever
heard of our former Commandant? No? Well, it isn't
saying too much if I tell you that the organization of the
whole penal colony is his work. We who were his friends
knew even before he died that the organization of the
colony was so perfect that his successor, even with a
thousand new schemes in his head, would find it impossible to alter anything, at least for many years to come.
And our prophecy has come true; the new Commandant
has had to acknowledge its truth. A pity you never met
the old Commandant!—But," the officer interrupted himself, "I am rambling on, and here stands his apparatus
before us. It consists, as you see, of three parts. In the
course of time each of these parts has acquired a kind
of popular nickname. The lower one is called the 'Bed,'
the upper one the 'Designer,' and this one here in the
middle that moves up and down is called the 'Harrow.' "
"The Harrow?" asked the explorer. He had not been
listening very attentively, the glare of the sun in the
shadeless valley was altogether too strong, it was difficult to collect one's thoughts. All the more did he admire
the officer, who in spite of his tight-fitting full-dress

uniform coat, amply befrogged and weighed down by epaulettes, was pursuing his subject with such enthusiasm and, besides talking, was still tightening a screw here and there with a spanner. As for the soldier, he seemed to be in much the same condition as the explorer. He had wound the prisoner's chain round both his wrists, propped himself on his rifle, let his head hang and was paying no attention to anything. That did not surprise the explorer, for the officer was speaking French, and certainly neither the soldier nor the prisoner understood a word of French. It was all the more remarkable, therefore, that the prisoner was none the less making an effort to follow the officer's explanations. With a kind of drowsy persistence he directed his gaze wherever the officer pointed a finger, and at the interruption of the explorer's question he, too, as well as the officer, looked round.

"Yes, the Harrow," said the officer, "a good name for it. The needles are set in like the teeth of a harrow and the whole thing works something like a harrow, although its action is limited to one place and contrived with much more artistic skill. Anyhow, you'll soon understand it. On the Bed here the condemned man is laid—I'm going to describe the apparatus first before I set it in motion. Then you'll be able to follow the proceedings better. Besides, one of the cog wheels in the Designer is badly worn; it creaks a lot when it's working; you can hardly hear yourself speak; spare parts, unfortunately, are difficult to get here.—Well, here is the Bed, as I told you. It is completely covered with a layer of cotton wool; you'll find out why later. On this cotton wool the condemned man is laid, face down, quite naked, of course; here are straps for the hands, here for the feet, and here

for the neck, to bind him fast. Here at the head of the
bed, where the man, as I said, first lays down his face,
is this little gag of felt, which can be easily regulated to
go straight into his mouth. It is meant to keep him from
screaming and biting his tongue. Of course the man is
forced to take the felt into his mouth, for otherwise his
neck would be broken by the strap." "Is that cotton
wool?" asked the explorer, bending forward. "Yes, certainly," said the officer, with a smile, "feel it for yourself." He took the explorer's hand and guided it over the
bed. "It's specially prepared cotton wool, that's why it
looks so different; I'll tell you presently what it's for."
The explorer already felt a dawning interest in the
apparatus; he sheltered his eyes from the sun with one
hand and gazed up at the structure. It was a huge affair.
The Bed and the Designer were of the same size and
looked like two dark wooden chests. The Designer hung
about two meters above the Bed; each of them was
bound at the corners with four rods of brass that almost
flashed out rays in the sunlight. Between the chests
shuttled the Harrow on a ribbon of steel.

The officer had scarcely noticed the explorer's previous indifference, but he was now well aware of his
dawning interest; so he stopped explaining in order to
leave a space of time for quiet observation. The condemned man imitated the explorer; since he could not
use a hand to shelter his eyes he gazed upwards without
shade.

"Well, the man lies down," said the explorer, leaning
back in his chair and crossing his legs.

"Yes," said the officer, pushing his cap back a little
and passing one hand over his heated face, "now listen!
Both the Bed and the Designer have an electric battery

each; the Bed needs one for itself, the Designer for the Harrow. As soon as the man is strapped down, the Bed is set in motion. It quivers in minute, very rapid vibrations, both from side to side and up and down. You will have seen similar apparatus in hospitals; but in our Bed the movements are all precisely calculated; you see, they have to correspond very exactly to the movements of the Harrow. And the Harrow is the instrument for the actual execution of the sentence."

"And how does the sentence run?" asked the explorer.

"You don't know that either?" said the officer in amazement, and bit his lips. "Forgive me if my explanations seem rather incoherent. I do beg your pardon. You see, the Commandant always used to do the explaining; but the new Commandant shirks this duty; yet that such an important visitor"—the explorer tried to deprecate the honor with both hands, the officer, however, insisted—"that such an important visitor should not even be told about the kind of sentence we pass is a new development, which—" He was just on the point of using strong language but checked himself and said only: "I was not informed, it is not my fault. In any case, I am certainly the best person to explain our procedure, since I have here"—he patted his breast pocket—"the relevant drawings made by our former Commandant."

"The Commandant's own drawings?" asked the explorer. "Did he combine everything in himself, then? Was he soldier, judge, mechanic, chemist and draughtsman?"

"Indeed he was," said the officer, nodding assent, with a remote, glassy look. Then he inspected his hands critically; they did not seem clean enough to him for touching the drawings; so he went over to the bucket and washed them again. Then he drew out a small leather wallet and said: "Our sentence does not sound severe. Whatever commandment the prisoner has disobeyed is written upon his body by the Harrow. This prisoner, for instance"—the officer indicated the man—"will have written on his body: HONOR THY SUPERIORS!"

The explorer glanced at the man; he stood, as the officer pointed him out, with bent head, apparently listening with all his ears in an effort to catch what was being said. Yet the movement of his blubber lips, closely pressed together, showed clearly that he could not understand a word. Many questions were troubling the explorer, but at the sight of the prisoner he asked only: "Does he know his sentence?" "No," said the officer, eager to go on with his exposition, but the explorer interrupted him: "He doesn't know the sentence that has been passed on him?" "No," said the officer again, pausing a moment as if to let the explorer elaborate his question, and then said: "There would be no point in telling him. He'll learn it on his body." The explorer intended to make no answer, but he felt the prisoner's gaze turned on him; it seemed to ask if he approved such ongoings. So he bent forward again, having already leaned back in his chair, and put another question: "But surely he knows that he has been sentenced?" "Nor that either," said the officer, smiling at the explorer as if expecting him to make further surprising remarks. "No," said the explorer, wiping his forehead, "then he can't know either whether his defense was effective?" "He has had no chance of putting up a defense," said the officer, turning his eyes away as if speaking to himself and so sparing the explorer the shame of hearing self-evident matters explained. "But he must have had some chance of defending himself," said the explorer, and rose from his seat.

The officer realized that he was in danger of having his exposition of the apparatus held up for a long time; so he went up to the explorer, took him by the arm, waved a hand towards the condemned man, who was standing very straight now that he had so obviously become the center of attention—the soldier had also given the chain a jerk—and said: "This is how the matter stands. I have been appointed judge in this penal colony. Despite my youth. For I was the former Commandant's assistant in all penal matters and know more about the apparatus than anyone. My guiding principle is this: Guilt is never to be doubted. Other courts cannot follow that principle, for they consist of several opinions and have higher courts to scrutinize them. That is not the case here, or at least, it was not the case in the former Commandant's time. The new man has certainly shown some inclination to interfere with my judgments, but so far I have succeeded in fending him off and will go on succeeding. You wanted to have the case explained; it is quite simple, like all of them. A captain reported to me this morning that this man, who had been assigned to him as a servant and sleeps before his door, had been asleep on duty. It is his duty, you see, to get up every time the hour strikes and salute the captain's door. Not an exacting duty, and very necessary, since he has to be a sentry as well as a servant, and must be alert in both functions. Last night the captain wanted to see if the man was doing his duty. He opened the door as the clock struck two and there was his man curled up asleep. He took his riding whip and lashed him across the face. Instead of getting up and begging pardon, the man caught hold of his master's legs, shook him and cried: 'Throw that whip away or I'll eat you alive.'—That's the evidence. The captain came to me an hour ago, I wrote down his statement and appended the sentence to it. Then I had the man put in chains. That was all quite simple. If I had first called the man before me and interrogated him, things would have got into a confused tangle. He would have told lies, and had I exposed these lies he would have backed them up with more lies, and so on and so forth. As it is, I've got him and I won't let him go.—Is that quite clear now? But we're wasting time, the execution should be beginning and I haven't finished explaining the apparatus yet." He pressed the explorer back into his chair, went up again to the apparatus and began: "As you see, the shape of the Harrow corresponds to the human form; here is the harrow for the torso, here are the harrows for the legs. For the head there is only this one small spike. Is that quite clear?" He bent amiably forward towards the explorer, eager to provide the most comprehensive explanations.

The explorer considered the Harrow with a frown. The explanation of the judicial procedure had not satisfied him. He had to remind himself that this was in any case a penal colony where extraordinary measures were needed and that military discipline must be enforced to the last. He also felt that some hope might be set on the new Commandant, who was apparently of a mind to bring in, although gradually, a new kind of procedure which the officer's narrow mind was incapable of understanding. This train of thought prompted his next question: "Will the Commandant attend the execution?"

"It is not certain," said the officer, wincing at the direct question, and his friendly expression darkened. "That is just why we have to lose no time. Much as I dislike it, I shall have to cut my explanations short. But of course tomorrow, when the apparatus has been cleaned—its one drawback is that it gets so messy—I can recapitulate all the details. For the present, then, only the essentials.—When the man lies down on the Bed and it begins to vibrate, the Harrow is lowered onto his body. It regulates itself automatically so that the needles barely touch his skin; once contact is made the steel ribbon stiffens immediately into a rigid band. And then the performance begins. An ignorant onlooker would see no difference between one punishment and another. The Harrow appears to do its work with uniform regularity. As it quivers, its points pierce the skin of the body which is itself quivering from the vibration of the Bed. So that the actual progress of the sentence can be watched, the Harrow is made of glass. Getting the needles fixed in the glass was a technical problem, but after many experiments we overcame the difficulty. No trouble was too great for us to take, you see. And now anyone can look through the glass and watch the inscription taking form on the body. Wouldn't you care to come a little nearer and have a look at the needles?"

The explorer got up slowly, walked across and bent over the Harrow. "You see," said the officer, "there are two kinds of needles arranged in multiple patterns. Each long needle has a short one beside it. The long needle does the writing, and the short needle sprays a jet of water to wash away the blood and keep the inscription clear. Blood and water together are then conducted here through small runnels into this main runnel and down a waste pipe into the pit." With his finger the officer traced the exact course taken by the blood and water. To make the picture as vivid as possible he held both hands below the outlet of the waste pipe as if to catch the outflow, and when he did this the explorer drew back his head and feeling behind him with one hand sought to return to his chair. To his horror he found that the condemned man too had obeyed the officer's invitation to examine the Harrow at close quarters and had followed him. He had pulled forward the sleepy soldier with the chain and was bending over the glass. One could see that his uncertain eyes were trying to perceive what the two gentlemen had been looking at, but since he had not understood the explanation he could not make head or tail of it. He was peering this way and that way. He kept running his eyes along the glass. The explorer wanted to drive him away, since what he was doing was probably culpable. But the officer firmly restrained the explorer with one hand and with the other took a clod of earth from the rampart and threw it at the soldier. He opened his eyes with a jerk, saw what the condemned man had dared to do, let his rifle fall, dug his heels into the ground, dragged his prisoner back so that he stumbled and fell immediately, and then stood looking down at him, watching him struggling and rattling in his chains. "Set him on his feet!" yelled the officer, for he noticed that the explorer's attention was being too much distracted by the prisoner. In fact he was even leaning right across the Harrow, without taking any notice of it, intent only on finding out what was happening to the prisoner. "Be careful with him!" cried the officer again. He ran round the apparatus, himself caught the condemned man under the shoulders and with the soldier's help got him up on his feet, which kept slithering from under him.

"Now I know all about it," said the explorer as the officer came back to him. "All except the most important thing," he answered, seizing the explorer's arm and pointing upwards: "In the Designer are all the cogwheels that control the movements of the Harrow, and this machinery is regulated according to the inscription demanded by the sentence. I am still using the guiding plans drawn by the former Commandant. Here they are"—he extracted some sheets from the leather wallet—"but I'm sorry I can't let you handle them, they are my most precious possessions. Just take a seat and I'll hold them in front of you like this, then you'll be able to see everything quite well." He spread out the first sheet of paper. The explorer would have liked to say something appreciative, but all he could see was a labyrinth of lines crossing and re-crossing each other, which covered the paper so thickly that it was difficult to discern the blank spaces between them. "Read it," said the officer. "I can't," said the explorer. "Yet it's clear enough," said the officer. "It's very ingenious," said the explorer evasively, "but I can't make it out." "Yes," said the officer with a laugh, putting the paper away again, "it's no calligraphy for school children. It needs to be studied closely. I'm quite sure that in the end you would understand it too. Of course the script can't be a simple one; it's not supposed to kill a man straight off, but only after an interval of, on an average, twelve hours; the turning point is reckoned to come at the sixth hour. So there have to be lots and lots of flourishes around the actual script; the script itself runs

round the body only in a narrow girdle; the rest of the
body is reserved for the embellishments. Can you appreciate now the work accomplished by the Harrow and
the whole apparatus?—Just watch it!" He ran up the
ladder, turned a wheel, called down: "Look out, keep
to one side!" and everything started working. If the
wheel had not creaked, it would have been marvelous.
The officer, as if surprised by the noise of the wheel,
shook his fist at it, then spread out his arms in excuse
to the explorer and climbed down rapidly to peer at the
working of the machine from below. Something perceptible to no one save himself was still not in order;
he clambered up again, did something with both hands
in the interior of the Designer, then slid down one of
the rods, instead of using the ladder, so as to get down
quicker, and with the full force of his lungs, to make
himself heard at all in the noise, yelled in the explorer's
ear: "Can you follow it? The Harrow is beginning to
write; when it finishes the first draft of the inscription
on the man's back, the layer of cotton wool begins to
roll and slowly turns the body over, to give the Harrow
fresh space for writing. Meanwhile the raw part that has
been written on lies on the cotton wool, which is specially prepared to staunch the bleeding and so makes
all ready for a new deepening of the script. Then these
teeth at the edge of the Harrow, as the body turns
further round, tear the cotton wool away from the
wounds, throw it into the pit, and there is more work
for the Harrow. So it keeps on writing deeper and
deeper for the whole twelve hours. The first six hours
the condemned man stays alive almost as before, he
suffers only pain. After two hours the felt gag is taken
away, for he has no longer strength to scream. Here, into

this electrically heated basin at the head of the bed, some warm rice pap is poured, from which the man, if he feels like it, can take as much as his tongue can lap. Not one of them ever misses the chance. I can remember none, and my experience is extensive. Only about the sixth hour does the man lose all desire to eat. I usually kneel down here at that moment and observe what happens. The man rarely swallows his last mouthful, he only rolls it round his mouth and spits it out into the pit. I have to duck just then or he would spit it in my face. But how quiet he grows at just about the sixth hour! Enlightenment comes to the most dull-witted. It begins around the eyes. From there it radiates. A moment that might tempt one to get under the Harrow oneself. Nothing more happens than that the man begins to understand the inscription, he purses his mouth as if he were listening. You have seen how difficult it is to decipher the script with one's eyes; but our man deciphers it with his wounds. To be sure, that is a hard task; he needs six hours to accomplish it. By that time the Harrow has pierced him quite through and casts him into the pit, where he pitches down upon the blood and water and the cotton wool. Then the judgment has been fulfilled, and we, the soldier and I, bury him."

The explorer had inclined his ear to the officer and with his hands in his jacket pockets watched the machine at work. The condemned man watched it too, but uncomprehendingly. He bent forward a little and was intent on the moving needles when the soldier, at a sign from the officer, slashed through his shirt and trousers from behind with a knife, so that they fell off; he tried to catch at his falling clothes to cover his nakedness, but the soldier lifted him into the air and shook the last remnants from him. The officer stopped the machine, and in the sudden silence the condemned man was laid under the Harrow. The chains were loosened and the straps fastened on instead; in the first moment that seemed almost a relief to the prisoner. And now the Harrow was adjusted a little lower, since he was a thin man. When the needle points touched him a shudder ran over his skin; while the soldier was busy strapping his right hand, he flung out his left hand blindly; but it happened to be in the direction towards where the explorer was standing. The officer kept watching the explorer sideways, as if seeking to read from his face the impression made on him by the execution, which had been at least cursorily explained to him.

The wrist strap broke; probably the soldier had drawn it too tight. The officer had to intervene, the soldier held up the broken piece of strap to show him. So the officer went over to him and said, his face still turned towards the explorer: "This is a very complex machine, it can't be helped that things are breaking or giving way here and there; but one must not thereby allow oneself to be diverted in one's general judgment. In any case, this strap is easily made good; I shall simply use a chain; the delicacy of the vibrations for the right arm will of course be a little impaired." And while he fastened the chains, he added: "The resources for maintaining the machine are now very much reduced. Under the former Commandant I had free access to a sum of money set aside entirely for this purpose. There was a store, too, in which spare parts were kept for repairs of all kinds. I confess I have been almost prodigal with them, I mean in the past, not now as the new Commandant pretends, always looking for an excuse to

attack our old way of doing things. Now he has taken
charge of the machine money himself, and if I send for
a new strap they ask for the broken old strap as evidence, and the new strap takes ten days to appear and
then is of shoddy material and not much good. But how
I am supposed to work the machine without a strap,
that's something nobody bothers about."

The explorer thought to himself: It's always a ticklish
matter to intervene decisively in other people's affairs.
He was neither a member of the penal colony nor a
citizen of the state to which it belonged. Were he to
denounce this execution or actually try to stop it, they
could say to him: You are a foreigner, mind your own
business. He could make no answer to that, unless he
were to add that he was amazed at himself in this connection, for he traveled only as an observer, with no
intention at all of altering other people's methods of
administering justice. Yet here he found himself strongly
tempted. The injustice of the procedure and the inhu-
manity of the execution were undeniable. No one could
suppose that he had any selfish interest in the matter, for
the condemned man was a complete stranger, not a fellow countryman or even at all sympathetic to him.
The explorer himself had recommendations from high
quarters, had been received here with great courtesy,
and the very fact that he had been invited to attend
the execution seemed to suggest that his views would
be welcome. And this was all the more likely since the
Commandant, as he had heard only too plainly, was no
upholder of the procedure and maintained an attitude
almost of hostility to the officer.

At that moment the explorer heard the officer cry
out in rage. He had just, with considerable difficulty,

forced the felt gag into the condemned man's mouth
when the man in an irresistible access of nausea shut
his eyes and vomited. Hastily the officer snatched him
away from the gag and tried to hold his head over the
pit; but it was too late, the vomit was running all over
the machine. "It's all the fault of that Commandant!"
cried the officer, senselessly shaking the brass rods in
front, "the machine is befouled like a pigsty." With
trembling hands he indicated to the explorer what had
happened. "Have I not tried for hours at a time to get
the Commandant to understand that the prisoner must
fast for a whole day before the execution. But our new,
mild doctrine thinks otherwise. The Commandant's
ladies stuff the man with sugar candy before he's led
off. He has lived on stinking fish his whole life long and
now he has to eat sugar candy! But it could still be
possible, I should have nothing to say against it, but
why won't they get me a new felt gag, which I have
been begging for the last three months. How should a
man not feel sick when he takes a felt gag into his
mouth which more than a hundred men have already
slobbered and gnawed in their dying moments?"

The condemned man had laid his head down and
looked peaceful, the soldier was busy trying to clean
the machine with the prisoner's shirt. The officer advanced towards the explorer, who in some vague presentiment fell back a pace, but the officer seized him
by the hand, and drew him to one side. "I should like
to exchange a few words with you in confidence," he
said, "may I?" "Of course," said the explorer, and
listened with downcast eyes.

"This procedure and method of execution, which you
are now having the opportunity to admire, has at the

moment no longer any open adherents in our colony. I
am its sole advocate, and at the same time the sole advocate of the old Commandant's tradition. I can no longer
reckon on any further extension of the method, it takes
all my energy to maintain it as it is. During the old
Commandant's lifetime the colony was full of his adherents; his strength of conviction I still have in some
measure, but not an atom of his power; consequently
the adherents have skulked out of sight, there are still
many of them but none of them will admit it. If you
were to go into the teahouse today, on execution day,
and listen to what is being said, you would perhaps
hear only ambiguous remarks. These would all be made
by adherents, but under the present Commandant and
his present doctrines they are of no use to me. And
now I ask you: because of this Commandant and the
women who influence him, is such a piece of work, the
work of a lifetime"—he pointed to the machine—"to
perish? Ought one to let that happen? Even if one has
only come as a stranger to our island for a few days?
But there's no time to lose, an attack of some kind is
impending on my function as judge; conferences are
already being held in the Commandant's office from
which I am excluded; even your coming here today
seems to me a significant move; they are cowards and
use you as a screen, you, a stranger.—How different an
execution was in the old days! A whole day before the
ceremony the valley was packed with people; they all
came only to look on; early in the morning the Commandant appeared with his ladies; fanfares roused the
whole camp; I reported that everything was in readiness;
the assembled company—no high official dared to absent
himself—arranged itself round the machine; this pile of

cane chairs is a miserable survival from that epoch. The machine was freshly cleaned and glittering, I got new spare parts for almost every execution. Before hundreds of spectators—all of them standing on tiptoe as far as the heights there—the condemned man was laid under the Harrow by the Commandant himself. What is left today for a common soldier to do was then my task, the task of the presiding judge, and was an honor for me. And then the execution began! No discordant noise spoilt the working of the machine. Many did not care to watch it but lay with closed eyes in the sand; they all knew: Now Justice is being done. In the silence one heard nothing but the condemned man's sighs, half muffled by the felt gag. Nowadays the machine can no longer wring from anyone a sigh louder than the felt gag can stifle; but in those days the writing needles let drop an acid fluid, which we're no longer permitted to use. Well, and then came the sixth hour! It was impossible to grant all the requests to be allowed to watch it from near by. The Commandant in his wisdom ordained that the children should have the preference; I, of course, because of my office had the privilege of always being at hand; often enough I would be squatting there with a small child in either arm. How we all absorbed the look of transfiguration on the face of the sufferer, how we bathed our cheeks in the radiance of that justice, achieved at last and fading so quickly! What times these were, my comrade!" The officer had obviously forgotten whom he was addressing; he had embraced the explorer and laid his head on his shoulder. The explorer was deeply embarrassed, impatiently he stared over the officer's head. The soldier had finished his cleaning job and was now pouring rice pap from a pot into the basin. As soon as the condemned man, who seemed to have recovered entirely, noticed this action he began to reach for the rice with his tongue. The soldier kept pushing him away, since the rice pap was certainly meant for a later hour, yet it was just as unfitting that the soldier himself should thrust his dirty hands into the basin and eat out of it before the other's avid face.

The officer quickly pulled himself together. "I didn't want to upset you," he said, "I know it is impossible to make those days credible now. Anyhow, the machine is still working and it is still effective in itself. It is effective in itself even though it stands alone in this valley. And the corpse still falls at the last into the pit with an incomprehensibly gentle wafting motion, even although there are no hundreds of people swarming round like flies as formerly. In those days we had to put a strong fence round the pit, it has long since been torn down."

The explorer wanted to withdraw his face from the officer and looked round him at random. The officer thought he was surveying the valley's desolation; so he seized him by the hands, turned him round to meet his eyes, and asked: "Do you realize the shame of it?"

But the explorer said nothing. The officer left him alone for a little; with legs apart, hands on hips, he stood very still, gazing at the ground. Then he smiled encouragingly at the explorer and said: "I was quite near you yesterday when the Commandant gave you the invitation. I heard him giving it. I know the Commandant. I divined at once what he was after. Although he is powerful enough to take measures against me, he doesn't dare to do it yet, but he certainly means to use your

verdict against me, the verdict of an illustrious foreigner. He has calculated it carefully: this is your second
day on the island, you did not know the old Commandant and his ways, you are conditioned by European ways of thought, perhaps you object on principle
to capital punishment in general and to such mechanical
instruments of death in particular, besides you will see
that the execution has no support from the public, a
shabby ceremony—carried out with a machine already
somewhat old and worn—now, taking all that into consideration, would it not be likely (so thinks the Commandant) that you might disapprove of my methods?
And if you disapprove, you wouldn't conceal the fact
(I'm still speaking from the Commandant's point of
view), for you are a man to feel confidence in your
own well-tried conclusions. True, you have seen and
learned to appreciate the peculiarities of many peoples,
and so you would not be likely to take a strong line
against our proceedings, as you might do in your own
country. But the Commandant has no need of that. A
casual, even an unguarded remark will be enough. It
doesn't even need to represent what you really think,
so long as it can be used speciously to serve his purpose.
He will try to prompt you with sly questions, of that
I am certain. And his ladies will sit around you and
prick up their ears; you might be saying something like
this: 'In our country we have a different criminal procedure,' or 'In our country the prisoner is interrogated
before he is sentenced,' or 'We haven't used torture
since the Middle Ages.' All these statements are as true
as they seem natural to you, harmless remarks that pass
no judgment on my methods. But how would the Commandant react to them? I can see him, our good

Commandant, pushing his chair away immediately and rushing on to the balcony, I can see his ladies streaming out after him, I can hear his voice—the ladies call it a voice of thunder—well, and this is what he says: 'A famous Western investigator, sent out to study criminal procedure in all the countries of the world, has just said that our old tradition of administering justice is inhumane. Such a verdict from such a personality makes it impossible for me to countenance these methods any longer. Therefore from this very day I ordain . . .' and so on. You may want to interpose that you never said any such thing, that you never called my methods inhumane, on the contrary your profound experience leads you to believe they are most humane and most in consonance with human dignity, and you admire the machine greatly—but it will be too late; you won't even get onto the balcony, crowded as it will be with ladies; you may try to draw attention to yourself; you may want to scream out; but a lady's hand will close your lips—and I and the work of the old Commandant will be done for."

The explorer had to suppress a smile; so easy, then, was the task he had felt to be so difficult. He said evasively: "You overestimate my influence; the Commandant has read my letters of recommendation, he knows that I am no expert in criminal procedure. If I were to give an opinion, it would be as a private individual, an opinion no more influential than that of any ordinary person, and in any case much less influential than that of the Commandant, who, I am given to understand, has very extensive powers in this penal colony. If his attitude to your procedure is as definitely hostile as you believe, then I fear the end of your tradition is at hand, even without any humble assistance from me."

Had it dawned on the officer at last? No, he still did not understand. He shook his head emphatically, glanced briefly round at the condemned man and the soldier, who both flinched away from the rice, came close up to the explorer and without looking at his face but fixing his eye on some spot on his coat said in a lower voice than before: "You don't know the Commandant; you feel yourself—forgive the expression—a kind of outsider so far as all of us are concerned; yet, believe me, your influence cannot be rated too highly. I was simply delighted when I heard that you were to attend the execution all by yourself. The Commandant arranged it to aim a blow at me, but I shall turn it to my advantage. Without being distracted by lying whispers and contemptuous glances—which could not have been avoided had a crowd of people attended the execution —you have heard my explanations, seen the machine and are now in course of watching the execution. You have doubtless already formed your own judgment; if you still have some small uncertainties the sight of the execution will resolve them. And now I make this request to you: help me against the Commandant!"

The explorer would not let him go on. "How could I do that," he cried, "it's quite impossible. I can neither help nor hinder you."

"Yes, you can," the officer said. The explorer saw with a certain apprehension that the officer had clenched his fists. "Yes, you can," repeated the officer, still more insistently. "I have a plan that is bound to succeed. You believe your influence is insufficient. I know that it is sufficient. But even granted that you are right, is it not necessary, for the sake of preserving this tradition, to try even what might prove insufficient? Listen

to my plan, then. The first thing necessary for you to
carry it out is to be as reticent as possible today regarding your verdict on these proceedings. Unless you
are asked a direct question you must say nothing at all;
but what you do say must be brief and general; let it
be remarked that you would prefer not to discuss the
matter, that you are out of patience with it, that if
you are to let yourself go you would use strong language. I don't ask you to tell any lies; by no means;
you should only give curt answers, such as: 'Yes, I saw
the execution,' or 'Yes, I had it explained to me.' Just
that, nothing more. There are grounds enough for any
impatience you betray, although not such as will occur
to the Commandant. Of course, he will mistake your
meaning and interpret it to please himself. That's what
my plan depends on. Tomorrow in the Commandant's
office there is to be a large conference of all the high
administrative officials, the Commandant presiding. Of
course the Commandant is the kind of man to have
turned these conferences into public spectacles. He has
had a gallery built that is always packed with spectators.
I am compelled to take part in the conferences, but they
make me sick with disgust. Now, whatever happens,
you will certainly be invited to this conference; if you
behave today as I suggest the invitation will become an
urgent request. But if for some mysterious reason you're
not invited, you'll have to ask for an invitation; there's
no doubt of your getting it then. So tomorrow you're
sitting in the Commandant's box with the ladies. He
keeps looking up to make sure you're there. After various trivial and ridiculous matters, brought in merely to
impress the audience—mostly harbor works, nothing
but harbor works!—our judicial procedure comes up

for discussion too. If the Commandant doesn't intro-
duce it, or not soon enough, I'll see that it's mentioned.
I'll stand up and report that today's execution has taken
place. Quite briefly, only a statement. Such a statement
is not usual, but I shall make it. The Commandant thanks
me, as always, with an amiable smile, and then he can't
restrain himself, he seizes the excellent opportunity. 'It
has just been reported,' he will say, or words to that
effect, 'that an execution has taken place. I should like
merely to add that this execution was witnessed by the
famous explorer who has, as you all know, honored our
colony so greatly by his visit to us. His presence at
today's session of our conference also contributes to the
importance of this occasion. Should we not now ask the
famous explorer to give us his verdict on our traditional
mode of execution and the procedure that leads up to
it?' Of course there is loud applause, general agreement,
I am more insistent than anyone. The Commandant
bows to you and says: 'Then in the name of the assembled company, I put the question to you.' And now
you advance to the front of the box. Lay your hands
where everyone can see them, or the ladies will catch
them and press your fingers.—And then at last you can
speak out. I don't know how I'm going to endure the
tension of waiting for that moment. Don't put any restraint on yourself when you make your speech, publish
the truth aloud, lean over the front of the box, shout,
yes indeed, shout your verdict, your unshakable conviction, at the Commandant. Yet perhaps you wouldn't
care to do that, it's not in keeping with your character, in your country perhaps people do these things
differently, well, that's all right too, that will be quite
as effective, don't even stand up, just say a few words,

even in a whisper, so that only the officials beneath you will hear them, that will quite enough, you don't even need to mention the lack of public support for the execution, the creaking wheel, the broken strap, the filthy gag of felt, no, I'll take all that upon me, and, believe me, if my indictment doesn't drive him out of the conference hall, it will force him to his knees to make the acknowledgment: Old Commandant, I humble myself before you.—That is my plan; will you help me to carry it out? But of course you are willing, what is more, you must." And the officer seized the explorer by both arms and gazed, breathing heavily, into his face. He had shouted the last sentence so loudly that even the soldier and the condemned man were startled into attending; they had not understood a word but they stopped eating and looked over at the explorer, chewing their previous mouthfuls.

From the very beginning the explorer had no doubt about what answer he must give; in his lifetime he had experienced too much to have any uncertainty here; he was fundamentally honorable and unafraid. And yet now, facing the soldier and the condemned man, he did hesitate, for as long as it took to draw one breath. At last, however, he said, as he had to: "No." The officer blinked several times but did not turn his eyes away. "Would you like me to explain?" asked the explorer. The officer nodded wordlessly. "I do not approve of your procedure," said the explorer then, "even before you took me into your confidence—of course I shall never in any circumstances betray your confidence—I was already wondering whether it would be my duty to intervene and whether my intervention would have the slightest chance of success. I realized to whom I ought

to turn: to the Commandant, of course. You have made
that fact even clearer, but without having strengthened
my resolution, on the contrary, your sincere conviction has touched me, even though it cannot influence my
judgment."

The officer remained mute, turned to the machine,
caught hold of a brass rod, and then, leaning back a
little, gazed at the Designer as if to assure himself that
all was in order. The soldier and the condemned man
seemed to have come to some understanding; the condemned man was making signs to the soldier, difficult
though his movements were because of the tight straps;
the soldier was bending down to him; the condemned
man whispered something and the soldier nodded.

The explorer followed the officer and said: "You
don't know yet what I mean to do. I shall tell the Commandant what I think of the procedure, certainly, but
not at a public conference, only in private; nor shall I
stay here long enough to attend any conference; I am
going away early tomorrow morning, or at least em-
barking on my ship."

It did not look as if the officer had been listening. "So
you did not find the procedure convincing," he said
to himself and smiled, as an old man smiles at childish
nonsense and yet pursues his own meditations behind
the smile.

"Then the time has come," he said at last, and suddenly looked at the explorer with bright eyes that held
some challenge, some appeal for co-operation. "The
time for what?" asked the explorer uneasily, but got no
answer.

"You are free," said the officer to the condemned man
in the native tongue. The man did not believe it at first.

"Yes, you are set free," said the officer. For the first time the condemned man's face woke to real animation. Was it true? Was it only a caprice of the officer's, that might change again? Had the foreign explorer begged him off? What was it? One could read these questions on his face. But not for long. Whatever it might be, he wanted to be really free if he might, and he began to struggle so far as the Harrow permitted him.

"You'll burst my straps," cried the officer, "lie still! We'll soon loosen them." And signing the soldier to help him, he set about doing so. The condemned man laughed wordlessly to himself, now he turned his face left towards the officer, now right towards the soldier, nor did he forget the explorer.

"Draw him out," ordered the officer. Because of the Harrow this had to be done with some care. The condemned man had already torn himself a little in the back through his impatience.

From now on, however, the officer paid hardly any attention to him. He went up to the explorer, pulled out the small leather wallet again, turned over the papers in it, found the one he wanted and showed it to the explorer. "Read it," he said. "I can't," said the explorer, "I told you before that I can't make out these scripts." "Try taking a close look at it," said the officer and came quite near to the explorer so that they might read it together. But when even that proved useless, he outlined the script with his little finger, holding it high above the paper as if the surface dared not be sullied by touch, in order to help the explorer to follow the script in that way. The explorer did make an effort, meaning to please the officer in this respect at least, but he was quite unable to follow. Now the officer began to spell it, letter by letter, and then read out the words. "'BE JUST!' is what is written there," he said, "surely you can read it now." The explorer bent so close to the paper that the officer feared he might touch it and drew it farther away; the explorer made no remark, yet it was clear that he still could not decipher it. "'BE JUST!' is what is written there," said the officer once more. "Maybe," said the explorer, "I am prepared to believe you." "Well, then," said the officer, at least partly satisfied, and climbed up the ladder with the paper; very carefully he laid it inside the Designer and seemed to be changing the disposition of all the cogwheels; it was a troublesome piece of work and must have involved wheels that were extremely small, for sometimes the officer's head vanished altogether from sight inside the Designer, so precisely did he have to regulate the machinery.

The explorer, down below, watched the labor uninterruptedly, his neck grew stiff and his eyes smarted from the glare of sunshine over the sky. The soldier and the condemned man were now busy together. The man's shirt and trousers, which were already lying in the pit, were fished out by the point of the soldier's bayonet. The shirt was abominably dirty and its owner washed it in the bucket of water. When he put on the shirt and trousers both he and the soldier could not help guffawing, for the garments were of course slit up behind. Perhaps the condemned man felt it incumbent on him to amuse the soldier, he turned round and round in his slashed garments before the soldier, who squatted on the ground beating his knees with mirth. All the same, they presently controlled their mirth out of respect for the gentlemen.

When the officer had at length finished his task aloft, he surveyed the machinery in all its details once more, with a smile, but this time shut the lid of the Designer, which had stayed open till now, climbed down, looked into the pit and then at the condemned man, noting with satisfaction that the clothing had been taken out, then went over to wash his hands in the water bucket, perceived too late that it was disgustingly dirty, was unhappy because he could not wash his hands, in the end thrust them into the sand—this alternative did not please him, but he had to put up with it—then stood upright and began to unbutton his uniform jacket. As he did this, the two ladies' handkerchiefs he had tucked under his collar fell into his hands. "Here are your handkerchiefs," he said, and threw them to the condemned man. And to the explorer he said in explanation: "A gift from the ladies."

In spite of the obvious haste with which he was discarding first his uniform jacket and then all his clothing, he handled each garment with loving care, he even ran his fingers caressingly over the silver lace on the jacket and shook a tassel into place. This loving care was certainly out of keeping with the fact that as soon as he had a garment off he flung it at once with a kind of unwilling jerk into the pit. The last thing left to him was his short sword with the sword belt. He drew it out of the scabbard, broke it, then gathered all together, the bits of the sword, the scabbard and the belt, and flung them so violently down that they clattered into the pit.

Now he stood naked there. The explorer bit his lips and said nothing. He knew very well what was going to happen, but he had no right to obstruct the officer in anything. If the judicial procedure which the officer cherished were really so near its end—possibly as a result of his own intervention, as to which he felt himself pledged—then the officer was doing the right thing; in his place the explorer would not have acted otherwise.

The soldier and the condemned man did not understand at first what was happening, at first they were not even looking on. The condemned man was gleeful at having got the handkerchiefs back, but he was not allowed to enjoy them for long, since the soldier snatched them with a sudden, unexpected grab. Now the condemned man in turn was trying to twitch them from under the belt where the soldier had tucked them, but the soldier was on his guard. So they were wrestling, half in jest. Only when the officer stood quite naked was their attention caught. The condemned man especially seemed struck with the notion that some great change was impending. What had happened to him was now going to happen to the officer. Perhaps even to the very end. Apparently the foreign explorer had given the order for it. So this was revenge. Although he himself had not suffered to the end, he was to be revenged to the end. A broad, silent grin now appeared on his face and stayed there all the rest of the time.

The officer, however, had turned to the machine. It had been clear enough previously that he understood the machine well, but now it was almost staggering to see how he managed it and how it obeyed him. His hand had only to approach the Harrow for it to rise and sink several times till it was adjusted to the right position for receiving him; he touched only the edge of the Bed and already it was vibrating; the felt gag came to meet his mouth, one could see that the officer was really reluctant to take it but he shrank from it only a moment, soon he submitted and received it. Everything was ready, only the straps hung down at the sides, yet they were obviously unnecessary, the officer did not need to be fastened down. Then the condemned man noticed the loose straps, in his opinion the execution was incomplete unless the straps were buckled, he gestured eagerly to the soldier and they ran together to strap the officer down. The latter had already stretched out one foot to push the lever that started the Designer; he saw the two men coming up; so he drew his foot back and let himself be buckled in. But now he could not reach the lever; neither the soldier nor the condemned man would be able to find it, and the explorer was determined not to lift a finger. It was not necessary; as soon as the straps were fastened the machine began to work; the Bed vibrated, the needles flickered above the skin, the Harrow rose and fell. The explorer had been staring at it quite a while before he remembered that a wheel in the Designer should have been creaking; but everything was quiet, not even the slightest hum could be heard.

Because it was working so silently the machine simply escaped one's attention. The explorer observed the soldier and the condemned man. The latter was the more animated of the two, everything in the machine interested him, now he was bending down and now stretching up on tiptoe, his forefinger was extended all the time pointing out details to the soldier. This annoyed the explorer. He was resolved to stay till the end, but he could not bear the sight of these two. "Go back home," he said. The soldier would have been willing enough, but the condemned man took the order as a punishment. With clasped hands he implored to be allowed to stay, and when the explorer shook his head and would not relent, he even went down on his knees. The explorer saw that it was no use merely giving orders, he was on the point of going over and driving them away. At that moment he heard a noise above him in the Designer. He looked up. Was that cogwheel going to make trouble after all? But it was something quite different. Slowly the lid of the Designer rose up and then clicked wide open. The teeth of a cogwheel showed themselves and rose higher, soon the whole wheel was visible, it was as if some enormous force were squeezing the Designer so that there was no longer room for the wheel, the wheel moved up till it came to the very edge of the Designer, fell down, rolled along the sand a little on its rim and then lay flat. But a second wheel was already rising after it, followed by many others, large and small and indistinguishably minute, the same thing happened to all of them, at every moment one imagined the Designer must now really be empty, but another complex of numerous wheels was already rising into sight, falling down, trundling along the sand and lying flat. This phenomenon made the condemned man completely forget the explorer's command, the cogwheels fascinated him, he was always trying to catch one and at the same time urging the soldier to help, but always drew back his hand in alarm, for another wheel always came hopping along which, at least on its first advance, scared him off.

The explorer, on the other hand, felt greatly troubled; the machine was obviously going to pieces; its silent working was a delusion; he had a feeling that he must now stand by the officer, since the officer was no longer able to look after himself. But while the tumbling cog-wheels absorbed his whole attention he had forgotten to keep an eye on the rest of the machine; now that the last cogwheel had left the Designer, however, he bent over the Harrow and had a new and still more unpleasant surprise. The Harrow was not writing, it was only jabbing, and the bed was not turning the body over but only bringing it up quivering against the needles. The explorer wanted to do something, if pos-sible, to bring the whole machine to a standstill, for this was no exquisite torture such as the officer desired, this was plain murder. He stretched out his hands. But at that moment the Harrow rose with the body spitted on it and moved to the side, as it usually did only when the twelfth hour had come. Blood was flowing in a hundred streams, not mingled with water, the water jets too had failed to function. And now the last action failed to fulfil itself, the body did not drop off the long needles, streaming with blood it went on hanging over the pit without falling into it. The Harrow tried to move back to its old position, but as if it had itself noticed that it had not yet got rid of its burden it stuck after all where it was, over the pit. "Come and help!" cried the explorer to the other two, and himself seized the officer's feet. He wanted to push against the feet while the others seized the head from the opposite side and so the officer might be slowly eased off the needles. But the other two could not make up their minds to come; the condemned man actually turned away; the explorer had to go over to them and force them into position at the officer's head. And here, almost against his will, he had to look at the face of the corpse. It was as it had been in life; no sign was visible of the promised redemption; what the others had found in the machine the officer had not found; the lips were firmly pressed together, the eyes were open, with the same expression as in life, the look was calm and convinced, through the forehead went the point of the great iron spike.

As the explorer, with the soldier and the condemned man behind him, reached the first houses of the colony, the soldier pointed to one of them and said: "There is the teahouse."

In the ground floor of the house was a deep, low, cavernous space, its walls and ceiling blackened with smoke. It was open to the road all along its length. Although this teahouse was very little different from the other houses of the colony, which were all very dilapidated, even up to the Commandant's palatial head-quarters, it made on the explorer the impression of a historic tradition of some kind, and he felt the power of past days. He went near to it, followed by his com-panions, right up between the empty tables which stood in the street before it, and breathed the cool, heavy air that came from the interior. "The old man's buried here," said the soldier, "the priest wouldn't let him lie in the churchyard. Nobody knew where to bury him for a while, but in the end they buried him here. The officer never told you about that, for sure, because of course that's what he was most ashamed of. He even tried several times to dig the old man up by night, but he was always chased away." "Where is the grave?" asked the explorer, who found it impossible to believe the soldier. At once both of them, the soldier and the

condemned man, ran before him pointing with outstretched hands in the direction where the grave should
be. They led the explorer right up to the back wall,
where guests were sitting at a few tables. They were
apparently dock laborers, strong men with short, glis-
tening, full black beards. None had a jacket, their
shirts were torn, they were poor, humble creatures. As
the explorer drew near, some of them got up, pressed
close to the wall, and stared at him. "It's a foreigner,"
ran the whisper around him, "he wants to see the
grave." They pushed one of the tables aside, and under
it there was really a gravestone. It was a simple stone,
low enough to be covered by a table. There was an
inscription on it in very small letters, the explorer had
to kneel down to read it. This was what it said: "Here
rests the old Commandant. His adherents, who now
must be nameless, have dug this grave and set up this
stone. There is a prophecy that after a certain number
of years the Commandant will rise again and lead his
adherents from this house to recover the colony. Have
faith and wait!" When the explorer had read this and
risen to his feet he saw all the bystanders around him
smiling, as if they too had read the inscription, had
found it ridiculous and were expecting him to agree
with them. The explorer ignored this, distributed a few
coins among them, waiting till the table was pushed
over the grave again, quitted the teahouse and made for
the harbor.

The soldier and the condemned man had found some
acquaintances in the teahouse, who detained them. But
they must have soon shaken them off, for the explorer
was only halfway down the long flight of steps leading
to the boats when they came rushing after him. Prob-

ably they wanted to force him at the last minute to take them with him. While he was bargaining below with a ferryman to row him to the steamer, the two of them came headlong down the steps, in silence, for they did not dare to shout. But by the time they reached the foot of the steps the explorer was already in the boat, and the ferryman was just casting off from the shore. They could have jumped into the boat, but the explorer lifted a heavy knotted rope from the floor boards, threatened them with it and so kept them from attempting the leap.

A HUNGER ARTIST

A Hunger Artist

First Sorrow

A TRAPEZE ARTIST—this art, practiced high in the
vaulted domes of the great variety theaters, is admittedly one of the most difficult humanity can achieve—
had so arranged his life that, as long as he kept working
in the same building, he never came down from his
trapeze by night or day, at first only from a desire to
perfect his skill, but later because custom was too strong
for him. All his needs, very modest needs at that, were
supplied by relays of attendants who watched from
below and sent up and hauled down again in specially
constructed containers whatever he required. This way
of living caused no particular inconvenience to the theatrical people, except that, when other turns were on
the stage, his being still up aloft, which could not be
dissembled, proved somewhat distracting, as also the
fact that, although at such times he mostly kept very
still, he drew a stray glance here and there from the
public. Yet the management overlooked this, because
he was an extraordinary and unique artist. And of course
they recognized that this mode of life was no mere
prank, and that only in this way could he really keep
himself in constant practice and his art at the pitch of
its perfection.

FRANZ KAFKA

Besides, it was quite healthful up there, and when in the warmer seasons of the year the side windows all round the dome of the theater were thrown open and sun and fresh air came pouring irresistibly into the dusky vault, it was even beautiful. True, his social life was somewhat limited, only sometimes a fellow acrobat swarmed up the ladder to him, and then they both sat on the trapeze, leaning left and right against the supporting ropes, and chatted, or builders' workmen repairing the roof exchanged a few words with him through an open window, or the fireman, inspecting the emergency lighting in the top gallery, called over to him something that sounded respectful but could hardly be made out. Otherwise nothing disturbed his seclusion; occasionally, perhaps, some theater hand straying through the empty theater of an afternoon gazed thoughtfully up into the great height of the roof, almost beyond eyeshot, where the trapeze artist, unaware that he was being observed, practiced his art or rested.

The trapeze artist could have gone on living peacefully like that, had it not been for the inevitable journeys from place to place, which he found extremely trying. Of course his manager saw to it that his sufferings were not prolonged one moment more than necessary; for town travel, racing automobiles were used, which whirled him, by night if possible or in the earliest hours of the morning, through the empty streets at breakneck speed, too slow all the same for the trapeze artist's impatience; for railway journeys, a whole compartment was reserved, in which the trapeze artist, as a possible though wretched alternative to his usual way of living, could pass the time up on the luggage rack; in the next town on their circuit, long before he arrived, the trapeze was already slung up in the theater and all the doors leading to the stage were flung wide open, all corridors kept free—yet the manager never knew a happy moment until the trapeze artist set his foot on the rope ladder and in a twinkling, at long last, hung aloft on his trapeze.

Despite so many journeys having been successfully arranged by the manager, each new one embarrassed him again, for the journeys, apart from everything else, got on the nerves of the artist a great deal.

Once when they were again traveling together, the trapeze artist lying on the luggage rack dreaming, the manager leaning back in the opposite window seat reading a book, the trapeze artist addressed his companion in a low voice. The manager was immediately all attention. The trapeze artist, biting his lips, said that he must always in future have two trapezes for his performance instead of only one, two trapezes opposite each other. The manager at once agreed. But the trapeze artist, as if to show that the manager's consent counted for as little as his refusal, said that never again would he perform on only one trapeze, in no circumstances whatever. The very idea that it might happen at all seemed to make him shudder. The manager, watchfully feeling his way, once more emphasized his entire agreement, two trapezes were better than one, besides it would be an advantage to have a second bar, more variety could be introduced into the performance. At that the trapeze artist suddenly burst into tears. Deeply distressed, the manager sprang to his feet and asked what was the matter, then getting no answer climbed up on the seat and caressed him, cheek to cheek, so that his own face was bedabbled by the trapeze artist's tears. Yet it took much questioning and soothing endearment until the trapeze artist sobbed: "Only the one bar in my hands—how can I go on living!" That made it somewhat easier for the manager to comfort him; he promised to wire from the very next station for a second trapeze to be installed in the first town on their circuit; reproached himself for having let the artist work so long on only one trapeze, and thanked and praised him warmly for having at last brought the mistake to his notice. And so he succeeded in reassuring the trapeze artist, little by little, and was able to go back to his corner. But he himself was far from reassured, with deep uneasiness he kept glancing secretly at the trapeze artist over the top of his book. Once such ideas began to torment him, would they ever quite leave him alone? Would they not rather increase in urgency? Would they not threaten his very existence? And indeed the manager believed he could see, during the apparently peaceful sleep which had succeeded the fit of tears, the first furrows of care engraving themselves upon the trapeze artist's smooth, childlike forehead.

A Little Woman

SHE IS a little woman; naturally quite slim, she is tightly laced as well; she is always in the same dress when I see her, it is made of grayish-yellow stuff something the color of wood and is trimmed discreetly with tassels or button-like hangings of the same color; she never wears a hat, her dull, fair hair is smooth and not untidy, but worn very loose. Although she is tightly laced she is quick and light in her movements, actually she rather overdoes the quickness, she loves to put her hands on her hips and abruptly turn the upper part of her body sideways with a suddenness that is surprising. The impression her hand makes on me I can convey only by saying that I have never seen a hand with the separate fingers so sharply differentiated from each other as hers; and yet her hand has no anatomical peculiarities, it is an entirely normal hand.

This little woman, then, is very ill-pleased with me, she always finds something objectionable in me, I am always doing the wrong thing to her, I annoy her at every step; if a life could be cut into the smallest of small pieces and every scrap of it could be separately assessed, every scrap of my life would certainly be an offense to her. I have often wondered why I am such an offense to her; it may be that everything about me outrages her sense of beauty, her feeling for justice, her habits, her traditions, her hopes, there are such completely incompatible natures, but why does that upset her so much? There is no connection between us that could force her to suffer because of me. All she has to do is to regard me as an utter stranger, which I am, and which I do not object to being, indeed I should welcome it, she only needs to forget my existence, which I have never thrust upon her attention, nor ever would, and obviously her torments would be at an end. I am not thinking of myself, I am quite leaving out of account the fact that I find her attitude of course rather trying, leaving it out of account because I recognize that my discomfort is nothing to the suffering she endures. All the same I am well aware that hers is no affectionate suffering; she is not concerned to make any real improvement in me, besides whatever she finds objectionable in me is not of a nature to hinder my development. Yet she does not care about my development either, she cares only for her personal interest in the matter, which is to revenge herself for the torments I cause her now and to prevent any torments that threaten her from me in the future. I have already tried once to indicate the best way of putting a stop to this perpetual resentment of hers, but my very attempt wrought her up to such a pitch of fury that I shall never repeat it.

I feel too a certain responsibility laid upon me, if you like to put it that way, for strangers as we are to each other, the little woman and myself, and however true it is that the sole connection between us is the vexation I cause her, or rather the vexation she lets me cause her, I ought not to feel indifferent to the visible physical suffering which this induces in her. Every now and then, and more frequently of late, information is brought to me that she has risen of a morning pale, unslept, oppressed by headache and almost unable to work; her family are worried about her, they wonder what can have caused her condition, and they have not yet found the answer. I am the only one who knows that it is her settled and daily renewed vexation with me. True, I am not so worried about her as her family; she is hardy and tough; anyone who is capable of such strong feeling is likely also to be capable of surviving its effects; I have even a suspicion that her sufferings—or some of them, at least—are only a pretense put up to bring public suspicion on me. She is too proud to admit openly what a torment my very existence is to her; to make any appeal to others against me she would consider beneath her dignity; it is only disgust, persistent and active disgust, that drives her to be preoccupied with me; to discuss in public this unclean affliction of hers would be too shameful. But to keep utterly silent about something that so persistently rankles would be also too much for her. So with feminine guile she steers a middle course; she keeps silent but betrays all the outward signs of a secret sorrow in order to draw public attention to the matter. Perhaps she even hopes that once public attention is fixed on me a general public rancor against me will rise up and use all its great powers to condemn me definitively much more effectively and quickly than her relatively feeble private rancor could do; she would then retire into the background, draw a breath of relief and turn her back on me. Well, if that is what her hopes are really set on, she is deluding herself. Public opinion will not take over her role; public opinion would never find me so infinitely objectionable, even under its most powerful magnifying glass. I am not so altogether useless a creature as she thinks; I don't want to boast and especially not in this connection; but if I am not conspicuous for specially useful qualities, I am certainly not conspicuous for the lack of them; only to her, only to her almost bleached eyes, do I appear so, she won't be able to convince anyone else. So in this respect I can feel quite reassured, can I? No, not at all; for if it becomes generally known that my behavior is making her positively ill, which some observers, those who most industriously bring me information about her, for instance, are not far from perceiving, or at least look as if they perceived it, and the world should put questions to me, why am I tormenting the poor little woman with my incorrigibility, and do I mean to drive her to her death, and when am I going to show some sense and have enough decent human feeling to stop such goings-on—if the world were to ask me that, it would be difficult to find an answer. Should I admit frankly that I don't much believe in these symptoms of illness, and thus produce the unfavorable impression of being a man who blames others to avoid being blamed himself, and in such an ungallant manner? And how could I say quite openly that even if I did believe that she were really ill, I should not feel the slightest sympathy for her, since she is a complete stranger to me and any connection between us is her own invention and entirely one-sided. I don't say that people wouldn't believe me; they wouldn't be interested enough to get so far as belief; they would simply note the answer I gave concerning such a frail, sick woman, and that would be little in my favor. Any answer I made would inevitably come up against the world's incapacity to keep down the suspicion that there must be a love affair behind such a case as this, although it is as clear as daylight that such a relationship does not exist, and that if it did it would come from my side rather than hers, since I should be really capable of admiring the little woman for the decisive quickness of her judgment and her persistent vitality in leaping to conclusions, if these very qualities were not always turned as weapons against me. She, at any rate, shows not a trace of friendliness towards me; in that she is honest and true; therein lies my last hope; not even to help on her campaign would she so far forget herself as to let any such suspicion arise. But public opinion which is wholly insensitive in such matters would abide by its prejudices and always denounce me.

So the only thing left for me to do would be to change myself in time, before the world could intervene, just sufficiently to lessen the little woman's rancor, not to wean her from it altogether, which is unthinkable.

And indeed I have often asked myself if I am so pleased
with my present self as to be unwilling to change it, and
whether I could not attempt some changes in myself,
even although I should be doing so not because I found
them needful but merely to propitiate the little woman.
And I have honestly tried, taking some trouble and care,
it even did me good, it was almost a diversion; some
changes resulted which were visible a long way off,
I did not need to draw her attention to them, she per-
ceives all that kind of thing much sooner than I do, she
can even perceive by my expression beforehand what I
have in mind; but no success crowned my efforts. How
could it possibly do so? Her objection to me, as I am
now aware, is a fundamental one; nothing can remove it,
not even the removal of myself; if she heard that I had
committed suicide she would fall into transports of rage.

Now I cannot imagine that such a sharp-witted woman
as she is does not understand as well as I do both the
hopelessness of her own course of action and the helplessness of mine, my inability, with the best will in the
world, to conform to her requirements. Of course she
understands it, but being a fighter by nature she forgets
it in the lust of battle, and my unfortunate disposition,
which I cannot help since it is mine by nature, conditions me to whisper gentle admonitions to anyone who
flies into a violent passion. In this way, naturally, we
shall never come to terms. I shall keep on leaving the
house in the gay mood of early morning only to meet
that countenance of hers, lowering at the sight of me, the
contemptuous curl of her lips, the measuring glance,
aware beforehand of what it is going to find, that
sweeps over me and however fleeting misses nothing, the
sarcastic smile furrowing her girlish cheek, the com-

plaining lift of the eyes to Heaven, the planting of the hands on the hips, to fortify herself, and then the access of rage that brings pallor with it and trembling.

Not long ago I took occasion, for the very first time as I realized with some astonishment, to mention the matter to a very good friend of mine, just in passing, casually, in a word or two, reducing it to even less than its just proportions, trivial as it is in essence when looked at objectively. It was curious that my friend all the same did not ignore it, indeed of his own accord he even made more of it than I had done, would not be side-tracked and insisted on discussing it. But it was still more curious that in one important particular he underesti-mated it, for he advised me seriously to go away for a short time. No advice could be less understandable; the matter was simple enough, anyone who looked closely at it could see right through it, yet it was not so simple that my mere departure would set all of it right, or even the greater part of it. On the contrary, such a departure is just what I must avoid; if I am to follow a plan at all it must be that of keeping the affair within its present narrow limits which do not yet involve the outside world, that is to say, I must stay quietly where I am and not let it affect my behavior as far as can be seen, and that includes mentioning it to no one, but not at all be-cause it is a kind of dangerous mystery, merely because it is a trivial, purely personal matter and as such to be taken lightly, and to be kept on that level. So my friend's remarks were not profitless after all, they taught me nothing new yet they strengthened my original reso-lution.

And on closer reflection it appears that the develop-ments which the affair seems to have undergone in the

course of time are not developments in the affair itself,
but only in my attitude to it, insofar as that has become
more composed on the one hand, more manly, penetrating nearer the heart of the matter, while on the other
hand, under the influence of the continued nervous
strain which I cannot overcome, however slight, it has
increased in irritability.

I am less upset by the affair now that I think I perceive how unlikely it is to come to any decisive crisis,
imminent as that sometimes seems to be; one is easily disposed, especially when one is young, to exaggerate the
speed with which decisive moments arrive; whenever my
small critic, grown faint at the very sight of me, sank
sideways into a chair, holding on to the back of it with
one hand and plucking at her bodice strings with the
other, while tears of rage and despair rolled down her
cheeks, I used to think that now the moment had come
and I was just on the point of being summoned to answer for myself. Yet there was no decisive moment, no
summons, women faint easily, the world has no time to
notice all their doings. And what has really happened
in all these years? Nothing except that such occasions
have repeated themselves, sometimes more and sometimes less violently, and that their sum total has increased accordingly. And that people are hanging
around in the offing and would like to interfere if they
could find some way of doing it; but they can find none,
so up till now they have had to rely on what they could
smell out, and although that by itself is fully qualified
to keep the owners of the noses busy it can't do anything more. Yet the situation was always like that, fundamentally, always provided with superfluous bystanders and nosy onlookers, who always justified their pres-

ence by some cunning excuse, for preference claiming to be relatives, always stretching their necks and sniffing trouble, but all they have achieved is to be still standing by. The only difference is that I have gradually come to recognize them and distinguish one face from another; once upon a time I believed that they had just gradually trickled in from outside, that the affair was having wider repercussions, which would themselves compel a crisis; today I think I know that these onlookers were always there from the beginning and have little or nothing to do with the imminence of a crisis. And the crisis itself, why should I dignify it by such a name? If it ever should happen—and certainly not tomorrow or the day after tomorrow, most likely never—that public opinion concerns itself with the affair, which, I must repeat, is beyond its competence, I certainly won't escape unharmed, but on the other hand people are bound to take into account that I am not unknown to the public, that I have lived for long in the full light of publicity, trustingly and trustworthily, and that this distressed little woman, this latecomer in my life, who, let me remark in passing, another man might have brushed off like a burr and privately trodden underfoot without a sound, that this woman at the very worst could add only an ugly little flourish to the diploma in which public opinion long ago certified me to be a respectable member of society. That is how things stand today, little likely to cause me any uneasiness.

The fact that in the course of years I have all the same become somewhat uneasy has nothing to do with the real significance of this affair; a man simply cannot endure being a continual target for someone's spite, even when he knows well enough that the spite is gratuitous;

he grows uneasy, he begins, in a kind of physical way only, to expect final decisions, even when like a sensible man he does not much believe that they are forthcoming. Partly, too, it is a symptom of increasing age; youth sheds a bloom over everything; awkward characteristics are lost to sight in the endless upwelling of youthful energy; if as a youth a man has a somewhat wary eye it is not counted against him, it is not noticed at all, even by himself; but the things that survive in old age are residues, each is necessary, none is renewed, each is under scrutiny, and the wary eye of an aging man is clearly a wary eye and is not difficult to recognize. Only, as also in this case, it is not an actual degeneration of his condition.

So from whatever standpoint I consider this small affair, it appears, and this I will stick to, that if I keep my hand over it, even quite lightly, I shall quietly continue to live my own life for a long time to come, untroubled by the world, despite all the outbursts of the woman.

A Hunger Artist

DURING THESE last decades the interest in professional fasting has markedly diminished. It used to pay very well to stage such great performances under one's own management, but today that is quite impossible. We live in a different world now. At one time the whole town took a lively interest in the hunger artist; from day to day of his fast the excitement mounted; everybody wanted to see him at least once a day; there were people who bought season tickets for the last few days and sat from morning till night in front of his small barred cage; even in the nighttime there were visiting hours, when the whole effect was heightened by torch flares; on fine days the cage was set out in the open air, and then it was the children's special treat to see the hunger artist; for their elders he was often just a joke that happened to be in fashion, but the children stood openmouthed, holding each other's hands for greater security, marveling at him as he sat there pallid in black tights, with his ribs sticking out so prominently, not even on a seat but down among straw on the ground, sometimes giving a courteous nod, answering questions with a constrained smile, or perhaps stretching an arm through the bars so that one might feel how thin it was, and then again withdrawing deep into himself, paying no attention to anyone or anything, not even to the all-important striking of the clock that was the only piece of furniture in his cage, but merely staring into vacancy with half-shut eyes, now and then taking a sip from a tiny glass of water to moisten his lips.

Besides casual onlookers there were also relays of permanent watchers selected by the public, usually butchers, strangely enough, and it was their task to watch the hunger artist day and night, three of them at a time, in case he should have some secret recourse to nourishment. This was nothing but a formality, instituted to reassure the masses, for the initiates knew well enough that during his fast the artist would never in any circumstances, not even under forcible compulsion, swallow the smallest morsel of food; the honor of his profession forbade it. Not every watcher, of course, was capable of understanding this, there were often groups of night watchers who were very lax in carrying out their duties and deliberately huddled together in a retired corner to play cards with great absorption, obviously intending to give the hunger artist the chance of a little refreshment, which they supposed he could draw from some private hoard. Nothing annoyed the artist more than such watchers; they made him miserable; they made his fast seem unendurable; sometimes he mastered his feebleness sufficiently to sing during their watch for as long as he could keep going, to show them how unjust their suspicions were. But that was of little use; they only wondered at his cleverness in being able to fill his mouth even while singing. Much more to his taste were the watchers who sat close up to the bars, who were not content with the dim night lighting of the hall but focused him in the full glare of the electric pocket torch given them by the impresario. The harsh light did not trouble him at all, in any case he could never sleep properly, and he could always drowse a little, whatever the light, at any hour, even when the hall was thronged with noisy onlookers. He was quite happy at the prospect of spending a sleepless night with such watchers; he was ready to exchange jokes with them, to tell them stories out of his nomadic life, anything at all to keep them awake and demonstrate to them again that he had no eatables in his cage and that he was fasting as not one of them could fast. But his happiest moment was when the morning came and an enormous breakfast was brought them, at his expense, on which they flung themselves with the keen appetite of healthy men after a weary night of wakefulness. Of course there were people who argued that this breakfast was an unfair attempt to bribe the watchers, but that was going rather too far, and when they were invited to take on a night's vigil without a breakfast, merely for the sake of the cause, they made themselves scarce, although they stuck stubbornly to their suspicions.

Such suspicions, anyhow, were a necessary accompaniment to the profession of fasting. No one could possibly watch the hunger artist continuously, day and night, and so no one could produce first-hand evidence that the fast had really been rigorous and continuous; only the artist himself could know that, he was therefore bound to be the sole completely satisfied spectator of his own fast. Yet for other reasons he was never satisfied; it was not perhaps mere fasting that had brought him to such skeleton thinness that many people had regretfully to keep away from his exhibitions, because the sight of him was too much for them, perhaps it was dissatisfaction with himself that had worn him down. For he alone knew, what no other initiate knew, how easy it was to fast. It was the easiest thing in the world. He made no secret of this, yet people did not believe him, at the best they set him down as modest, most of them, however, thought he was out for publicity or else was some kind of cheat who found it easy to fast because he had discovered a way of making it easy, and then had the impudence to admit the fact, more or less. He had to put up with all that, and in the course of time had got used to it, but his inner dissatisfaction always rankled, and never yet, after any term of fasting—this must be granted to his credit—had he left the cage of his own free will. The longest period of fasting was fixed by his impresario at forty days, beyond that term he was not allowed to go, not even in great cities, and there was good reason for it, too. Experience had proved that for about forty days the interest of the public could be stimulated

by a steadily increasing pressure of advertisement, but
after that the town began to lose interest, sympathetic
support began notably to fall off; there were of course
local variations as between one town and another or one
country and another, but as a general rule forty days
marked the limit. So on the fortieth day the flower-
bedecked cage was opened, enthusiastic spectators filled
the hall, a military band played, two doctors entered
the cage to measure the results of the fast, which were
announced through a megaphone, and finally two young
ladies appeared, blissful at having been selected for the
honor, to help the hunger artist down the few steps leading to a small table on which was spread a carefully
chosen invalid repast. And at this very moment the artist
always turned stubborn. True, he would entrust his
bony arms to the outstretched helping hands of the ladies
bending over him, but stand up he would not. Why stop
fasting at this particular moment, after forty days of it?
He had held out for a long time, an illimitably long time;
why stop now, when he was in his best fasting form, or
rather, not yet quite in his best fasting form? Why
should he be cheated of the fame he would get for fasting longer, for being not only the record hunger artist
of all time, which presumably he was already, but for
beating his own record by a performance beyond human imagination, since he felt that there were no limits
to his capacity for fasting? His public pretended to admire him so much, why should it have so little patience
with him; if he could endure fasting longer, why
shouldn't the public endure it? Besides, he was tired, he
was comfortable sitting in the straw, and now he was
supposed to lift himself to his full height and go down to
a meal the very thought of which gave him a nausea

that only the presence of the ladies kept him from be-
traying, and even that with an effort. And he looked up
into the eyes of the ladies who were apparently so
friendly and in reality so cruel, and shook his head,
which felt too heavy on its strengthless neck. But then
there happened yet again what always happened. The
impresario came forward, without a word—for the band
made speech impossible—lifted his arms in the air above
the artist, as if inviting Heaven to look down upon its
creature here in the straw, this suffering martyr, which
indeed he was, although in quite another sense; grasped
him round the emaciated waist, with exaggerated cau-
tion, so that the frail condition he was in might be appreciated; and committed him to the care of the blench-
ing ladies, not without secretly giving him a shaking so
that his legs and body tottered and swayed. The artist
now submitted completely; his head lolled on his breast
as if it had landed there by chance; his body was hol-
lowed out; his legs in a spasm of self-preservation clung
close to each other at the knees, yet scraped on the
ground as if it were not really solid ground, as if they
were only trying to find solid ground; and the whole
weight of his body, a featherweight after all, relapsed
onto one of the ladies, who, looking round for help and
panting a little—this post of honor was not at all what
she had expected it to be—first stretched her neck as far
as she could to keep her face at least free from contact
with the artist, then finding this impossible, and her
more fortunate companion not coming to her aid but
merely holding extended on her own trembling hand the
little bunch of knucklebones that was the artist's, to the
great delight of the spectators burst into tears and had
to be replaced by an attendant who had long been sta-

tioned in readiness. Then came the food, a little of which the impresario managed to get between the artist's lips, while he sat in a kind of half-fainting trance, to the accompaniment of cheerful patter designed to distract the public's attention from the artist's condition; after that, a toast was drunk to the public, supposedly prompted by a whisper from the artist in the impresario's ear; the band confirmed it with a mighty flourish, the spectators melted away, and no one had any cause to be dissatisfied with the proceedings, no one except the hunger artist himself, he only, as always.

So he lived for many years, with small regular intervals of recuperation, in visible glory, honored by the world, yet in spite of that troubled in spirit, and all the more troubled because no one would take his trouble seriously. What comfort could he possibly need? What more could he possibly wish for? And if some good-natured person, feeling sorry for him, tried to console him by pointing out that his melancholy was probably caused by fasting, it could happen, especially when he had been fasting for some time, that he reacted with an outburst of fury and to the general alarm began to shake the bars of his cage like a wild animal. Yet the impresario had a way of punishing these outbreaks which he rather enjoyed putting into operation. He would apologize publicly for the artist's behavior, which was only to be excused, he admitted, because of the irritability caused by fasting; a condition hardly to be understood by well-fed people; then by natural transition he went on to mention the artist's equally incomprehensible boast that he could fast for much longer than he was doing; he praised the high ambition, the good will, the great self-denial undoubtedly implicit in such a statement; and then quite simply countered it by bringing out photographs, which were also on sale to the public, showing the artist on the fortieth day of a fast lying in bed almost dead from exhaustion. This perversion of the truth, familiar to the artist though it was, always unnerved him afresh and proved too much for him. What was a consequence of the premature ending of his fast was here presented as the cause of it! To fight against this lack of understanding, against a whole world of non-understanding, was impossible. Time and again in good faith he stood by the bars listening to the impresario, but as soon as the photographs appeared he always let go and sank with a groan back on to his straw, and the reassured public could once more come close and gaze at him.

A few years later when the witnesses of such scenes called them to mind, they often failed to understand themselves at all. For meanwhile the aforementioned change in public interest had set in; it seemed to happen almost overnight; there may have been profound causes for it, but who was going to bother about that; at any rate the pampered hunger artist suddenly found himself deserted one fine day by the amusement seekers, who went streaming past him to other more favored attractions. For the last time the impresario hurried him over half Europe to discover whether the old interest might still survive here and there; all in vain; everywhere, as if by secret agreement, a positive revulsion from professional fasting was in evidence. Of course it could not really have sprung up so suddenly as all that, and many premonitory symptoms which had not been sufficiently remarked or suppressed during the rush and glitter of success now came retrospectively to mind, but it was now too late to take any countermeasures. Fasting would

surely come into fashion again at some future date, yet
that was no comfort for those living in the present.
What, then, was the hunger artist to do? He had been
applauded by thousands in his time and could hardly
come down to showing himself in a street booth at
village fairs, and as for adopting another profession,
he was not only too old for that but too fanatically
devoted to fasting. So he took leave of the impresario,
his partner in an unparalleled career, and hired himself
to a large circus; in order to spare his own feelings he
avoided reading the conditions of his contract.

A large circus with its enormous traffic in replacing
and recruiting men, animals and apparatus can always
find a use for people at any time, even for a hunger
artist, provided of course that he does not ask too much,
and in this particular case anyhow it was not only the
artist who was taken on but his famous and long-known
name as well, indeed considering the peculiar nature of
his performance, which was not impaired by advancing age, it could not be objected that here was an artist
past his prime, no longer at the height of his professional skill, seeking a refuge in some quiet corner of a
circus, on the contrary, the hunger artist averred that he
could fast as well as ever, which was entirely credible,
he even alleged that if he were allowed to fast as he
liked, and this was at once promised him without more
ado, he could astound the world by establishing a record
never yet achieved, a statement which certainly provoked a smile among the other professionals, since it
left out of account the change in public opinion, which
the hunger artist in his zeal conveniently forgot.

He had not, however, actually lost his sense of the
real situation and took it as a matter of course that he

and his cage should be stationed, not in the middle of
the ring as a main attraction, but outside, near the animal cages, on a site that was after all easily accessible.
Large and gaily painted placards made a frame for the
cage and announced what was to be seen inside it.
When the public came thronging out in the intervals
to see the animals, they could hardly avoid passing the
hunger artist's cage and stopping there for a moment,
perhaps they might even have stayed longer had not
those pressing behind them in the narrow gangway,
who did not understand why they should be held up
on their way towards the excitements of the menagerie,
made it impossible for anyone to stand gazing quietly
for any length of time. And that was the reason why the
hunger artist, who had of course been looking forward
to these visiting hours as the main achievement of his
life, began instead to shrink from them. At first he
could hardly wait for the intervals; it was exhilarating
to watch the crowds come streaming his way, until only
too soon—not even the most obstinate self-deception,
clung to almost consciously, could hold out against the
fact—the conviction was borne in upon him that these
people, most of them, to judge from their actions, again
and again, without exception, were all on their way to
the menagerie. And the first sight of them from the
distance remained the best. For when they reached his
cage he was at once deafened by the storm of shouting
and abuse that arose from the two contending factions,
which renewed themselves continuously, of those who
wanted to stop and stare at him—he soon began to dislike them more than the others—not out of real interest
but only out of obstinate self-assertiveness, and those
who wanted to go straight on to the animals. When

the first great rush was past, the stragglers came along, and these, whom nothing could have prevented from stopping to look at him as long as they had breath, raced past with long strides, hardly even glancing at him, in their haste to get to the menagerie in time. And all too rarely did it happen that he had a stroke of luck, when some father of a family fetched up before him with his children, pointed a finger at the hunger artist and explained at length what the phenomenon meant, telling stories of earlier years when he himself had watched similar but much more thrilling performances, and the children, still rather uncomprehending, since neither inside nor outside school had they been sufficiently prepared for this lesson—what did they care about fasting?—yet showed by the brightness of their intent eyes that new and better times might be coming. Perhaps, said the hunger artist to himself many a time, things would be a little better if his cage were set not quite so near the menagerie. That made it too easy for people to make their choice, to say nothing of what he suffered from the stench of the menagerie, the animals' restlessness by night, the carrying past of raw lumps of flesh for the beasts of prey, the roaring at feeding times, which depressed him continually. But he did not dare to lodge a complaint with the management; after all, he had the animals to thank for the troops of people who passed his cage, among whom there might always be one here and there to take an interest in him, and who could tell where they might seclude him if he called attention to his existence and thereby to the fact that, strictly speaking, he was only an impediment on the way to the menagerie.

A small impediment, to be sure, one that grew steadily

less. People grew familiar with the strange idea that they could be expected, in times like these, to take an interest in a hunger artist, and with this familiarity the verdict went out against him. He might fast as much as he could, and he did so; but nothing could save him now, people passed him by. Just try to explain to anyone the art of fasting! Anyone who has no feeling for it cannot be made to understand it. The fine placards grew dirty and illegible, they were torn down; the little notice board telling the number of fast days achieved, which at first was changed carefully every day, had long stayed at the same figure, for after the first few weeks even this small task seemed pointless to the staff; and so the artist simply fasted on and on, as he had once dreamed of doing, and it was no trouble to him, just as he had always foretold, but no one counted the days, no one, not even the artist himself, knew what records he was already breaking, and his heart grew heavy. And when once in a time some leisurely passer-by stopped, made merry over the old figure on the board and spoke of swindling, that was in its way the stupidest lie ever invented by indifference and inborn malice, since it was not the hunger artist who was cheating, he was working honestly, but the world was cheating him of his reward.

Many more days went by, however, and that too came to an end. An overseer's eye fell on the cage one day and he asked the attendants why this perfectly good cage should be left standing there unused with dirty straw inside it; nobody knew, until one man, helped out by the notice board, remembered about the hunger artist. They poked into the straw with sticks and found him in it. "Are you still fasting?" asked the overseer, "when on earth do you mean to stop?" "Forgive me, everybody," whispered the hunger artist; only the overseer, who had his ear to the bars, understood him. "Of course," said the overseer, and tapped his forehead with a finger to let the attendants know what state the man was in, "we forgive you." "I always wanted you to admire my fasting," said the hunger artist. "We do admire it," said the overseer, affably. "But you shouldn't admire it," said the hunger artist. "Well then we don't admire it," said the overseer, "but why shouldn't we admire it?" "Because I have to fast, I can't help it," said the hunger artist. "What a fellow you are," said the overseer, "and why can't you help it?" "Because," said the hunger artist, lifting his head a little and speaking, with his lips pursed, as if for a kiss, right into the overseer's ear, so that no syllable might be lost, "because I couldn't find the food I liked. If I had found it, believe me, I should have made no fuss and stuffed myself like you or anyone else." These were his last words, but in his dimming eyes remained the firm though no longer proud persuasion that he was still continuing to fast.

"Well, clear this out now!" said the overseer, and they buried the hunger artist, straw and all. Into the cage they put a young panther. Even the most insensitive felt it refreshing to see this wild creature leaping around the cage that had so long been dreary. The panther was all right. The food he liked was brought him without hesitation by the attendants; he seemed not even to miss his freedom; his noble body, furnished almost to the bursting point with all that it needed, seemed to carry freedom around with it too; somewhere in his jaws it seemed to lurk; and the joy of life streamed with such ardent passion from his throat that for the onlookers it was not easy to stand the shock of it. But they braced themselves, crowded round the cage, and did not want ever to move away.

Josephine the Singer, or the Mouse Folk

OUR SINGER is called Josephine. Anyone who has not heard her does not know the power of song. There is no one but is carried away by her singing, a tribute all the greater as we are not in general a music-loving race. Tranquil peace is the music we love best; our life is hard, we are no longer able, even on occasions when we have tried to shake off the cares of daily life, to rise to anything so high and remote from our usual routine as music. But we do not much lament that; we do not get even so far; a certain practical cunning, which admittedly we stand greatly in need of, we hold to be our greatest distinction, and with a smile born of such cunning we are wont to console ourselves for all shortcomings, even supposing—only it does not happen—that we were to yearn once in a way for the kind of bliss which music may provide. Josephine is the sole exception; she has a love for music and knows too how to transmit it; she is the only one; when she dies, music—who knows for how long—will vanish from our lives.

I have often thought about what this music of hers really means. For we are quite unmusical; how is it that we understand Josephine's singing or, since Josephine denies that, at least think we can understand it. The simplest answer would be that the beauty of her singing is so great that even the most insensitive cannot be deaf to it, but this answer is not satisfactory. If it were really so, her singing would have to give one an immediate and lasting feeling of being something out of the ordinary, a feeling that from her throat something is sounding which we have never heard before and which we are not even capable of hearing, something that Josephine alone and no one else can enable us to hear. But in my opinion that is just what does not happen, I do not feel this and have never observed that others feel anything of the kind. Among intimates we admit freely to one another that Josephine's singing, as singing, is nothing out of the ordinary.

Is it in fact singing at all? Although we are unmusical we have a tradition of singing; in the old days our people did sing; this is mentioned in legends and some songs have actually survived, which, it is true, no one can now sing. Thus we have an inkling of what singing is, and Josephine's art does not really correspond to it. So is it singing at all? Is it not perhaps just a piping? And piping is something we all know about, it is the real artistic accomplishment of our people, or rather no mere accomplishment but a characteristic expression of our life. We all pipe, but of course no one dreams of making out that our piping is an art, we pipe without thinking of it, indeed without noticing it, and there are even many among us who are quite unaware that piping is one of our characteristics. So if it were true that Josephine does not sing but only pipes and perhaps, as it seems to me at least, hardly rises above the level of our usual piping—yet, perhaps her strength is not even quite equal to our usual piping, whereas an ordinary farmhand can keep it up effortlessly all day long, besides doing his work—if that were all true, then indeed Josephine's alleged vocal skill might be disproved, but that would merely clear the ground for the real riddle which needs solving, the enormous influence she has.

After all, it is only a kind of piping that she produces. If you post yourself quite far away from her and listen, or, still better, put your judgment to the test, whenever she happens to be singing along with others, by trying to identify her voice, you will undoubtedly distinguish nothing but a quite ordinary piping tone, which at most differs a little from the others through being delicate or weak. Yet if you sit down before her, it is not merely a piping; to comprehend her art it is necessary not only to hear but to see her. Even if hers were only our usual workaday piping, there is first of all this peculiarity to consider, that here is someone making a ceremonial performance out of doing the usual thing. To crack a nut is truly no feat, so no one would ever dare to collect an audience in order to entertain it with nut-cracking. But if all the same one does do that and succeeds in entertaining the public, then it cannot be a matter of simple nut-cracking. Or it is a matter of nut-cracking, but it turns out that we have overlooked the art of cracking nuts because we were too skilled in it and that this newcomer to it first shows us its real nature, even finding it useful in making his effects to be rather less expert in nut-cracking than most of us.

Perhaps it is much the same with Josephine's singing; we admire in her what we do not at all admire in ourselves; in this respect, I may say, she is of one mind with us. I was once present when someone, as of course often happens, drew her attention to the folk piping everywhere going on, making only a modest reference to it, yet for Josephine that was more than enough. A smile so sarcastic and arrogant as she then assumed I

have never seen; she, who in appearance is delicacy itself, conspicuously so even among our people who are
prolific in such feminine types, seemed at that moment
actually vulgar; she was at once aware of it herself, by
the way, with her extreme sensibility, and controlled
herself. At any rate she denies any connection between
her art and ordinary piping. For those who are of the
contrary opinion she has only contempt and probably
unacknowledged hatred. This is not simple vanity, for
the opposition, with which I too am half in sympathy,
certainly admires her no less than the crowd does, but
Josephine does not want mere admiration, she wants
to be admired exactly in the way she prescribes, mere
admiration leaves her cold. And when you take a seat
before her, you understand her; opposition is possible
only at a distance, when you sit before her, you know:
this piping of hers is no piping.

Since piping is one of our thoughtless habits, one
might think that people would pipe up in Josephine's
audience too; her art makes us feel happy, and when
we are happy we pipe; but her audience never pipes, it
sits in mouselike stillness; as if we had become par-
takers in the peace we long for, from which our own
piping at the very least holds us back, we make no
sound. Is it her singing that enchants us or is it not
rather the solemn stillness enclosing her frail little voice?
Once it happened while Josephine was singing that some
silly little thing in all innocence began to pipe up too.
Now it was just the same as what we were hearing from
Josephine; in front of us the piping sound that despite
all rehearsal was still tentative and here in the audience
the unself-conscious piping of a child; it would have
been impossible to define the difference; but yet at once

we hissed and whistled the interrupter down, although
it would not really have been necessary, for in any case
she would certainly have crawled away in fear and
shame, whereas Josephine struck up her most triumphal
notes and was quite beyond herself, spreading her arms
wide and stretching her throat as high as it could reach.

That is what she is like always, every trifle, every
casual incident, every nuisance, a creaking in the par-
quet, a grinding of teeth, a failure in the lighting incites
her to heighten the effectiveness of her song; she believes anyhow that she is singing to deaf ears; there is
no lack of enthusiasm and applause, but she has long
 learned not to expect real understanding, as she con-
ceives it. So all disturbance is very welcome to her;
whatever intervenes from outside to hinder the purity of
her song, to be overcome with a slight effort, even with
no effort at all, merely by confronting it, can help to
awaken the masses, to teach them not perhaps understanding but awed respect.

And if small events do her such service, how much
more do great ones. Our life is very uneasy, every day
brings surprises, apprehensions, hopes and terrors, so
that it would be impossible for a single individual to
bear it all did he not always have by day and night the
support of his fellows; but even so it often becomes very
difficult; frequently as many as a thousand shoulders
are trembling under a burden that was really meant
only for one pair. Then Josephine holds that her time
has come. So there she stands, the delicate creature,
shaken by vibrations especially below the breastbone, so
that one feels anxious for her, it is as if she has concentrated all her strength on her song, as if from everything in her that does not directly subserve her singing

all strength has been withdrawn, almost all power of
life, as if she were laid bare, abandoned, committed
merely to the care of good angels, as if while she is so
wholly withdrawn and living only in her song a cold
breath blowing upon her might kill her. But just when
she makes such an appearance, we who are supposed
to be her opponents are in the habit of saying: "She
can't even pipe; she has to put such a terrible strain on
herself to force out not a song—we can't call it song—
but some approximation to our usual customary piping."
So it seems to us, but this impression although, as I said,
inevitable is yet fleeting and transient. We too are soon
sunk in the feeling of the mass, that, warmly pressed
body to body, listens with indrawn breath.

And to gather around her this mass of our people who
are almost always on the run and scurrying hither and
thither for reasons that are often not very clear,
Josephine mostly needs to do nothing else than take up
her stand, head thrown back, mouth half open, eyes
turned upwards, in the position that indicates her intention to sing. She can do this where she likes, it need
not be a place visible a long way off, any secluded
corner pitched on in a moment's caprice will serve as
well. The news that she is going to sing flies round at
once and soon whole processions are on the way there.
Now, sometimes, all the same, obstacles intervene,
Josephine likes best to sing just when things are most
upset, many worries and dangers force us then to take
devious ways, with the best will in the world we cannot assemble ourselves as quickly as Josephine wants,
and on occasion she stands there in ceremonial state for
quite a time without a sufficient audience—then indeed
she turns furious, then she stamps her feet, swearing in

most unmaidenly fashion; she actually bites. But even
such behavior does no harm to her reputation; instead
of curbing a little her excessive demands, people exert
themselves to meet them; messengers are sent out to
summon fresh hearers; she is kept in ignorance of the
fact that this is being done; on the roads all around
sentries can be seen posted who wave on newcomers
and urge them to hurry; this goes on until at last a
tolerably large audience is gathered.

What drives the people to make such exertions for
Josephine's sake? This is no easier to answer than the
first question about Josephine's singing, with which it
is closely connected. One could eliminate that and combine them both in the second question, if it were possible to assert that because of her singing our people are
unconditionally devoted to Josephine. But this is simply not the case; unconditional devotion is hardly
known among us; ours are people who love slyness beyond everything, without any malice, to be sure, and
childish whispering and chatter, innocent, superficial
chatter, to be sure, but people of such a kind cannot go
in for unconditional devotion, and that Josephine herself certainly feels, that is what she is fighting against
with all the force of her feeble throat.

In making such generalized pronouncements, of
course, one should not go too far, our people are all
the same devoted to Josephine, only not unconditionally.
For instance, they would not be capable of laughing at
Josephine. It can be admitted: in Josephine there is
much to make one laugh; and laughter for its own sake
is never far away from us; in spite of all the misery of
our lives quiet laughter is always, so to speak, at our
elbows; but we do not laugh at Josephine. Many a time

I have had the impression that our people interpret their relationship to Josephine in this way, that she, this frail creature, needing protection and in some way remarkable, in her own opinion remarkable for her gift of song, is entrusted to their care and they must look after her; the reason for this is not clear to anyone, only the fact seems to be established. But what is entrusted to one's care one does not laugh at; to laugh would be a breach of duty; the utmost malice which the most malicious of us wreak on Josephine is to say now and then: "The sight of Josephine is enough to make one stop laughing."

So the people look after Josephine much as a father takes into his care a child whose little hand—one cannot tell whether in appeal or command—is stretched out to him. One might think that our people are not fitted to exercise such paternal duties, but in reality they discharge them, at least in this case, admirably; no single individual could do what in this respect the people as a whole are capable of doing. To be sure, the difference in strength between the people and the individual is so enormous that it is enough for the nursling to be drawn into the warmth of their nearness and he is sufficiently protected. To Josephine, certainly, one does not dare mention such ideas. "Your protection isn't worth an old song," she says then. Sure, sure, old song, we think. And besides her protest is no real contradiction, it is rather a thoroughly childish way of doing, and childish gratitude, while a father's way of doing is to pay no attention to it.

Yet there is something else behind it which is not so easy to explain by this relationship between the people and Josephine. Josephine, that is to say, thinks just the opposite, she believes it is she who protects the people.

When we are in a bad way politically or economically, her singing is supposed to save us, nothing less than that, and if it does not drive away the evil, at least gives us the strength to bear it. She does not put it in these words or in any other, she says very little anyhow, she is silent among the chatterers, but it flashes from her eyes, on her closed lips—few among us can keep their lips closed, but she can—it is plainly legible. Whenever we get bad news—and on many days bad news comes thick and fast at once, lies and half-truths included— she rises up at once, whereas usually she sits listlessly on the ground, she rises up and stretches her neck and tries to see over the heads of her flock like a shepherd before a thunderstorm. It is certainly a habit of children, in their wild, impulsive fashion, to make such claims, but Josephine's are not quite so unfounded as children's. True, she does not save us and she gives us no strength; it is easy to stage oneself as a savior of our people, in- ured as they are to suffering, not sparing themselves, swift in decision, well acquainted with death, timorous only to the eye in the atmosphere of reckless daring which they constantly breathe, and as prolific besides as they are bold—it is easy, I say, to stage oneself after the event as the savior of our people, who have always somehow managed to save themselves, although at the cost of sacrifices which make historians—generally speaking we ignore historical research entirely—quite horror-struck. And yet it is true that just in emergen- cies we hearken better than at other times to Josephine's voice. The menaces that loom over us make us quieter, more humble, more submissive to Josephine's domina- tion; we like to come together, we like to huddle close to each other, especially on an occasion set apart from the

troubles preoccupying us; it is as if we were drinking in
all haste—yes, haste is necessary, Josephine too often
forgets that—from a cup of peace in common before
the battle. It is not so much a performance of songs as
an assembly of the people, and an assembly where except for the small piping voice in front there is complete stillness; the hour is much too grave for us to
waste it in chatter.

A relationship of this kind, of course, would never
content Josephine. Despite all the nervous uneasiness
that fills Josephine because her position has never been
quite defined, there is still much that she does not see,
blinded by her self-conceit, and she can be brought
fairly easily to overlook much more, a swarm of flatterers is always busy about her to this end, thus really
doing a public service—and yet to be only an incidental,
unnoticed performer in a corner of an assembly of the
people, for that, although in itself it would be no small
thing, she would certainly not make us the sacrifice of
her singing.

Nor does she need to, for her art does not go unnoticed. Although we are at bottom preoccupied with
quite other things and it is by no means only for the
sake of her singing that stillness prevails and many a
listener does not even look up but buries his face in his
neighbor's fur, so that Josephine up in front seems to
be exerting herself to no purpose, there is yet something—it cannot be denied—that irresistibly makes its
way into us from Josephine's piping. This piping, which
rises up where everyone else is pledged to silence, comes
almost like a message from the whole people to each
individual; Josephine's thin piping amidst grave decisions
is almost like our people's precarious existence amidst

the tumult of a hostile world. Josephine exerts herself, a mere nothing in voice, a mere nothing in execution, she asserts herself and gets across to us; it does us good to think of that. A really trained singer, if ever such a one should be found among us, we could certainly not endure at such a time and we should unanimously turn away from the senselessness of any such performance. May Josephine be spared from perceiving that the mere fact of our listening to her is proof that she is no singer. An intuition of it she must have, else why does she so passionately deny that we do listen, only she keeps on singing and piping her intuition away.

But there are other things she could take comfort from: we do really listen to her in a sense, probably much as one listens to a trained singer; she gets effects which a trained singer would try in vain to achieve among us and which are only produced precisely because her means are so inadequate. For this, doubtless, our way of life is mainly responsible.

Among our people there is no age of youth, scarcely the briefest childhood. Regularly, it is true, demands are put forward that the children should be granted a special freedom, a special protection, that their right to be a little carefree, to have a little senseless giddiness, a little play, that this right should be respected and the exercise of it encouraged; such demands are put forward and nearly everyone approves them, there is nothing one could approve more, but there is also nothing, in the reality of our daily life, that is less likely to be granted, one approves these demands, one makes attempts to meet them, but soon all the old ways are back again. Our life happens to be such that a child, as soon as it can run about a little and a little distinguish one thing from another, must look after itself just like an adult; the areas on which, for economic reasons, we have to live in dispersion are too wide, our enemies too numerous, the dangers lying everywhere in wait for us too incalculable—we cannot shelter our children from the struggle for existence, if we did so, it would bring them to an early grave. These depressing considerations are reinforced by another, which is not depressing: the fertility of our race. One generation—and each is numerous—treads on the heels of another, the children have no time to be children. Other races may foster their children carefully, schools may be erected for their little ones, out of these schools the children may come pouring daily, the future of the race, yet among them it is always the same children that come out day after day for a long time. We have no schools, but from our race come pouring at the briefest intervals the innumerable swarms of our children, merrily lisping or chirping so long as they cannot yet pipe, rolling or tumbling along by sheer impetus so long as they cannot yet run, clumsily carrying everything before them by mass weight so long as they cannot yet see, our children! And not the same children, as in those schools, no, always new children again and again, without end, without a break, hardly does a child appear than it is no more a child, while behind it new childish faces are already crowding so fast and so thick that they are indistinguishable, rosy with happiness. Truly, however delightful this may be and however much others may envy us for it, and rightly, we simply cannot give a real childhood to our children. And that has its consequences. A kind of unexpended, ineradicable childishness pervades our people; in direct opposition to what is best in us, our

No room for development [handwritten marginal note]

infallible practical common sense, we often behave with
the utmost foolishness, with exactly the same foolishness as children, senselessly, wastefully, grandiosely, ir-
responsibly, and all that often for the sake of some
trivial amusement. And although our enjoyment of it
cannot of course be so wholehearted as a child's enjoyment, something of this survives in it without a doubt.
From this childishness of our people Josephine too has
profited since the beginning.

Yet our people are not only childish, we are also in a
sense prematurely old. Childhood and old age come
upon us not as upon others. We have no youth, we are
all at once grown-up, and then we stay grown-up too
long, a certain weariness and hopelessness spreading
from that leaves a broad trail through our people's nature, tough and strong in hope that it is in general. Our
lack of musical gifts has surely some connection with
this; we are too old for music, its excitement, its rapture do not suit our heaviness, wearily we wave it away;
we content ourselves with piping; a little piping here and
there, that is enough for us. Who knows, there may be
talents for music among us; but if there were, the character of our people would suppress them before they
could unfold. Josephine on the other hand can pipe as
much as she will, or sing or whatever she likes to call
it, that does not disturb us, that suits us, that we can
well put up with; any music there may be in it is reduced to the least possible trace; a certain tradition of
music is preserved, yet without making the slightest demand upon us.

But our people, being what they are, get still more
than this from Josephine. At her concerts, especially in
times of stress, it is only the very young who are in-

terested in her singing as singing, they alone gaze in astonishment as she purses her lips, expels the air between her pretty front teeth, swoons in sheer wonderment at the sounds she herself is producing and after such a lying away swells her performance to new and more incredible heights, whereas the real mass of the people—this is plain to see—are quite withdrawn into themselves. Here in the brief intervals between their struggles our people dream, it is as if the limbs of each were loosened, as if the harried individual once in a while could relax and stretch himself at ease in the great, warm bed of the community. And into these dreams Josephine's piping drops note by note; she calls it pearl-like, we call it staccato; but at any rate here it is in its right place, as nowhere else, finding the moment wait for it as music scarcely ever does. Something of our poor brief childhood is in it, something of lost happiness that can never be found again, but also something of active daily life, of its small gaieties, unaccountable and yet springing up and not to be obliterated. And indeed this is all expressed not in full round tones but softly, in whispers, confidentially, sometimes a little hoarsely. Of course it is a kind of piping. Why not? Piping is our people's daily speech, only many a one pipes his whole life long and does not know it, where here piping is set free from the fetters of daily life and it sets us free too for a little while. We certainly should not want to do without these performances.

But from that point it is a long, long way to Josephine's claim that she gives us new strength and so on and so forth. For ordinary people, at least, not for her train of flatterers. "What other explanation could there be?"—they say with quite shameless sauciness—"how

else could you explain the great audiences, especially
when danger is most imminent, which have even often
enough hindered proper precautions being taken in time
to avert danger." Now, this last statement is unfortunately true, but can hardly be counted as one of
Josephine's titles to fame, especially considering that
when such large gatherings have been unexpectedly
flushed by the enemy and many of our people left lying
for dead, Josephine, who was responsible for it all, and
indeed perhaps attracted the enemy by her piping, has
always occupied the safest place and was always the
first to whisk away quietly and speedily under cover of
her escort. Still, everyone really knows that, and yet
people keep running to whatever place Josephine decides on next, at whatever time she rises up to sing. One
could argue from this that Josephine stands almost beyond the law, that she can do what she pleases, at the
risk of actually endangering the community, and will
be forgiven for everything. If this were so, even
Josephine's claims would be entirely comprehensible,
yes, in this freedom to be allowed her, this extraordinary
gift granted to her and to no one else in direct contra-
vention of the laws, one could see an admission of the
fact that the people do not understand Josephine, just
as she alleges, that they marvel helplessly at her art, feel
themselves unworthy of it, try to assuage the pity she
rouses in them by making really desperate sacrifices for
her and, to the same extent that her art is beyond their
comprehension, consider her personality and her wishes
to lie beyond their jurisdiction. Well, that is simply not
true at all, perhaps as individuals the people may sur-
render too easily to Josephine, but as a whole they sur-
render unconditionally to no one, and not to her either.

For a long time back, perhaps since the very beginning of her artistic career, Josephine has been fighting
for exemption from all daily work on account of her
singing; she should be relieved of all responsibility for
earning her daily bread and being involved in the general struggle for existence, which—apparently—should be
transferred on her behalf to the people as a whole. A
facile enthusiast—and there have been such—might argue
from the mere unusualness of this demand, from the
spiritual attitude needed to frame such a demand, that it
has an inner justification. But our people draw other conclusions and quietly refuse it. Nor do they trouble much
about disproving the assumptions on which it is based.
Josephine argues, for instance, that the strain of working
is bad for her voice, that the strain of working is of
course nothing to the strain of singing, but it prevents
her from being able to rest sufficiently after singing and
to recuperate for more singing, she has to exhaust her
strength completely and yet, in these circumstances,
can never rise to the peak of her abilities. The people
listen to her arguments and pay no attention. Our people, so easily moved, sometimes cannot be moved at all.
Their refusal is sometimes so decided that even Josephine is taken aback, she appears to submit, does her
proper share of work, sings as best she can, but all only
for a time, then with renewed strength—for this purpose her strength seems inexhaustible—she takes up the
fight again.

Now it is clear that what Josephine really wants is not
what she puts into words. She is honorable, she is not
work-shy, shirking in any case is quite unknown among
us, if her petition were granted she would certainly live
the same life as before, her work would not at all get

in the way of her singing nor would her singing grow
any better—what she wants is public, unambiguous, permanent recognition of her art, going far beyond any
precedent so far known. But while almost everything
else seems within her reach, this eludes her persistently.
Perhaps she should have taken a different line of attack
from the beginning, perhaps she herself sees that her
approach was wrong, but now she cannot draw back,
retreat would be self-betrayal, now she must stand or
fall by her petition.

If she really had enemies, as she avers, they could get
much amusement from watching this struggle, without
having to lift a finger. But she has no enemies, and
even though she is often criticized here and there, no
one finds this struggle of hers amusing. Just because
of the fact that the people show themselves here in their
cold, judicial aspect, which is otherwise rarely seen
among us. And however one may approve it in this
case, the very idea that such an aspect might be turned
upon oneself some day prevents amusement from breaking in. The important thing, both in the people's refusal and in Josephine's petition, is not the action itself,
but the fact that the people are capable of presenting a
stony, impenetrable front to one of their own, and that
it is all the more impenetrable because in other respects
they show an anxious paternal care, and more than
paternal care, for this very member of the people.

Suppose that instead of the people one had an individual to deal with: one might imagine that this man
had been giving in to Josephine all the time while nurs-
ing a wild desire to put an end to his submissiveness one
fine day; that he had made superhuman sacrifices for
Josephine in the firm belief that there was a natural limit

to his capacity for sacrifice; yes, that he had sacrificed
more than was needful merely to hasten the process,
merely to spoil Josephine and encourage her to ask for
more and more until she did indeed reach the limit
with this last petition of hers; and that he then cut her
off with a final refusal which was curt because long held
in reserve. Now, this is certainly not how the matter
stands, the people have no need of such guile, besides,
their respect for Josephine is well tried and genuine,
and Josephine's demands are after all so far-reaching
that any simple child could have told her what the outcome would be; yet it may be that such considerations
enter into Josephine's way of taking the matter and so
add a certain bitterness to the pain of being refused.

But whatever her ideas on the subject, she does not
let them deter her from pursuing the campaign. Recently she has even intensified her attack; hitherto she
has used only words as her weapons but now she is
beginning to have recourse to other means, which she
thinks will prove more efficacious but which we think
will run her into greater dangers.

Many believe that Josephine is becoming so insistent
because she feels herself growing old and her voice
falling off, and so she thinks it high time to wage the
last battle for recognition. I do not believe it. Josephine
would not be Josephine if that were true. For her there
is no growing old and no falling off in her voice. If
she makes demands it is not because of outward circumstances but because of an inner logic. She reaches for
the highest garland not because it is momentarily hanging a little lower but because it is the highest; if she
had any say in the matter she would have it still higher.

This contempt for external difficulties, to be sure,

does not hinder her from using the most unworthy methods. Her rights seem beyond question to her; so what does it matter how she secures them; especially since in this world, as she sees it, honest methods are bound to fail. Perhaps that is why she has transferred the battle for her rights from the field of song to another which she cares little about. Her supporters have let it be known that, according to herself, she feels quite capable of singing in such a way that all levels of the populace, even to the remotest corners of the opposition, would find it a real delight, a real delight not by popular standards, for the people affirm that they have always delighted in her singing, but a delight by her own standards. However, she adds, since she cannot falsify the highest standards nor pander to the lowest, her singing will have to stay as it is. But when it comes to her campaign for exemption from work, we get a different story; it is of course also a campaign on behalf of her singing, yet she is not fighting directly with the priceless weapon of her song, so any instrument she uses is good enough. Thus, for instance, the rumor went round that Josephine meant to cut short her grace notes if her petition were not granted. I know nothing about grace notes, and have never noticed any in Josephine's singing. But Josephine is going to cut short her grace notes, not, for the present, to cut them out entirely, only to cut them short. Presumably she has carried out her threat, although I for one have observed no difference in her performance. The people as a whole listened in the usual way without making any pronouncement on the grace notes, nor did their response to her petition vary by a jot. It must be admitted that Josephine's way of thinking, like her figure, is often very charming.

And so, for instance, after that performance, just as if
her decision about the grace notes had been too severe
or too sudden a move against the people, she announced
that next time she would put in all the grace notes again.
Yet after the next concert she changed her mind once
more, there was to be definitely an end of these great
arias with the grace notes, and until her petition was
favorably regarded they would never recur. Well, the
people let all these announcements, decisions and coun-
terdecisions go in at one ear and out at the other, like a
grown-up person deep in thought turning a deaf ear to
a child's babble, fundamentally well disposed but not
accessible.

Josephine, however, does not give in. The other day,
for instance, she claimed that she had hurt her foot at
work, so that it was difficult for her to stand up to
sing; but since she could not sing except standing up,
her songs would now have to be cut short. Although
she limps and leans on her supporters, no one believes
that she is really hurt. Granted that her frail body is
extra sensitive, she is yet one of us and we are a race
of workers; if we were to start limping every time we
got a scratch, the whole people would never be done
limping. Yet though she lets herself be led about like a
cripple, though she shows herself in this pathetic condition oftener than usual, the people all the same listen
to her singing thankfully and appreciatively as before,
but do not bother much about the shortening of her
songs.

Since she cannot very well go on limping forever, she
thinks of something else, she pleads that she is tired, not
in the mood for singing, feeling faint. And so we get
a theatrical performance as well as a concert. We see

Josephine's supporters in the background begging and imploring her to sing. She would be glad to oblige, but she cannot. They comfort and caress her with flatteries, they almost carry her to the selected spot where she is supposed to sing. At last, bursting inexplicably into tears, she gives way, but when she stands up to sing, obviously at the end of her resources, weary, her arms not widespread as usual but hanging lifelessly down, so that one gets the impression that they are perhaps a little too short—just as she is about to strike up, there, she cannot do it after all, an unwilling shake of the head tells us so and she breaks down before our eyes. To be sure, she pulls herself together again and sings, I fancy, much as usual; perhaps, if one has an ear for the finer shades of expression, one can hear that she is singing with unusual feeling, which is, however, all to the good. And in the end she is actually less tired than before, with a firm tread, if one can use such a term for her tripping gait, she moves off, refusing all help from her supporters and measuring with cold eyes the crowd which respectfully makes way for her.

That happened a day or two ago; but the latest is that she has disappeared, just at a time when she was supposed to sing. It is not only her supporters who are looking for her, many are devoting themselves to the search, but all in vain; Josephine has vanished, she will not sing; she will not even be cajoled into singing, this time she has deserted us entirely.

Curious, how mistaken she is in her calculations, the clever creature, so mistaken that one might fancy she has made no calculations at all but is only being driven on by her destiny, which in our world cannot be anything but a sad one. Of her own accord she abandons

her singing, of her own accord she destroys the power
she has gained over people's hearts. How could she ever
have gained that power, since she knows so little about
these hearts of ours? She hides herself and does not sing,
but our people, quietly, without visible disappointment,
a self-confident mass in perfect equilibrium, so consti-
tuted, even although appearances are misleading, that
they can only bestow gifts and not receive them, even
from Josephine, our people continue on their way.

Josephine's road, however, must go downhill. The
time will soon come when her last notes sound and die
into silence. She is a small episode in the eternal history
of our people, and the people will get over the loss of
her. Not that it will be easy for us; how can our gatherings take place in utter silence? Still, were they not
silent even when Josephine was present? Was her actual
piping notably louder and more alive than the memory
of it will be? Was it even in her lifetime more than a
simple memory? Was it not rather because Josephine's
singing was already past losing in this way that our
people in their wisdom prized it so highly?

So perhaps we shall not miss so very much after all,
while Josephine, redeemed from the earthly sorrows
which to her thinking lay in wait for all chosen spirits,
will happily lose herself in the numberless throng of the
heroes of our people, and soon, since we are no historians,
will rise to the heights of redemption and be forgotten
like all her brothers.

APPENDIX

The First Long Train Journey

BY MAX BROD AND FRANZ KAFKA

OF THE travel diary we had planned to do together only one chapter was written, which was published in the *Herderblätter* (Prague 1912). The following foreword served as introduction:

Under the title "Richard and Samuel—A Short Journey through Central European Regions," the parallel traveling diaries of two friends of widely differing character are to be included in one small volume.

Samuel is a young man of the world who takes very seriously his ambition to acquire knowledge in the grand style and an informed judgment on all matters of life and art, without becoming dry or in any way pedantic. Richard has no definite sphere of interest, lets himself drift along at the mercy of unaccountable feelings and still more of his weakness, but within his limited and casual experience shows so much intensity and naïve independence that he never declines into a whimsical comic figure. By profession Samuel is the secretary of an art society, Richard a bank clerk. Samuel has private means, and has taken up a profession only because he thinks he cannot stand an idle life; Richard has to support himself by his work, which is incidentally successful and much appreciated.

This particular journey is the first occasion on which these two, although schoolfellows, have been alone together for any length of time. They appreciate each other, although they seem incomprehensible to each other. They are attracted and repelled in varying ways. A description is given of how this relationship first flares up into a feverish intimacy, then after many incidents in the dangerous setting of Milan and Paris quietens down into a mutual manly understanding and becomes firmly established. The journey concludes with both friends pooling their talents in a new, original, artistic venture.

The purpose of this work is to describe the many gradations possible in a friendship between two men and at the same time to turn a double light, from two different angles, upon the countries traveled through, and by this means to present them with a freshness and significance too often unjustly reserved for exotic regions only.

Prague—Zurich

SAMUEL: Departure 26.VIII.1911, 1.2 P.M.

RICHARD: The sight of Samuel making some brief entry in his usual tiny pocket diary suggests again my good old idea that each of us should keep a journal of this expedition. I mention it to him. He first dissents, then agrees, each time giving reasons which each time I have the vaguest understanding of, but that doesn't matter, if only we keep the journals.—Now he's having another good laugh at my notebook which, being bound all in black linen, new, very big, squarish, does look rather like a school exercise book. I know beforehand that it's going to be difficult and in any case a nuisance to carry this book in my pocket all through the journey. Still, I can buy a handier one in Zurich along with him. He has a fountain pen, too. I'll borrow that now and then.

SAMUEL: In a station just opposite our window a carriage full of peasant women. On the lap of one who is laughing another is sleeping. Wakening up, she waves to us, suggestively, in her half-asleep state, "Come on." As if she were mocking us for not being able to get across. In the next compartment a dark, heroic type, quite immobile. Her head is leaning right back and she looks out along the windowpane. Delphic sibyl.

RICHARD: But what I don't like is the way he greets the peasant women, in a wheedling, falsely gallant, almost toadying manner. Now the train is moving off, and Samuel is left in the lurch waving his cap and cracking his face in a much too wide smile.—Or am I exaggerating?—Samuel reads me the note he has just made, it impresses me a lot. I should have paid more attention to the peasant women.—The guard asks, and does it very indistinctly, as if he expects all the passengers to have traveled this stretch of the line often, whether anyone wants a coffee at Pilsen. If you order one, he sticks a small green ticket for each order on the compartment window, like what they used to do in Misdroy, before there was a landing jetty, when the steamers, far off, ran up pennants to show how many boats would be needed to land passengers. Samuel does not know Misdroy at all. Pity I didn't go there with him. That time was lovely. This time will be marvelous too. The journey is too fast, it passes too quickly; what a yearning I have now for long journeys!—How out-of-date is the comparison I have just made, for there has been a jetty at Misdroy the last five years.—Coffee in Pilsen on the platform. You don't need to take it if you have a ticket and you can get it without a ticket at all.

SAMUEL: From the platform we see an unknown girl looking out from our compartment, who turns out later to be a Dora Lippert. Pretty, broad-nosed, small neck-opening in a white lace blouse. First mutual experience as journey goes on; her large hat in its paper bag lightly floats off the rack and comes down on my head. —We learn that she is the daughter of an officer transferred to Innsbruck and is traveling to visit her parents, whom she hasn't seen for a long time. She works in an engineering office in Pilsen, all day long, has a lot to do, but she enjoys it, she is very happy in her life. In the office they call her: our pet chicken, our little swallow. She's the youngest there among a lot of men. Oh, it's great fun in the office! You change people's hats in the cloakroom, nail morning rolls to the desk or glue pens to the writing block. We too have the chance to play such a "gorgeous" trick. She is writing a postcard to her colleagues in the office, which says: "Sorry to say the worst has happened after all. I got into the wrong train and here I am in Zurich. Warmest greetings." We are to post the card in Zurich. But since we are "men of honor" she trusts us to add nothing to it. In the office they will be worried, of course, they will send telegrams and God knows what else.—She is a Wagner devotee, never misses a Wagner performance, "You should have seen Kurz the other day as Isolde," she's

just reading the Wagner-Wesendonck letters, she's
taking the book with her to Innsbruck, a gentleman
lent it to her, the one who plays her all the piano scores,
of course. She herself unfortunately has little talent for
the piano, but we know that already since she has
hummed over some leitmotifs to us.—She collects choco-
late papers, and she's making a big ball of silver paper,
which she has with her too. This ball is to be given to a
girl friend, its further use not stated. And she collects
cigar bands, quite certainly for a tray.—The appearance
of the first Bavarian train guard prompts her to give us
the benefit of her opinions on Austrian soldiers and soldiers in general, briefly and most dogmatically, somewhat contradictory and ambiguous opinions for an officer's daughter. She regards not only the Austrian Army
as slack, but the German Army too, and all army men
anywhere. But doesn't she rush to the office window
when a military band goes past? She just doesn't, because they're not really military. Her youngest sister,
now, is quite different. She's always dancing in the
Innsbruck Officers' Casino. But as for herself, uniforms
don't impress her in the very least and officers don't
mean a thing to her. Obviously the gentleman who lends
her the piano scores is partly responsible for this, but
partly too our strolling up and down together on the
platform at the Fürth station, for she feels it so refreshing to walk after sitting still and smooths her hips
down with the palms of her hands. Richard sticks up for
the Army, but quite seriously.—Her favorite expres-
sions: gorgeous—with 0.5 acceleration—to fire out—
prompt—slack.

RICHARD: Dora L. has round cheeks with much blond
down on them; but they are so bloodless that one would

have to press them a long time with one's fingers before they showed a flush. Her corset is bad, the edge of it across her bosom rumples her blouse; one has to overlook that.

I am glad to be sitting opposite and not beside her, since I can't talk to anyone who is sitting beside me. Samuel, for instance, rather prefers to sit beside me; he likes sitting beside Dora, too. I on the other hand feel it like an inquisition when anyone sits beside me. After all, one doesn't have an eye in readiness for such a person, one has first to turn one's eyes round to meet his. True, I am sometimes left out of the conversation between Dora and Samuel because I'm on the opposite seat, especially when the train is in motion; one can't have all the advantages. Still, I've already seen them sitting side by side in silence, though only a moment or two at a time; of course, through no fault of mine.

I admire her; she is so musical. Samuel, I know, seems to be smiling ironically as she hums something over to him. Perhaps it wasn't quite correct, but anyhow, is it not admirable for a girl all on her own in a big city to be so warmly interested in music? She has even rented a piano and had it brought to her room, which is just a rented room too. Only imagine: such a complicated transaction as the transport of a piano (piano-forte!), which makes difficulties even for whole families, and one frail girl! How much independence and decision that involves!

I ask her about her living arrangements. She lives with two girl friends, one of them always buys their supper in a provision shop, they have a good time together and laugh a lot. That this all takes place by the light of a petrol lamp strikes me as queer when I hear it, but I don't like to say so. Evidently the bad lighting can't matter to her, for with energy like hers she could certainly extort a better light from the landlady if it ever once occurred to her.

Since in the course of conversation she has to show us everything in her handbag, we see a medicine bottle too with something nasty and yellow in it. It turns out now that she is not quite well, was even ill for a long time. And after the illness she was still rather run-down. The Chief himself advised her (they are so decent to her) that she should come to the office only for half-days. She's getting on better now, but she has to take this iron mixture. I counsel her rather to throw it out of the window. She quite agrees with me (for the stuff has an abominable taste) but cannot be brought to take me seriously, although I, bending forward to her nearer than before, try to expound my ideas, which in this respect are clear enough, about nature treatment for the human organism, and all with the honest intention of being helpful, or at least of saving from harm a girl who knows no better, and so for a long moment feel myself as a lucky Providence for this girl.—Since she keeps on laughing, I stop. It didn't do me any good either that Samuel has been shaking his head all through my lecture. I know him. He believes in doctors and thinks nature cure treatment ridiculous. I understand very well why: he has never needed a doctor and so has never had serious thoughts of his own about such things, for instance he can't put himself in the place of anyone taking this disgusting mixture.—If I had been alone with the girl, I'd have convinced her all right. For: if I'm not right in this, I'm right in nothing!

The cause of her anemia has been clear enough to

me from the very beginning. The office. Like everything else, an office life can be taken as a joke (and the girl honestly sees it as a joke, she is completely taken in), but in its essence, in its unhappy consequences!?—I know for myself what I'm talking about. And think of a poor girl sitting in an office, her very skirt isn't made for the job, what a strain is put upon it having to shift to and fro all the time for hours on a hard wooden chair. And so these round bottoms are galled, and the breasts too against the edge of the desk.—An exaggeration?—Well, a girl in an office is a depressing sight to me at any time.

Samuel has already become fairly intimate with her. He has even induced her, which I should never have thought of, to come into the dining car with us. We go walking into the dining car among the unknown passengers with a quite incredible air of belonging together, all three of us. This is to be noted, that one should try a new environment for strengthening a friendship. I am now actually sitting beside her, we drink wine, our arms touch, our mutual holiday spirit really turns us into a family.

This fellow Samuel, in spite of her lively resistance, backed up by the fact that it is raining, has overborne her into joining us in a motor ride through Munich during our half-hour's wait there. While he is finding a car, she says to me in the station hall, and takes me by the arm as she says it: "Please, don't let us go. I mustn't do it. It's quite out of the question. I'm telling you, because I trust you. It's no use talking to your friend. He's quite crazy!"—We climb into the car, the whole affair is painful to me, and reminds me closely of a film called "The White Slave," in which the innocent heroine is forced into a car by strange men just outside a railway station in the dark and carried off. Samuel on the other hand is in good spirits. Since the big hood of the car cuts off our view, we really see only as far as the first floor of all the buildings, with an effort. It is night. Cellar-like perspectives. But Samuel draws fantastic deductions from them about the height of the castles and churches. Since Dora in her dark seat at the back keeps on saying nothing and I am almost afraid of a scene, he is somewhat taken aback at last and inquires, rather too conventionally for my taste: "Why, you're not angry with me, are you, Fraülein? Have I done anything to you?" and so on. She answers: "Since I am here, I don't want to spoil your fun. But you shouldn't have made me come. If I say 'No,' it's because I have my reasons. I ought not to be in the car." "Why?" he asks. "I can't tell you. You ought to see for yourself that it's not a thing for a girl to do, to ride round in a car at night with gentlemen. Besides, there's another reason. Suppose that I'm already engaged. . . ." We divine, each of us, with hushed respect, that the Wagner gentleman has something to do with this. Well, I have nothing to reproach myself with, but I try all the same to cheer her up. Samuel too, who has been inclined to patronize her a little until now, seems to repent it and confines himself to talking about the journey. The driver, at our request, calls out the names of the invisible buildings that one ought to be sight-seeing. The tires whir on the wet asphalt like the apparatus in a cinema. Again I think of "The White Slave." These long, lone, washed black streets. Our clearest impression is of the great, uncurtained windows of the "Vier Jahreszeiten," a restaurant which we heard of as among the most elegant there are. A waiter in livery bowing before a table full of guests. Passing a monument which we have the happy idea of hailing as the Wagner Memorial, she begins to take an interest. We are allowed to stop for a moment only at the Freedom Monument with its fountains spouting in the rain. The bridge over the Isar, which we can only surmise is there. Fine gentlemen's villas all along the English Garden. Ludwigstrasse, Theatiner Church, Feldherrn Hall, Pschorr brewery. I don't know how it happens: but I recognize nothing, although I have been several times in Munich before. Sendlinger Gate. Station, which I was anxious (especially on Dora's account) to reach in time. So, like a spring wound up for just the right distance, we have gone whizzing through the town in precisely twenty minutes by the taxi meter.

We escort our Dora, just as if we were her Munich relations, into a through compartment for Innsbruck, where a lady in black, much more to be feared than we are, offers her protection for the night. Only now am I aware that the two of us can safely be trusted with a girl.

SAMUEL: The affair with Dora has been a complete failure. The farther it went, the worse it got. I meant to break the journey and spend the night in Munich. Until we had supper, at about Regensburg, I was sure it would be all right. I tried to let Richard know by slipping a few words to him on a note. He seems not to have read it at all, thinking only of tucking it away in his pocket. After all, it doesn't matter, I didn't give two pins for the insipid creature. Only Richard made so much fuss about her, with his ceremonious advice and gallantry. That made her put on more of her silly airs than ever, until finally in the car they became quite unbearable. When we said goodbye she went all sentimental, as was to be expected. Richard, who was of course carrying her suitcase, behaved as if she had conferred undeserved favors on him, I had only an embarrassed feeling. To put it shortly: women who travel alone or want in some way or other to be regarded as independent, have no business to indulge in the usual coquetry, perhaps already out-of-date, first leading a man on and then fending him off, and taking advantage of his consequent confusion. It can be seen through too easily and makes one soon happy to be fended off, a good deal farther than was probably intended.

We got into the compartment where to Richard's anxiety we had left our luggage lying. Richard makes his usual preparations for sleep, rolling his rug under his head for a pillow and hanging up his greatcoat so that its skirts make a canopy over his face. It pleases me that at least where his sleep comes in question, he acts inconsiderately, for instance he darkens the light without asking me, although he knows that I cannot sleep in a train. He stretches himself out on the seat as if he had a better right to it than his fellow travelers. And falls asleep peacefully at once. And yet the man is always complaining about sleeplessness.

Besides us there are two young French lads in the compartment (high-school students from Geneva). One of them, a black-haired one, laughs all the time, even over the fact that Richard has left him hardly room to sit down (his legs stretch so far), and then later because he seizes the chance when Richard gets up for a minute and begs everyone not to smoke so much, of recovering some part of Richard's bedstead. Such small disputes between people of different languages are carried on silently and so with the utmost lightness, no

excuses made and no reproaches.—The French boys help
the night to pass by handing back and forth a tin of
biscuits or twisting up cigarettes or going every other
minute into the corridor, calling each other out, and
then coming back again. In Lindau (they say "Lendó")
they laugh heartily and with surprising loudness, considering the time of night, at the Austrian guard. A foreign country's train guards seem irresistibly comical, as
the Bavarian one in Fürth seemed to us, with his huge
red bag that flapped low down about his legs.—A long-
continued view of the Lake of Constance glittering and
smooth under the lights from the train, right across to
the distant lights on the opposite shore, dark and misty.
An old poem I learned at school comes into my mind:
"The Rider over the Lake of Constance." I spend a fair
time trying to reconstruct it from memory.—Three
Swiss come pushing in. One of them is smoking. One,
who stays behind after the other two have gone out,
is at first insubstantial but becomes visible towards
morning. He has put an end to the dispute between
Richard and the black-haired French boy by setting
them both equally in the wrong, planting himself stiffly between them for all the rest of the night, his
mountaineering stick between his knees. Richard shows
that he can sleep just as well sitting.

Switzerland surprises me because of the houses standing separately and therefore with an air of apparently
sturdy and emphatic independence in all the little towns
and villages along the whole stretch of the railway line.
In St. Gall none are joined together into streets. Perhaps
this is an expression of good German individuality—
helped out by the inequalities of the ground. Each
house with its dark green window shutters and much

green color on the woodwork of the eaves and the railings looks rather like a villa. And yet accommodates a firm, only *one*, the family and the business premises seem to be the same. This arrangement, carrying on business in villas, reminds me strongly of R. Walser's novel *The Assistant*.

It is Sunday, five o'clock in the morning, 27th August. All the windows are still shut, everyone is asleep. Haunted by the feeling that we, imprisoned in this train, are breathing the only bad air there is far and wide, while the landscape outside unveils itself in a natural fashion which cannot properly be observed except from a night express under a continuously burning light. Dark mountains first shoulder it this way between them and the train as an extremely narrow valley, then the morning mist diffuses a white radiance as if through fanlights, the meadows gradually appear, fresh as if untouched, green and full of sap, which amazes me in this year of drought, finally as the sun rises the grass pales in a slow transmutation.—Trees with great heavy branches loaded with needles that sweep down to the very foot of the trunks.

One often sees shapes like these in the pictures of Swiss artists, and until today I took them to be merely stylized forms.

A mother with her children is beginning to take a Sunday walk along the clean road. That reminds me of Gottfried Keller who was brought up by his mother.

All over the pasture land the most carefully fashioned fences; many are made of gray logs sharpened at the point like pencils, often out of such logs split in two. We used to split our pencils like that when we were children, to get the lead out. I have never seen fences

like that before. So every country has novelties to show
in the ordinary objects of daily life, and in rejoicing
over such impressions one must be careful not to miss
what is extraordinary.

RICHARD: Switzerland in the first morning hours left to
itself. Samuel wakens me ostensibly to show me a bridge
worth looking at, which however is already past before
I peer up, and this direct action of his procures him
perhaps his first strong impression of Switzerland. I see
it at first, for too long a time, from an inner as an outer
crepuscular dimness.

I have slept uncommonly well this night, as nearly
always in a train. My going to sleep in a train is literally
a tidy piece of work. I ease myself down, my head last
of all, make brief trials of various positions as a prelim-
inary, isolate myself from the whole company, however
they may all stare at me from all sides, by covering my
face with my overcoat or my traveling cap, and in the
comfort that begins to steal over my body from having
taken up a new position I am floated into sleep. In the
beginning darkness is of course a great help, later on it
becomes almost superfluous. People could go on talking,
too, just as before, only in the nature of things a person
who is sleeping in earnest is a reminder that even a
chatterer sitting at several removes cannot ignore. For
there is hardly a place where utterly opposing ways
of life are thrown into such close, direct and surprising
proximity as in a railway carriage, and as a result of
continuous mutual observation they begin to exert an
influence upon each other in the shortest of times. So
even if a sleeper does not immediately lull the others to
sleep, he makes them quieter or much against his own
will heightens their meditativeness to the point of smok-

ing, as unfortunately happened on this journey, where in the good atmosphere of unobtrusive dreams I had to inhale clouds of cigarette smoke.

My good sleep in a train I can explain in this way, that my nervousness, arising from overwork, usually keeps me from sleeping because of the noise it sets up within me, which is so exacerbated by every stray sound in the night from the large dwelling house and from the street, by the rolling of every wheel coming from a distance, the brawling of every drunkard, the echo of every step on the staircase, that often in my irritation I lay all the blame of my sleeplessness on these external noises— whereas in a train the monotonous regularity of the noises of the journey, whether from the action of the carriage springs, the friction of the wheels, the collision of the rail points, or the vibration of the whole wooden, glass and iron structure, makes a level as of the utmost tranquillity on which I can sleep, to all appearance like a healthy man. This appearance of course is not proof against a penetrating whistle from the engine, for instance, or an alteration in the speed of the train, or quite definitely the sensation of coming into a station, which transmits itself through the whole of my sleep just as through the whole body of the train until it makes me wake up. Then I hear, without any surprise, the names of the places called out which I had never expected to pass, as on this journey Lindau, Constance, I think also Romanshorn, and I get less pleasure from them than if I had only dreamed about them, on the contrary merely annoyance. If I am awakened during the journey the shock is the greater because it is like an offense against the nature of train sleep. I open my eyes and turn for a moment to the window. There I

don't see much, and what I see is perceived with the
lazy faculties of a dreamer. Yet I could swear that
somewhere in Württemberg, just as if I had known
Württemberg intimately, at about two in the morning I
saw a man leaning over the railings on the verandah of
his country house. Behind him was the half-open door
of his study, all lit up, as if he had just come out to
cool his head before going to bed. In Lindau the night
was filled with the sound of singing in the station, but
also on the way in and out again, and though on such
a journey overnight between Saturday and Sunday one
is generally bound to sweep along much night life for
long stretches, which disturbs one's sleep only slightly,
the sleep seems all the deeper and the disturbance outside all the louder. The conductors too, whom I often
saw trotting past my clouded windowpane and who
were only doing their duty and not trying to awaken
anyone, called out with extra loudness in the empty sta-
tions one syllable of the place name into our compartment and the other syllables farther on. My fellow
travelers were then tempted to reconstruct the name,
or they got up to wipe the window clear once more
and read the name itself through it; but my head was
already back on its wooden rest again.

Still, when one can sleep so well in a train as I can—
Samuel sits up all night with his eyes open, so he says—
one should be allowed to sleep right on until reaching
one's destination, and not find oneself, in the very moment of waking out of a sound sleep, cramped up in a
corner of a compartment, with a greasy face, sweating
body, hair rumpled in all directions, in clothes and body
linen that have been exposed to railway grit for twenty-
four hours without brushing or airing, and condemned

to go on traveling in this condition. If one had the energy one would execrate such a sleep, but as it is, one secretly envies people like Samuel who have perhaps slept only for snatches yet have been able to pay more attention to themselves, have made nearly the whole journey in full consciousness and have kept their minds inviolate and clear through all the oppression of sleep which they must have been liable to as well. I was indeed completely at Samuel's mercy in the morning.

We were standing side by side at the window, I only to please him, and while he showed me what was visible of Switzerland and told me about all I had missed seeing while asleep, I nodded and admired accordingly. It's a good thing that when I'm in such a condition either he doesn't notice it or doesn't understand it, for just at these times he is friendlier to me than when I am more deserving. But in all seriousness I was thinking only of the Lippert girl. It's hard for me to form a true judgment about brief encounters with new acquaintances, especially with women. For while the acquaintance is progressing, I am inclined rather to observe myself, where there is much to occupy me, and so harvest only a ridiculously small part of all that I have sensed fleetingly and lost at once during the course of it. In recollection, on the other hand, these acquaintances immediately grow to large and adorable figures, since there they are silent, attend only to their own affairs and show their indifference to us through their complete forgetfulness of our presence. Yet I had another reason for yearning so much after Dora, the girl nearest to me in memory. On this morning Samuel fell short of what I needed. He was willing to travel with me as my friend, but that was not much. That meant merely my having a fully clothed man beside me on all the days of this journey, whose body I could see only in bathing, without even having the faintest desire for such a spectacle. Samuel, to be sure, would let me lay my head on his breast if I wanted to weep there, but in his presence, at the sight of his masculine face, his neat pointed beard wagging, his tightly shut mouth—I need say no more—could the tears of deliverance ever rise to my eyes at all?

The Aeroplanes at Brescia *

La sentinella bresciana of September 9, 1909, announces with delight: "In Brescia we have a throng of people such as we have never had before, not even at the time of the great automobile races; visitors from Venice, Liguria, Piedmont, Tuscany, Rome, even from as far away as Naples; indeed, the big men of France, England, and America are crowding our squares, our hotels, every nook and corner of our private houses: all prices are rising splendidly; the means of transport are insufficient to carry the crowds to the 'circuito aerio'; the restaurants at the aerodrome can serve two thousand people excellently, confronted with several thousand they could not but break down. The militia was needed to protect the buffets. In the cheap places fifty thousand people are standing the whole day."

As my two friends and I read this news we were filled with courage and fear simultaneously. Courage, because where there are such fearful crowds, things are generally done in a beautifully democratic way, and where there is no room, one needn't look for it. Fear—fear of

---

* Translated by G. Humphreys Roberts.

the way Italians organize such undertakings; fear of the committee that will take us in hand; fear of the journey by trains of which the *Sentinella* proudly boasts that they are four hours late. All expectations are false, all one's memories of Italy get completely mixed up with each other as soon as we get back home; they fade, and we cannot rely on them.

As we drive into the black hole of the station at Brescia, where people are screaming as if the ground were on fire under their feet, we are still earnestly warning each other that whatever happens we must stick together. Aren't we going with a kind of hostility?

We get out; a carriage that hardly manages to stay on its wheels accepts us; the driver is in a very good temper; we drive through almost empty streets up to the palace of the committee, where they overlook our inward wickedness, as if it were not there; we find out everything we need to know. The inn we are directed to seems to us at first sight to be the dirtiest we have ever seen, but after a while it is not at all so exaggeratedly bad. It is dirt which is just there, that's all, and about which no more is said; dirt which will never change any more, which has made itself at home, which in a certain sense makes life more tangible, more earthly; dirt out of which our host hurries forth, proud towards himself, humble towards us, continually stroking his elbows, and casting new and ever new shadows on his face with his hands—every finger is a compliment—bowing from the waist all the time in a way we recognize later at the aerodrome, in Gabriele d'Annunzio, for instance. Who, one must ask, could still have anything on his mind against this dirt?

The aerodrome is at Montechiari, and can be reached

in a bare hour by the local line that goes to Mantua. This local line has reserved itself a length of rail along the general highway, on which it lets its trains travel with all modesty neither higher nor lower than the rest of the traffic, between the cyclists who ride into the dust with their eyes almost closed, between the completely unusable carriages from the whole province— which pick up as many passengers as you like, and are besides so quick, you can't believe it—and between the motorcars which are often huge, and which, given their head, are deliberately trying to run into each other at every moment, with their manifold hootings which, at the speed, have become one noise. At times one gives up hope altogether of ever coming to the *circuito* with this wretched train. But people are laughing all around you, and to the right and to the left people are laughing into the train. I am standing on a platform, squeezed up against an enormous man who is standing with his legs stretched wide apart over the buffers of two carriages, in a shower of soot and dust that falls from the roofs of the gently shaking carriages. Twice the train stops and waits for a train coming in the opposite direction, as long and as patiently as if it were waiting only for a chance meeting. A few villages pass slowly by, wild posters announcing the last automobile race appear on the walls here and there, all growth on the side of the road is unrecognizable under the olive-leaf color of the white dust. At last the train stops, because it can't go any farther. A group of cars put their brakes on at the same moment, through the clouds of dust that arise we see not far away a lot of little flags; a herd of cattle which has got out of all control, swaying on the bumpy ground and deliberately charging the automobiles, holds us up still.

We have arrived. In front of the aerodrome lies a great square with suspicious-looking little wooden houses, on which we should have expected to see quite different things written up than, "Garage," "Grand Buffet International" and so on. Enormous beggars grown fat in their little gocarts stretch their arms out across one's path, one is tempted in one's haste to leap over them. We catch up with a lot of people, a lot of people catch up with us. We look up, at the sky, which is, after all, the thing that matters here. Thank God, nobody is flying! We refuse to get out of the way and yet we are not run over. Between and behind, and advancing to meet the thousands of vehicles, plunges the Italian cavalry. Order and accidents seem equally impossible.

Once, in Brescia, late in the evening, we wanted to get to a certain street in a hurry and we thought it was rather far. A cab driver wanted three liras, we offered two. The driver wouldn't take us, and only out of friendliness, described to us how frightfully far this street really was. We began to be ashamed of our offer. All right, three liras. We got in, the cab made three turns through short streets; we were there. Otto, more energetic than we two, explained that he had no intention, of course, of paying three liras for a journey that took one minute. One lira was more than enough. There was a lira. It was already night, the little street was empty, the cabby was strong. He flew into a passion immediately, as though the quarrel had been going on for an hour already. What?—That was swindling. What were we thinking of, then? Three liras was the bargain, three liras we must pay. Out with the three liras, or we should be surprised. . . . Otto: "The tariff or the police!" Tariff? There wasn't any tariff. How should there be a tariff for things like that! It was a special price for

a night fare, but if we would give him two liras he
would let us go. OTTO, enough to scare anybody: "The
tariff or the police!" A little more shouting and search-
ing, then a tariff was produced, on which nothing was
to be seen but dirt. So we agreed on one lira fifty, and
the cabby went off down the narrow street in which he
could not turn, not only raging, but also saddened as I
can't help thinking. For our behavior was, alas, not the
right behavior; one doesn't behave that way in Italy.
In other countries that may be all right, but not here.
Well, who thinks of all that when he is in a hurry!
There is nothing to complain about in that, one can't
become an Italian in a short week's holiday tour.

But repentance shall not spoil our pleasure at the aerodrome, that would only give ground for fresh repentance, and we jump into the aerodrome rather than walk,
in this enthusiasm of all our limbs which sometimes suddenly seizes us, one after the other, in this country,
under this sun.

We pass the hangars, which, with their curtains
drawn, look like the closed-up stages of a touring dra-
matic company. On their pediments are written the
names of the aviators whose machines they house, and
over that fly the colors of their countries. We read the
names of Cobianchi, Cagno, Rougier, Curtiss, Moucher
(a "Tridentiner" flying Italian colors, he trusts them
more than he does ours), Anzani, the Club of Roman
Aviators. *And Blériot?* we ask. Blériot, of whom we
have been thinking all the time, where is Blériot?

In the fenced-in ground in front of his hangar,
Rougier, a little man with a conspicuous nose, is dashing
about in his shirt sleeves. He is extremely, if somewhat
obscurely, busy, he waves his arms about, his hands in

violent gesticulation, feels himself all over as he walks, sends his workmen behind the curtain of his hangar, calls them back, goes in himself, thrusting them all on one side, while his wife stands to one side in a tight, white dress, a little black hat pressed firmly into her hair, her legs under a short skirt, gently outstretched, she is gazing into the empty heat, a business woman, with all the cares of business in her little head.

In front of the next hangar Curtiss is sitting all alone. Through the curtains, slightly drawn back, his machine can be seen; it is bigger than we had heard. As we were passing, Curtiss was holding up the *New York Herald* in front of him, and reading a line on the top of a page. After half an hour we pass him again, he has already got to the middle of this page; another half an hour and he has finished the page and begun another. Obviously he is not going to fly today. We turn and look at the broad field. It is so big that everything on it looks forlorn: the guide posts near us, the signaling mast in the distance, the catapult for starting somewhere to the right, a committee car, that, with little yellow flags fluttering in the wind, describes a curve about the field, stops in its own dust, and then goes on again. An artificial desert has been created here in an almost tropical land, and the aristocracy of Italy, sparkling ladies from Paris, and all the other thousands of people are here to look at this sunny desert with harrowed eyes for many hours. In this place there is none of the distractions that are otherwise provided on other sports fields. One misses the beautiful hurdles of the racecourse, the white lines of the tennis court, the fresh green meadow of the football ground, the stony up-and-down of the automobile and cycle tracks. Only two or three times during the afternoon a troop of colorful horsemen rides straight across the plain. The horses' hoofs are invisible in the dust, the steady light of the sun doesn't change until about five o'clock in the afternoon. And, that nothing may disturb the view of this plain, there is also no music at all, only the whistling of the crowds in the cheap places tries to meet the demands of the ear and of impatience. From the expensive, tall grandstands which stand behind us, all this crowd, it is true, probably melts into the empty plain without any difference.

On one side of the wooden fence a lot of people are standing together. "How tiny," a group of Frenchmen cries, like a sigh. What's the matter then? We push our way through. But look, here there is indeed, on the field, quite near, with real yellow coloring, a small flying machine that they are getting ready for flight. Now, too, we see Blériot's hangar, and next it that of his pupil Leblanc; they have been built on the flying ground itself. Standing, leaning against one of the two wings of his machine is Blériot, whom we immediately recognize, with his head set firmly on his shoulders, watching the fingers of his mechanics as they work at the engine.

Is he going to go up in the air in this tiny thing? Then people on the water, for instance, have an easier job after all. They can practice in puddles first, then in ponds, and not venture out to sea until much later, for this man there is only the sea.

Blériot is in his seat already, holding some kind of lever in his hand, but he lets his mechanics do their best, as if they were over-diligent children. He looks slowly over in our direction, looks away from us and again in another direction, but keeps his look to himself always. He is going to fly now, nothing is more natural. This feeling of naturalness, with the simultaneous, general feeling of the extraordinary that cannot be withheld from him, lends him this attitude.

A workman grasps one of the blades of the screw, in order to turn it, tugs at it, it gives a jerk, too; one hears something like the gasp of a strong man in his sleep, but the screw doesn't move any farther. Once again they try, ten times they try, sometimes the screw stops immediately, sometimes it lets itself go round for a few turns. It's the fault of the engine. Work is begun on it afresh, the onlookers get more tired than those who are taking close part. The engine is oiled on every side, hidden screws are loosened and tightened up; one man runs into the hangar and brings out a spare part; that doesn't fit again; he hurries back, and sitting on his haunches on the floor of the hangar, he holds it between his knees, and hammers away at it. Blériot changes his seat with a mechanic, the mechanic with Leblanc. Now this man, now that, tugs away at the screw. But the engine is intractable, like a schoolboy one always helps, the whole class prompts him; no, he doesn't know it, he stops again and again, he breaks down. For a while Blériot sits quite still in his seat: his six assistant workers stand round him without moving, they all seem to be dreaming.

The onlookers can breathe again, and look around. The young Mrs. Blériot passes by with a motherly face, two children behind her. If her husband can't fly, that does not suit her, and if he flies, she is afraid; moreover her lovely dress is a little heavy for this temperature.

Once again the screw is given a turn, perhaps a better one than before, perhaps just the same. The engine comes to life with a roar, as if it were a different thing; four men hold the machine from behind and in the middle of the complete calm all around, the gusts from the swinging screw go in thrusts through the overalls of these men. One doesn't hear a word, only the noise of the screw seems to give orders, eight hands release the machine, which rolls a long way over the waving ground like a clumsy man on a polished floor.

Many such attempts are made, and all of them end without result. Each one sends the public rushing up to the bundles of hay on which one stretches one's arms out partly to keep one's balance, and partly to express hope, fear, and joy. In the intervals, however, the Italian aristocracy walks along the grandstands. They say good day to each other, bow, recognize each other once again, they embrace each other, they walk up and down the gangways of the grandstand. People point out to each other Princess Laetitia Savoia Bonaparte, Princess Borghese, an elderly woman whose face is the color of dark yellow grapes, Countess Morosini. Marcello Borghese is in every lady's company and no lady's company; from a distance he seems to have an understanding face, but when you get close to him, his cheeks overlap the corners of his mouth in the oddest way. Gabriele d'Annunzio, short and weakly, dances attendance, apparently shyly, before Count Oldofredi, one of the most important men on the committee. Over the railings of the stand peers the strong face of Puccini, with a nose that one might well call a drinker's nose.

But you see these people only if you look for them. Otherwise one sees everywhere, depreciating everything, the tall ladies of the present fashion! They prefer walking to sitting, in their clothes sitting doesn't go very easily. All their faces, veiled like Asiatics, are borne in a faint twilight; the dress, loose on the bust, gives the whole figure a kind of fainthearted appearance; a kind of mixed, restless feeling overcomes one when such ladies look fainthearted. The bodice is low-cut, one can hardly reach it; the waist seems broader than usual because everything else is narrow; these women want to be embraced lower down.

It was only Leblanc's machine that had been shown so far. But now comes the machine in which Blériot flew over the Channel; nobody says so, everybody knows it. A long pause, and Blériot is in the air. One sees his straight body over the wings, his legs are stretched down like a part of the engine. The sun is sinking, and under the baldachin of the grandstands, throws its light on the hovering wings. Devotedly everybody looks up to him, there is no room in anybody's heart for anyone else. And everybody looks with outstretched neck at the monoplane, as it falls, is seized by Blériot, and even climbs. What is happening? Here, above us, there is a man twenty meters above the earth, imprisoned in a wooden box, and pitting his strength against an invisible danger which he has taken on of his own free will. But we are standing below, thrust right back out of the way, without existence, and looking at this man.

Everything goes well, the signaling mast at the same time shows that the wind has got more favorable, and that Curtiss is going to fly for the Grand Prix of Brescia. Is he really going to, after all? One has hardly finished finding out whether he is or not when Curtiss's engine roars, and one has hardly had time to look at it before he is flying away from us, flying over the plains that widen in front of him, towards the woods in the distance that seem to be rising out of the ground for the first time. His flight extends far over these woods; he disappears from sight; we are gazing at the woods, not at him. From behind some houses, God knows where, he comes out at the same height as before, and races towards us; when he climbs, you can see the under-surfaces of his biplane dipping darkly; when he descends, the upper surfaces glisten in the sun. He makes a turn round the signal mast and, indifferent to the roars of welcome, turns straight back to where he has come from, only to become speedily tiny and lonely again. He does five rounds like this, flies fifty kilometers in forty-nine minutes twenty-four seconds, and so wins the Grand Prix of Brescia—30,000 liras. It is a perfect achievement; but perfect achievements cannot be appreciated; everyone, when you come to think of it, thinks he is capable of a perfect achievement, no courage seems to be needed for perfect achievements. And while Curtiss is working all on his own there above the woods, while his wife, whom everybody knows, is worried about him, the crowd has almost forgotten him. All one hears on every side is complaining because Calderara is not going to fly—his machine was smashed; Rougier has been tinkering about with his Voisin for two whole days without letting go of it; and *Zodiac*, the Italian navigable balloon, has not yet arrived. The rumors running around about Calderara's accident are so full of his glory that one is ready to believe the love of the nation would raise him into the air more securely than his Wright.

Curtiss had not yet finished his flight before the engines in three hangars were tuning up, as if out of enthusiasm. Wind and dust are driven together from opposite directions. One pair of eyes is not enough. One twists and turns in one's seat, loses one's balance, clutches somebody or other firmly, apologizes; somebody or other loses his balance, drags somebody else after him, is thanked. The early evening of the Italian autumn is beginning; it is impossible to see everything clearly in the field any longer.

Just as Curtiss passes over us after his winning flight, and takes his cap off with a slight smile without looking at us, Blériot begins a little round trip which everybody is immediately confident will be successful. Now, one doesn't know whether one is applauding Curtiss or Blériot, whose big heavy machine is now hurling itself into the air. Rougier sits at his levers like a great man at a writing desk which one climbs up to by a couple of steps behind his back. He climbs in small circles, flies above Blériot, turns him into an onlooker, and continues to climb without stopping.

If we want to get a carriage back again, it is high time to get going; there are already a lot of people pushing past us. One knows, of course, that this is only a trial flight; as it is already getting on to seven, it would not be counted officially any longer. In the approach to the aerodrome the chauffeurs and attendants are standing on their seats and pointing to Rougier; on Rougier's account three trains crowded to the last buffers refuse to move. We are lucky enough to get a carriage; the coachman squats down in front of us—there is no box—and, having at last become independent existences once more, we set off. Max very rightly remarks that one could and should arrange something of this kind in Prague too. It wouldn't have to be a prize race, he thought, although that would also be worth while, but to invite an airman would certainly be an easy matter after all, and none of the participants would have any grounds for regrets. The thing would be so simple, in fact; Wright was now flying in Berlin; all you would have to do, then, would be to persuade the people to come a little out of their way. We two others didn't answer a word, first of all because we were tired, and secondly because we had no objections anyway. The road turned, and Rougier appeared, so high in the air that one thought that soon his course would have to be determined only by the stars that were soon about to shine in the sky, which had already grown dark. We couldn't stop turning round; Rougier was still climbing straight up, but our way led with finality deeper into the Campagna.

Three Critical Pieces *

A Novel about Youth

FELIX STERNHEIM: Die Geschichte des jungen Oswald.
Hyperionverlag Hans von Weber, Munich, 1910.

WHETHER IT intends to or not, this is a book to make
young people happy.

As he begins reading this novel, which is in epistolary
form, the reader perhaps must needs assume a certain
naivety, for a reader does not fare so well when at the
very outset he has to bend his head immediately over the
unchanging stream of an emotion. And perhaps this
naivety on the reader's part is what makes the author's
weaknesses appear to him, right at the beginning, in such
a clear morning light: a limited vocabulary hovered over
by Werther's shadow, painful to the ears with its constant "sweet" and constant "lovely." An ever recurring
rapture, whose fulness is never abated but which pro-
ceeds through these pages stillborn, often just barely
clinging to the words.

But when the reader feels more at home, when he
reaches a sheltered spot whose ground trembles in accord
with the ground of the story, then it is no longer difficult
to perceive that the novel's epistolary form needs the
author almost more than he needs it. The epistolary form

* Translated by Clement Greenberg.

permits sudden change to be depicted as in the midst of a permanent situation, yet without depriving the sudden change of its suddenness: it permits a permanent situation to be made known by an outcry, and its permanency, moreover, continues to prevail. It permits the action to be delayed with no harm done, for while the man by whose justified ardor we are moved writes his letters, all the powers that be shield him, the curtain is lowered and with his whole body at rest he moves his hand evenly over the letter paper. The writing goes on at night in a half-sleep; the wider one's eyes are open to all this the sooner do they fall shut. Two letters are written in succession to different addressees, and the second with a mind that thinks only about the first. Letters are written in the evening, at night and in the morning, and in the morning one's face looks past one's nocturnal face, which is already unrecognizable, into one's evening face with eyes still filled with understanding. The words, "Dearest, dearest Gretchen!" emerge hidden from between two big sentences and, taking them both by surprise, push them aside and win complete freedom.

And we abandon everything, fame, the art of fiction, music, and lose ourselves as we are in that summery country where the fields and meadows "are traversed, Dutch-fashion, by dark, narrow waterways," where in the company of grown-up girls, small children and a clever woman, Oswald falls in love with Gretchen to the tic-tac of briefly uttered sentences. This Gretchen inhabits the still center of the novel; we rush towards her, continually, from every direction. Now and then we even lose sight of Oswald, but not of her; we see her even amid the loudest laughter of her little circle, as if through a thicket. Yet hardly do we see her, see her simple form, than we are so near her that we cannot see her any more; hardly do we feel her near than we are snatched away and see her small in the distance. "She leaned her little head on the birchwood railings, so that half her face was bathed in moonlight."

Admiration in one's heart for this summer—who would venture to say or, better, who would venture the demonstration that from here on the book along with its hero, along with love, faithfulness and all good things, destroys itself outright, while only the writer's art of its hero triumphs, a circumstance not questionable only because it is indifferent. And thus it happens that the reader, the closer he comes to the novel's end, the more he wishes he were back in the summer with which it begins, and finally, instead of following the hero onto the cliffs of suicide, joyfully turns back to that summer, content to stay there forever.

On Kleist's "Anecdotes"

WHAT A joy to see how the great works, even when arbitrarily cut up, continue to live on out of their indivisible inner essences—then, in all likelihood, striking our jaded eyes in an altogether special way. This is the explanation for the real merit possessed by every special edition that calls our attention once and for all to some limited part of an author's complete works, especially when, like this collection of Kleist's anecdotes, it respects a new unity and thus actually enlarges the scope of Kleist's work. It enlarges this scope even when we already know all these anecdotes—which, however, happily cannot be the case for many. The expert of course will be able to explain why many of these anecdotes are lacking in various complete editions of Kleist's works, even in the Tempel one; the layman will not understand and for this reason will hold all the more tightly to this new text provided him by the Verlag Rowohlt in clear type and dignified format (the paper, which is a bit tinted, seems particularly appropriate to me) for the small matter of two marks.

Hyperion

HALF UNDER compulsion and half by free choice, the magazine *Hyperion* has ended its work, and its twelve white volumes, big as stone slabs, are now all there is. Only the Hyperion Almanacs of 1910 and 1911, which the public now scrambles for like the diverting relics of some disagreeable corpse, still reminds one of it directly. Its real editor was Franz Blei, that admirable man who was driven into the thick of literature by the impetuosity and, even more, the variety of his talents; being unable, however, to liberate or maintain himself there, he escaped with transformed energies into the founding of literary magazines. Its publisher was Hans von Weber, whose house, though at first completely overshadowed by *Hyperion*, has today become one of the German publishing houses most aware of where they are going, and that without running off down some byway of literature, and at the same time without making a great to-do with sweeping programs.

The aim of these founders of *Hyperion* was to have it fill that gap in the literary magazine field which *Pan* was the first to recognize, *Insel* tried to fill subsequently, and which since then has apparently remained unfilled. Here already was the beginning of *Hyperion*'s error, and hardly ever indeed did a literary magazine err more nobly. *Pan* in its time brought to Germany the benefit of a dismay that branched out from the magazine a thousandfold, by uniting the forces that were really contemporary but still unknown and enabling them to give aid and comfort to one another; *Insel,* in the lack of such an urgent necessity, wheedled itself one of another, if inferior, sort; *Hyperion* had none. It wanted to grant a representation, a great and vital one, to those who dwelled on the peripheries of literature; but these people were not entitled to it nor at bottom did they want it.

Those whose natures keep them at a distance from the community cannot appear regularly without damage in a magazine where they feel placed in a kind of limelight next to the rest of the contents and look stranger than they are; nor do they need defending, for incomprehension cannot hurt them, since they are dark and love will find them anywhere; nor do they need encouragement, for if they want to remain authentic they can live only off themselves, and so they cannot be helped without being harmed first. However, while the possibilities open to other magazines—the possibilities of representing, showing, defending, strengthening—were denied to *Hyperion,* it could not at the same time avoid painful liabilities; a collection of literature like that put together in *Hyperion* has a strong attraction for dishonest things and is powerless to defend itself against them; and, on the other hand, where the best in general literature and art did enter *Hyperion* there was by no means a complete harmony always, and anyhow there was no special gain that could not have been got elsewhere.

Yet all these doubts could not spoil one's enjoyment of

Hyperion during those two years, for the excitement of the venture, which was barbaric only to the extent that everything heroic is, caused all else to be forgotten; but for *Hyperion* itself these doubts were indeed a matter of life and death, and as self-reproaches they would certainly have brought about its disappearance had not the incomprehension of the public (which did not consciously aim at doing this) forestalled them. They would have made it disappear like a spirit whose night had expired and which was by no means any more important than are all other good spirits in this life of ours which, without at all asking for permission, it tried to put into order by a new confusion. Its memory, however, will be unable to disappear, if only because there will be no one, certainly, in the coming generations with the will, the power, the self-sacrificial courage and the enthusiastic self-delusion to start a similar undertaking again; and therefore the unforgotten *Hyperion* has already begun to put itself beyond the reach of any hostility, and in ten or twenty years it will be nothing less than a bibliographical treasure.

Epilogue

THIS VOLUME brings together everything that Franz Kafka himself published; none of his other works, it would appear, was intended for publication.

"The Stoker," however, although it was originally published as a separate story by Kafka, is omitted because it is the first chapter of the novel *Amerika*. Of the two dialogues from the story entitled "Description of a Struggle"—"Conversation with the Supplicant" and "Conversation with the Drunken Man," both published in 1909 in the eighth number of *Hyperion* (Munich)— only the former is included because its text differs slightly from the text of the dialogue as it appears in the story.

The following stories later published in the collection, *A Country Doctor*, were first printed in two Jewish magazines: "A Dream" appeared in *Selbstwehr*; "Jackals and Arabs" and "A Report to an Academy" in *Der Jude*. Kafka had intended to take "The Bucket Rider," too, into *A Country Doctor*; it was first published in the *Prager Presse* on December 25, 1921 and has as its background the Prague coal famine of the winter of 1916-1917.

"The Aeroplanes at Brescia" was first published by the Prague newspaper *Bohemia* on September 28, 1909.

Three critical pieces are also added, of which only the first was printed; as well as a chapter from a novel planned together with myself, called "Richard and Samuel," which appeared in the *Herderblätter* (edited by Willi Haas) in Prague, 1912. No further instalments of this novel were published.

The dates of the various publications are as follows: "Meditation," 1913, in the Ernst Rowohlt Verlag, Leipzig, with the dedication "For M.B."; "The Judgment," 1913, in the annual *Arkadia*, Verlag Kurt Wolff, Leipzig, with the dedication "For Miss Felice B.," in a later edition "For F."; "The Metamorphosis," November 1915, as Volume 22/23 of a series called "Judgment Day" (*Der Jüngste Tag*), with a title page by Othmar Starke, Verlag Kurt Wolff, Leipzig (in the same series the stories "The Judgment" and "The Stoker" were also published); *A Country Doctor*, at the end of 1919 in the Verlag Kurt Wolff, Munich and Leipzig, with the dedication "To my Father"; "In the Penal Colony," as the fourth of the new series of Drugulin editions of the Verlag Kurt Wolff, May 1919; *A Hunger Artist*, 1924, in the Verlag "Die Schmiede," Berlin. The first proofs of this last book were read by Kafka on his final sickbed; further corrections were supervised by myself.

I have left the prose pieces grouped and arranged in the same order in which Franz Kafka himself published them in the aforesaid books. Insofar as these books go to make a set of collected works, the arrangement of the parts cannot be regarded as accidental. Each book as compiled, too, made its effect as a unity, and so belongs in its original form to the history of literature. For this reason "Before the Law" and "An Imperial Message" have been left in their original places within the compilation, *A Country Doctor*, although the former appears again in *The Trial* and the latter in the story "The Great Wall of China." Kafka did not use the title of this present volume for any collection of his writings, but only for the one story. MAX BROD